Disobedience By Design

Harwell Heirs Book 2

Regina Kammer

Viridium Press

Published by: Viridium Press, Friday Harbor, Washington
ISBN-13: 978-0-9910166-5-5 (paperback)
ISBN-10: 0-9910166-5-3 (paperback)
ISBN-13: 978-0-9910166-6-2 (ebook)
ISBN-10: 0-9910166-6-1 (ebook)

The Harwell Heirs

iii

Victorian aristocracy has very strict rules concerning marital connections and familial obligations. But the Harwell heirs—Helena, Sophia, and Arthur—discover love doesn't always follow the rules. Scandalous affairs force these scions of society to choose between duty and desire, deference and destiny.

Book 1: *The Pleasure Device*
Book 2: *Disobedience By Design*
Book 3: *Where Destiny Plays*

Acknowledgments

Thank you to my family—especially my parents—and friends for their enthusiastic and continued encouragement, and to my colleagues for their advice, knowledge, and support. Special thanks to my husband for transportation and investment scheme research—and for his advice, patience, and love.

Dedication

To Curtis and Susan, wherever you are. Thank you for reading with such enthusiasm.

CHAPTER ONE

Lincolnshire, 24 March 1860

Boring. Boring. Dreadful. Taken.

Lady Sophia Harwell sat upright in a baroque high-backed chair, her hands folded primly in her lap, affecting a polite demeanor as she surveyed the guests attending her eighteenth-birthday ball...and decided that the eligible men Mama had picked out for her were, each one of them, somehow *ineligible.*

Of course that might have been Mama's plot all along. She and Papa were quite adamant Sophia marry the rather dull Duke of Royston, which must have been the reason they decided to hold her party on the first Saturday of spring—the very same day as the queen's first Drawing Room of the year. Thus, it seemed, all the truly handsome, interesting men were attending their sisters and cousins during their presentations at Court.

Sophia simply could not see herself as the Duchess of Royston—well, really could not see herself as a duchess at all, it seemed such a boring fate—but especially could not see herself marrying Royston.

The man had to be well over fifty—he was older than her parents, of that she was sure. His hair was almost all gray, the hair he had left anyway. And he was—well, the most polite thing she could say was *paunchy* and that didn't seem very polite at all. She would not mind so much his portly physique and lack of hair if such things meant he was jolly and wise. She could see herself raising a couple of chubby babies with a man such as that, and then being widowed by the time she was twenty-five. But Royston was boorish, arrogant, condescending and sometimes quite vile, especially to the servants. Being married to him even for a day would most certainly not be very pleasant, and having to give him children was an odious notion, even if doing so meant she would end up a young widow who could eventually marry for love.

But according to her parents—and her brother—being the daughter of the Marquess of Richmond meant she had a responsibility to marry a peer—the higher the better—and give him a son. They all spoke of familial obligation, of duty to the crown and how they, as the heirs to the Richmond Marquessate, were above sentimentality and romantic notions.

Yet somehow her brother Arthur, the actual heir to the marquessate, was allowed his sentiment and romance.

That just boiled her blood.

She loved Arthur, she really did. He was the best brother in the world. Why, at that very moment he danced with his fiancée Henrietta—Henny—her full skirts swinging like a bell in perfect rhythm to his lead, their faces flushed and smiling. His countenance reflected the swell of pride he felt toward Henny, hers how absolutely besotted she was with him. They were a perfect couple and Sophia did not wish them ill will in the slightest, but she did take umbrage over the fact that Arthur was allowed to marry for love and she was not.

Or maybe she was just annoyed because when Henny, the beautiful, charming daughter of the Earl of Bloxholme, fell in love with the rather handsome—she had to admit, even though he was her brother—Lord Petersham, she had decided Sophia's fate.

Because for a short while, Henny had been considered a possible wife for the Duke of Royston. He was her mother's cousin and so when Henny came of age and Royston was still unmarried, all concerned—except Henny of course—discussed their possible union. Then she met Arthur at a grand social occasion where he was all dressed to the nines and dashing. After that, Henny was no longer considered a match for Royston.

She must have breathed a sigh of relief. And it wasn't as if her decision was intentional. No. Henny just had reasonable parents who preferred their precious daughter marry for love.

Whereas Sophia was somehow expendable in the service of queen and country.

She drew in a deep breath and forced a smile as the music ended and Arthur and Henny came toward the dais where Sophia sat.

"Are you feeling well, Sophie?" Arthur's forehead furrowed in concern.

"Oh, I'm just tired, is all. I need a little respite."

"Arthur, your sister has been dancing all night and with some dreadful partners, I should add." Henny touched Sophia's shoulder. "Darling, shall we go to the refreshment room?"

"That would be wonderful, Henny."

The best thing about Arthur getting engaged was Sophia suddenly gaining an older sister. Mama had her limitations as a confidante and friend. With Henny, Sophia finally had someone to gossip with, someone to talk to about men with, someone to tell her all about kissing. Someone who was actually on her side in the whole Royston affair.

"I think it's ghastly that your parents are even considering such a match, Sophie," Henny had said. "Let's make sure we find you someone else, shall we?"

Unfortunately Sophia's birthday party was not the night to find that someone else.

"You know I think I saw Geoffrey over by the champagne earlier. Perhaps he's still there." Henny raised a suggestive brow and offered her arm.

Sophia stifled a smile but she couldn't hide a blush. She and Geoffrey Peel were partners in the sinfully delightful pastime of kissing. She wasn't in love with him—he was far too interested in boring pursuits like hunting and fishing. But that didn't mean they couldn't divert each other when the opportunity presented itself. And as a good friend of Arthur's who lived two hills over, Geoffrey was around quite a bit and opportunities were more plentiful than they really ought to be.

The path to the refreshment room was fraught with guests pausing to bestow birthday greetings, introducing Sophia to bachelors and widowers, or stopping for pleasant chitchat. When they finally arrived, Geoffrey was nowhere to be seen. Royston, however, chatted loudly with the Countess Asterby and her extraordinarily pretty daughter Maude—who was certainly only sixteen—all the while brandishing disgustingly lascivious leers in the poor girl's direction.

Henny gently pulled Sophia back into the oak-paneled passageway.

"Looks as if we'll have to try our luck in the ballroom," Henny said.

On the return journey once again they had to feign sociability and gaiety. Sophia's head hurt from offering false smiles and tedious pleasantries to people she barely knew.

She steered them up the stairs to the ladies' retiring suite. There maids attended their ladies, arranging hair and dresses. In the back room a gaggle of girls gossiped—probably complaining about the dearth of handsome suitors. They greeted Sophia then quickly filed out. Sophia plopped on a padded bench, her crinolines poofing up her skirt inelegantly. She patted the spot next to her. Henny sat with the same indecorous flair.

Sophia giggled. "Henny, it's after midnight and so, I suppose, no longer my birthday—"

"And it's not really your birthday anyway, darling."

Henny was right. Sophia's birthday was in February but February was far too cold a month for a coming-out party. Although the first Saturday of spring was only slightly warmer.

"Yes, well, I mean, I don't think I should have to stay until the end, right? I'm frightfully bored."

"Sophie—" Henny scolded.

"I just want to find Geoffrey and take a stroll."

Henny laughed her very contagious laugh then squeezed Sophia's hand. "All right but don't stay away too long or your parents will go searching. You don't want them catching you."

Maybe I do. Then she would have to marry Geoffrey and not the horrid Royston.

"Sophie." Henny's voice raised in rebuke.

"No one will see me. I'll take the servants' stairs."

Henny shook her head. "All right. But I know nothing about what you are doing, remember?" She kissed Sophia's cheek then stood and left with a nonchalant air.

Sophia waited a moment then glided down the back stairs, through the corridor behind the ballroom, and exited into the Great Courtyard. She crossed to the private passageway that led to the Great Wood where Geoffrey always waited for her and inhaled the air of temporary freedom.

Joseph Phillips sank into the button-back, leather club chair and gazed in admiration at Arthur's billiard room, the dark luster of the wood paneling and box-beamed ceiling evoking a refined manliness a world away from the crude virility of the New York docks. He swirled the brandy in his crystal snifter, the rich amber liquid reflecting the golden glow of the fire in the marble-trimmed hearth, and sucked on his cigar, exhaling the fragrant smoke with a sigh. A man could get used to such a life very easily. Too easily. Especially a man enervated from spending almost three weeks traveling three thousand miles, using every damn mode of transportation in existence. Joseph swigged a mouthful of liquor with a bitter blasphemy for being part of such an exhausting industry.

The departure of the steamship *Telemachus* from the Port of New York had been delayed due to a dispute with the captain of a merchant ship left short-handed with landing his cargo. For Joseph, a former stevedore, the episode was the height of irony, empathetic frustration mounting as he stood idly by, inconspicuous in a crowd of other first-class passengers waiting along South Street. He was a modern man of business now, his future in railroads not waterways, yet his status was in stark opposition to his sympathies.

Of course the lost time was made up during the Atlantic crossing, the proud distinction of the steamship's snub of the vicissitudes of the wind. His rather beat-up copy of *The Odyssey* provided an intellectual refuge from vacuous, polite conversation during the fifteen days at sea. The smiles of young women were especially diverting. But the daughters of the wealthy were not the lusty damsels of the docks and only served to remind him of his probable upcoming abstinence while ensconced among the aristocracy.

Liverpool was as chaotic a port as New York and he wanted to linger but he was not a tourist. Then, lo and behold, the train was delayed due to rain. Good heavens above! How did the British do anything in their blasted country if their railways could be delayed by *rain*? At least he got his day in Liverpool. He sent a letter to Arthur explaining his predicament, then received a reply that very same afternoon. There was to be a grand social occasion on the night Joseph was to arrive but Arthur was certain Joseph would not be interested in such an event and he should simply proceed to Arthur's entrance and his man would take care of him.

The missive in his hand begged the question—why couldn't Joseph simply ride with the damn postman?

The next day he took the London & North Western from Liverpool to Manchester, transferred to the Manchester, Sheffield & Lincolnshire line to Retford, transferring once again to the Great Northern to Little Bytham. The choice of routes was staggering, competition among the various railway companies creating a system of hatch marks to shade the contours of England. One day the map of the United States would be equally crisscrossed with its transcontinental system.

The station-master at Retford telegraphed his colleague at Little Bytham to expect Joseph's arrival but the message had failed to be delivered to Arthur's man, and when Joseph arrived at the tiny station in the middle of the night he had to shake a local wretch out of bed, promising money he did not have but assuring the man that the Earl of Petersham—his very good friend indeed—would be able to pay any amount. Darkness and drowsiness made the nearly two-hour dogcart ride dull. By the time the half-asleep driver found himself on the gravel approach to the great Tudor hall that was the estate of the Marquess of Richmond, he was wide awake. And by the time the man stood on the carved stone stoop of the east wing, his jaw dropping at the sight of the elegantly dressed butler, he said no fare was required, that the privilege was "all mine, milord," and wished Joseph a very good night.

Joseph would have to send the man an appropriate sum in the morning.

As it was well past midnight all he wanted to do was sleep. Unfortunately his body was still agitated from his travels, his thoughts spinning and reeling from nerves or anticipation or both. The earl's valet—because gentlemen had such things—showed him to his rooms—not "room" singular—and had indicated where the billiards and library were, that both had been laid with fires and were quite comfortable, and then had left Joseph to his own devices.

So he threw off his jacket and waistcoat, tore off his tie and stiff collar, unbuttoned his shirt to mid-chest then staggered downstairs to the billiard room.

Once comfortably settled in the masculine haven, the glow of the fire burnishing the rich oak paneling, he said a quiet prayer of thanks to the gods who sent Arthur Harwell, the Earl of Petersham—and his cigars and brandy—into his life. He snorted a chuckle. Life was truly amazing when a poor American dock worker could be sipping brandy in the billiard room of an English earl.

Geoffrey Peel downed his champagne a little too quickly then grabbed another glass from a passing tray. He should have known Sophia would be busy with more eligible suitors. But—*blast it*—he was her brother's best friend and solicitor. He deserved a courtesy dance.

Because then he could exhaust her with far too much turning so they'd have to take a reprieve outside. There they would walk to a dark corner in the woods and tire each other out in far more delicious pursuits.

He grew hard just thinking about the possibilities. Ambling back to the ballroom should take care of that. The perfumes and décolletages of other women would be distracting.

He followed two such distractions as they babbled in what they thought was confidence. The advantage of being a tall man meant not only a good view of plunging necklines but the opportunity to eavesdrop undetected.

"Poor dear. Did you see her? She looked simply enervated."

Sophia?

"And it being her debut—"

Yes. Sophia.

"She should have all the vigor of youth."

Geoffrey looked down at the woman who spoke. She was not much older than thirty.

"Well, I think I saw her go upstairs. And not to the ladies' room. Across the courtyard."

"Probably to her bedroom for a nap. The final dance isn't for a couple of hours. Poor dear."

Bedroom? He knew precisely where that was—from the outside at least. He knew at which window to toss a pebble as a signal to meet him in the woods. He'd only been on the inside once, having been invited to see a new dress, which turned out to be a high-collared day dress or riding habit or something equally unrevealing that her maid and the seamstress were fussing over. Of course he had followed her mother from the morning room so hadn't come upon her bedroom from the courtyard, but no matter. He was fairly certain her room must be next to Arthur's old bedroom, which Geoffrey had been in a few times before Arthur moved to the east wing. Surely he could find Sophia's suite without too much trouble?

He sauntered casually out of the ballroom, through the French doors, across the flagstone courtyard to the family's private staircase. He removed his gloves, pulled up the black collar of his evening jacket to shield the white of his shirt then ducked into the dark, furtively glancing around before he took the stairs to the first floor.

Torchlight from the Great Courtyard spilled through the diamond-shaped windowpanes of the gallery, illuminating his way. He kept to the shadowed wall along the bedrooms, peering at the bottoms of the doors to see if light shone through underneath.

A swoosh of skirts, pale gray in the dark, swirled not twenty feet away before him out of the gallery and into a room. The door clicked shut.

Sophia.

It must be her. Her dress was white—with a shockingly low-cut neckline. And if he remembered correctly, he'd just passed the door to Arthur's old bedroom with its puppy claw scratches along the base.

Geoffrey drew in a breath as he reached her door. Accosting a woman in her bedroom was perhaps not the best of plans. But it was Sophia and they had an understanding. She might be surprised but she'd definitely be willing.

He turned the knob stealthily and went in.

The room was dark with a nip in the air. He let his eyes adjust and took a moment to scan the space. A sitting room, most likely, as the bed was nowhere to be seen.

He spied her at the mantel, a little hunched, perhaps warming herself at the dying fire. He was behind her in three strides.

"Sophie, darling, I've a present for you."

And then she was in his arms, his lips caressing hers, she a little startled, pushing him back. He held her more tightly and she relented, allowing his tongue to delve into the warm recesses of her mouth, her hands encircling his neck as she moaned meekly against him.

His body flared with desire. His hand spanned her upper back, a support for her arch, the fine linen of her dress heated from the excitement of their embrace—

Except Sophia had been wearing a silk dress and it certainly did not extend up her back.

She wasn't Sophia.

Geoffrey pulled away, mortified, releasing his partner with a gasp.

Her breaths puffed excitedly. "Mr. Peel?"

Anna. Sophia's maid.

He fell to his knees. "My apologies, Anna. I…I… Oh, God, I hardly know what to say. This is unconscionable. You must think me a brute."

She remained silent and still, a grotesque counterpoint to his thudding heart and shaking hands. Waiting for her reaction—any reaction—was excruciating.

"Say something, Anna. Please. Anything."

"I'm sorry, sir, but my lady is not in her rooms. I believe her to be at the ball. Were you thinking otherwise?"

He calmed his breath. "I was under the impression she had retired for a spell before the final dance."

"Oh."

He stood. "I now understand I have been given incorrect information. Please forgive me. I find myself in the most awkward of positions. I have just divulged a confidence of my relationship with Lady Sophia and I have just insulted you."

"In truth, sir, I have known about you and my lady." Her sigh held a slight shudder. "And I have not been insulted."

"Thank you, Anna. You do me a service." He dragged his fingers through his hair. "I'll take my leave."

"Yes, sir."

His lips still tingled as he retraced his path to the ballroom. *That* had been an absolutely fantastic kiss. Possibly better than Sophia's.

The stepping stones embedded in the grass came to an end. Sophia halted. Before her rolled a vast lawn receding into the darkness. Above, the moon shone in barely a sliver, obscuring what was most likely a very wet and muddy trudge to reach the woods. Her dancing shoes and ball gown would not survive such a venture unscathed. Besides, there was no sign of Geoffrey surreptitiously waiting for her as she had hoped or, rather, sort of vaguely imagined as one way of alleviating the frustrations of the evening. She sighed. She'd have to turn back and face her fate.

Or perhaps not.

She could spend a moment or two in Arthur's library. Even better, she knew where he kept his spirits. A glass of sherry and a few lines of poetry sounded ideal. Surely Arthur wouldn't mind? And she would return to the ballroom, really she would. She'd be expected to dance one last dance with Royston. She'd need another glass of sherry just for that.

She tugged off her gloves and headed to the east wing. As she approached Arthur's apartments from the stone path along the perimeter of the manor, signs of occupation caught her eye. The bright glow of an oil lamp spilled onto the Small Court from the billiard room above. She chortled to herself. Arthur had made his escape before she had. Well, he'd have to put up with his little sister for a while.

She entered the house via the gardener's entrance and climbed the narrow staircase, quite a difficult task in her cage crinoline and stiff petticoats. At the landing she heard billiard balls crashing together, followed by a muttered oath.

Not Arthur. No, that was not Arthur's voice at all. Not only was it a bit deeper and growlier, the profanity twanged with a heavy accent. Not Continental. Maybe…American?

Of course. Arthur's American. Her brother was expecting the man and had warned Sophia—and apologized to Henny—that he would be preoccupied with the American on business matters, that Sophia should not meddle nor ask too many questions as she was wont to do. Arthur hated it when she asked a lot of questions. She really did have a curious nature but sometimes she played it up just to annoy him.

She chewed on her lip thoughtfully. Meeting this American promised to be far more interesting a diversion than necking and toying with Geoffrey. She'd get to ask the Yankee about all sorts of things then startle Arthur with her knowledge. Why, the old gent would probably be flattered to have a young girl talk to him about whatever it was he did—something with railways, if she remembered correctly.

The door to the billiard room stood ajar. She peered in. And froze.

She hadn't expected to see a young man, much less a handsome man with tousled light-brown hair, bent over the billiard table, his intense gray eyes boring down the length of the cue then flickering up to the red object ball on the felt. And he wasn't dressed—well he was, just not properly. He wore only his shirt, the placket unbuttoned, emphasizing the brawny bulk of his chest, and his sleeves rolled up, exposing the fine hair on his thick arms. She had never seen so much bared male flesh before in her life.

A delicious heat melted her insides, sliding an audible sigh down her throat, quashed quickly by a gasp of embarrassment.

Joseph looked up, his concentration on the aim of the cue broken by a melodic, breathy sound at the door. A spark of surprise shot through him at the sight of an angelic vision in white, a spectacularly beautiful young woman who slowly entered the room as he pulled himself up from his bent position over the billiard table. Her auburn hair framed a perfect face, radiating a glow of youthful innocence only slightly marred—or perhaps enhanced—by an obvious inquisitiveness bordering on deviousness reflected in her mossy eyes.

She seemed stunned into silence by his presence so he broke the spell.

"Hullo." He took a puff of his cigar to calm his body's growing interest in the girl.

"Are you Arthur's American?"

God, her accent was utterly charming.

He chuckled. "I suppose I am. You look like you were just at that shindig."

"I beg your pardon?"

"Party," he explained, giving her the once-over. "I guess it was a formal affair."

The bodice of her ball gown fit perfectly on her shapely form, a row of pale-pink silk roses demarcating the low-cut neckline from the ivory flesh of her steadily heaving bosom. A damn distracting sight. He ripped his gaze away unwillingly.

She walked farther into the room. "Yes, I was at that 'shindig'," she said, pronouncing the word with an exaggerated and clumsy American accent.

She drew her finger along the polished edge of the billiard table, awakening his brain to fantasies of her finger stroking a part of him in need of attention at that very moment.

"I found it rather boring," she added.

"Boring?" A room full of women as beautiful as she couldn't possibly be boring. "How so?"

"For one, there were not very many attractive men." She bit her lip, her apparent abashment profoundly provocative.

Aha. So he had a chance. Sort of. She was clearly far above his laboring-class background. Still, a man should always try his luck where women were concerned. "How might the presence of attractive men have made the party more interesting?"

She cocked her head. "I would have had far more distractions." She drew out the last word as if implying something indecent.

His unruly prick stirred. "And how would you like a man to distract you?"

She glanced up through long lashes. "First, he would bring me a refreshment."

Joseph grabbed his brandy snifter and handed it to her. Her eyes widened and she took a sip. Her choking gag revealed her innocence as far as liquor was concerned. She blushed sheepishly. He chuckled and downed the rest of the drink.

"Then after a refreshment," she said, clearing her throat, "he would offer his arm for a walk to the ballroom."

Joseph gallantly held out his right arm. She wrapped her delicate, warm hand around him, blushing at the touch of bare skin on bare skin. His cock livened again.

"Of course he would be a fine dancer," she said.

Joseph extended his arms in a waltz stance. She flushed again as she grasped his left hand and placed her other hand on his right shoulder, his state of undress rather conspicuous in such a position as her gaze met his chest. Her breathing noticeably quickened.

He placed his right hand at her waist and it took every ounce of his willpower to not pull her into his arms and kiss her senseless.

Instead, he led her in a waltz around the billiard table. She moved with him in perfect rhythm, as if they had danced together before, as if they were meant to dance with one another. She was so precious in her inability to decide where to focus. She stared at the opening of his unbuttoned shirt with a mixture of fascination and alarm then looked askance with a blush. Tried to meet his eyes, then shied away.

Shit. She had to be a virgin. Perhaps the most precocious and intriguing virgin he had ever met but he'd have to be careful.

"And when the dance ended?" he inquired, slowing his pace after a turn around the table.

"He would suggest we go for a walk."

He offered his arm and once again she took it willingly. He led her beyond the French doors out onto the terrace. A breeze tried to cool him but his flesh was far too heated from her closeness.

He dipped his head toward hers. "And then?"

She smiled alluringly. "He would flatter me."

"In what way?"

The beguiling smile turned into a grin. "By comparing my beauty to the stars or some such poetic silliness."

Joseph chuckled softly then walked her to the balustrade at the edge of the terrace where the light of the billiard room could not reach. He looked up at the stars.

"Do you see that formation over there?" He pointed at the sky.

"You mean the Plough?"

"Plough?" He hadn't heard it called that before. "It's also known as Ursa Major, which means Great Bear in Latin."

"Are you comparing me to a bear, sir?" she asked with feigned shock.

He chuckled. "During the time of the gods and goddesses," he began with a seductive drawl, "there was a beautiful princess named Callisto. She was a companion of Artemis, the virgin goddess of the hunt, and as such Callisto took a vow to remain a virgin. Callisto's beauty was unsurpassed, even by the goddess herself, and Zeus, the god of all gods, wanted her desperately."

The virgin on the terrace shivered slightly from the chilly night. Joseph positioned himself behind her, shielding her from the breeze with the warmth of his body.

"Zeus was a devious seducer. He assumed the form of Artemis and approached Callisto while she picked flowers alone in the woods. He convinced her that he was the huntress, and as Artemis he made love to the virgin princess."

"Two women making love?" She sounded genuinely astonished. "Is that possible?"

He bent down and watched the pulse quicken in her neck, breathing in her delicate perfume intensified by her skin's heated arousal. "Yes…and what a wondrous act to behold," he said softly in her ear. He straightened to stare at the sky again. "Callisto bore a son and was banished by Artemis. Zeus' wife Hera was filled with jealous rage. To protect his lover and his son, Zeus turned them into bears and put them in the sky out of reach from both goddesses."

"Ursa Major and Ursa Minor."

"Yes." He lowered his head to murmur in her ear. "Your beauty is as Callisto's, tempting both man and woman but only within reach to one man, a lucky man, a god among men to have your love, a man for whom you are a shining beacon in his otherwise dreary life."

Despite the mawkish mixed metaphors she seemed deliciously agitated. She turned toward him. "And after such poetic words I think I should like him to kiss me," she said with a boldness he had only hoped she had.

Every nerve in his body tingled with anticipation. "Kiss you?" he queried gently. "Where?"

"Well, a terrace would be far too public. So perhaps a dark corner of the garden."

He grinned. "I meant what part of your anatomy."

He knew she flushed at that and he cursed the night and his shadow for obscuring her reaction. She returned her attention to the sky then looked at him with an innocent coquettishness that inflamed certain parts of *his* anatomy.

"Sir, you are very wicked." She broke out in a grin and laughed a stunningly melodic laugh.

There was no possible way he could kiss her. She was clearly someone of high rank from her manner, her dress, and the fact she had shown up at the Earl of Petersham's house in the middle of the night. But kiss her was what he wanted to do. He fought every instinct to pull her into his arms and give her the most memorable of kisses.

"Phillips." Arthur's felicitous call came from the terrace doors. "I'm glad to see you arrived safely." He walked across the terrace to heartily shake Joseph's hand then looked down at the young woman. "I suppose you kept yourself well occupied. It looks as if you were about to ravish my sister."

Shit. "Your sister?" Joseph immediately stepped back.

His beautiful virgin crossed her arms to fend off the cold, plumping her distracting breasts in the process.

"Yes, my sister." Arthur gave the young woman a chastising look. "I was trying to find her. The guests were rather upset she had disappeared from her own birthday party," he scolded.

"Arthur," she complained. "You know only one guest in particular would make such a fuss."

"One very important guest."

Joseph cleared his throat.

Arthur sighed. "I suppose you two didn't bother introducing yourselves?"

"It seemed more freeing somehow that we did not," Joseph offered as he stole a glance at the girl.

"Joseph, may I present to you my very incorrigible sister, Lady Sophia Harwell." Arthur turned to his now-smirking sibling. "Sophie, may I introduce my business partner in a new American venture, Mr. Joseph Phillips."

Sophia. Wisdom. She should have been named Circe, an island seductress tempting unsuspecting travelers. "Pleased to make your acquaintance, my lady." He bowed slightly as he imagined one did when one met nobility.

She curtsied with a smile. "And yours, Mr. Phillips."

"Arthur, I've looked everywhere—"

The second most beautiful woman Joseph had ever seen approached them on the terrace. What heaven had he been dropped into?

She stopped and surveyed the scene, flashing a glance between him and Lady Sophia. "Oh, I see you've found her," she said, her voice dripping with insinuation. Blonde hair framed a face beautiful in its perfection but, much like the sister, colored by an intriguing mischievousness.

She grabbed Arthur's arm and he immediately took possession of her by placing the arm around her waist instead. They clearly belonged together but all the while she regarded Joseph—and his state of undress—with keen interest.

"Have we been introduced?" she asked.

"My apologies," Arthur exclaimed. "Mr. Joseph Phillips, meet my fiancée, Lady Henrietta Langley."

She held out her hand and Joseph took it lightly and bowed.

"So you're the American," Lady Henrietta said as if quite impressed. "Arthur, you didn't tell me how handsome he was."

She flashed a look at Lady Sophia, who blushed.

"Arthur talks about you quite a bit," Lady Henrietta added.

"And he talked about you quite a bit last fall in New York. However, his effusions were no match for your beauty in person."

"Oh, goodness. Are all American men as handsome and charming as you, Mr. Phillips?"

He chuckled. "I would like to think so. But next time Arthur will have to bring you along so you can find out for yourself."

"Before we start talking about America, I have to return Sophie to the ballroom," Arthur said, eying his sister with a scowl. "The Duke of Royston is waiting."

"Yes, Arthur," Lady Sophia pouted with resignation and disappointment, no longer the enchantingly seductive virgin, instead the whiny little sister.

"Well, I should probably get some sleep myself," Joseph announced. "Ladies, it has been a pleasure." He bowed again.

Lady Sophia Harwell smiled sweetly at him, a smile he knew would bedevil him in his dreams all night long.

* * * * *

After having returned Sophie to the ballroom, Arthur kept a watchful eye on her from the fringes of the dance floor, rocking back and forth on his heels, his hands clasped behind his back. She was marvelous at feigning having a grand time at her party. She'd be waltzing with the duke next, an obligation she loathed but which she'd have to get used to. If it wasn't the duke, it would be some other friend or associate of Father's. And unfortunately Father did not have interesting or young friends.

"Arthur, stop fidgeting," scolded Henny at his side. "You're like a boy at his first ball."

"I *am* like a boy," he said, bending down to her ear. "A boy on Christmas morning who's waited far too long to open his presents. No one will notice if we leave, my darling, so now would be the time to get away."

She caught his eye with a start. "You devil."

"I'll give you just enough time for your lady's maid to fiddle with that contraption under your skirt and take it off."

"You don't intend for Adele to join us, do you, love?" she inquired flippantly.

"They do that sort of thing in France, don't they?"

"I wouldn't know, Arthur. Do they?"

He chuckled. "Fifteen minutes, Henny."

She pursed her lips to stifle a giggle and walked away casually.

Arthur tried to tamp down the excitement growing inside. Fifteen minutes was an eternity to his unruly cock. He and Henny hadn't had much time to do anything during her stay, as she had been trifling with Sophie over clothes and men and all sorts of things young girls concern themselves about.

He sighed. Henny was going to be the best sister-in-law Sophie could imagine.

He looked up from his reverie, certain fifteen minutes had gone by. He glanced around cautiously, seeing all eyes on Sophie and the duke, and sauntered away to the first floor of the guest wing.

Her door was unlocked as he knew it would be. He didn't give a damn if the servants saw him slip inside.

Henny stood in the middle of her bedroom in her chemise, the soft glow of an oil lamp exaggerating every shadow made by her curvaceous figure, her pretty, pink-tipped breasts buoyant under the filmy linen.

He started toward her.

"Uh-uh," she said, holding out her hand. "You have to take off your clothes, Arthur darling, before you can touch."

"Termagant."

He held her gaze as he hastily shed his clothing, her smirk dissolving into lust as each article dropped to the floor. And when he stood before her utterly nude she stared at his exuberant cock bobbing in the air, the tip of her tongue flicking over her lips.

He had no time for games. He peeled off her chemise, picked her up and deposited her on the bed, bouncing onto the mattress beside her. She squealed in delight as he pecked her face, her neck, her shoulder. He cupped a firm, round breast, eliciting a breathy sigh, then pressed his mouth to hers. She yielded under him with a soft moan, her body growing more pliant with every caress, letting him slip between her legs, allowing his cock to rub against her quim. He rolled his hips, nestling his erection in her wetness.

She stiffened and grabbed his face between her hands. "Arthur, I'm not ready."

He kissed her cheek. "I understand, darling." He only sort of did. "We'll wait. There's no hurry." Except his balls were at bursting. What a shame girls were taught to wait until their wedding night, even worse that they should expect a horrific, painful event.

She relaxed. "Thank you, love." She pecked the tip of his nose. "I'm just too old-fashioned." She kissed his lips. "Maybe we should have gone to Scotland. No one would have known and we could still have a church wedding. And I wouldn't have these silly qualms."

"It would have raised a great deal of suspicion had you and I gone to Lamberton together." He laughed. "Your qualms aren't silly. I've asked far too much of you already. You're too generous."

He slid down to kiss her breasts, pressing them together as he licked her excited nipples, drawing one into his mouth. He sucked relentlessly while working the other peak, pinching the tender tip. She writhed under him, threading her fingers through his hair, pulling at the strands, moaning gently, encouraging him to move lower.

He trailed gentle kisses down her body, nipped her belly, still kneading her soft bosom. He reached the hair of her mons and she breathed her consent.

"Oh, darling. Yes please."

He was rock hard. He pushed her knees up and out, exposing her, and became harder still. He ground his cock into the mattress, expecting to spend at any moment.

He licked his lips then delved in, slipping his tongue through her plump sex. She was deliciously sticky, growing wetter as he feasted on her, squirming beneath him, mewling entreaties. He nibbled on her clit and she thrashed ecstatically, heaving her hips against his mouth.

God, he needed release.

He reached for his rampant cock, moving abruptly as he did so, breaking the spell she was under. Henny lifted her head then curled and curved on the mattress.

"Let me," she said.

He twisted around to meet her, straddling her, his erection pointing toward her face. She gripped him and slowly drew him into her mouth.

He uttered an oath against her quim as heated wetness surrounded his cock, then practically came as she sucked the full length deeper, her tongue stroking along the shaft, her lips tightening and loosening as she moved her head up and down. He no longer knew what he was doing to her but she continued to moan around him, the delectable vibrations stimulating even more. He was going to spend but for an even sweeter climax, he needed her to spend too.

He sucked on her clitoris, frantically flicking his tongue against the nub. Her breaths puffed unevenly, her attentions to his pleasure grew chaotic. Her hips undulated in a frenetic cadence, every thrust against his mouth brusque and jerky, when suddenly she pressed up and screamed around his cock. But he did not stop, he could not stop.

He sucked on her clit as his orgasm welled within, propelling him forward in a whirlwind of bliss to erupt without warning, emptying his seed in her willing mouth as he tumbled down into a rapturous abyss.

They lay in a tangle of limbs and satisfaction, panting, until she pushed him off with a friendly groan. Arthur gathered her in his arms and nuzzled his nose into her hair.

"That was marvelous, Henny."

She sighed, her breath hot on his chest. "I can't wait until we're married. It will be so much fun, won't it?"

He chuckled and gave her a squeeze. Henny had proved over and over how much she enjoyed bed sport. "Yes it will."

Sophia had to admit the Duke of Royston was at least a good dancer. His carriage in the waltz was strong, his steps practiced, his lead unwavering—so much so she could practically close her eyes and think about Mr. Joseph Phillips.

And two hours later—far too much of that time spent with Anna undressing her with painstaking care, fretting about fashion as she removed Sophia's elaborate underwear—and finally in bed, Sophia could fantasize about Mr. Phillips freely. She imagined the kiss they almost shared, pondered how two women could possibly make love, wondered how on earth Mr. Phillips could have been a witness to such a "wondrous act".

She pulled up her nightgown and cupped her hand over the hair between her legs. Whenever she and Geoffrey kissed, a pleasurable heat grew there. Pressing her palm into her mound and her fingers against the dampness always relieved her agitation. But tonight her body yearned for a satisfaction she did not understand. She needed something more than just a press of her hand. She squeezed her thighs together, finding a momentary release. She did it again and again, each squeeze resulting only in increased desire.

Fantasies of Mr. Joseph Phillips apparently required desperate measures.

She had never dared to delve a finger inside. Virginity was too much of a prize. But what if she fondled herself just a little? Surely touching just the outside would not be harmful?

She stroked the plump outer flesh, tangling in the damp hair, then ever so tentatively slid a finger over the slit, working her way slowly between the folds. She was stickier than she had ever been. She drew her finger back and forth through the wetness, wishing desperately she could insert a finger to relieve the pulsating throb vexing her deep inside.

She closed her eyes and sighed.

Joseph.

He was looking down at her, his gray gaze flicking between her eyes and her mouth, his lips parted ever so slightly, enough that the tip of his tongue toyed with the lower lip, wetting it. He placed his hands on her shoulders, slid them down her arms to her elbows, his touch exciting her, stiffening her nipples. He grasped her at the waist, his hold secure and strong.

"Where shall I kiss you?" he murmured, lowering his head. "In the garden?" His head tilted slightly to the right. "Or on your lips?"

And then his mouth covered hers, his body enveloped hers. Her mouth fell open, yearning for his tongue, her nipples ached, yearning for his touch. And then she was Callisto, among the stars, spinning in the heavens and he was dancing with her, surrounding her, on top of her. Her feminine passage flexed and squeezed, yearning to be filled. And then he was inside her and she squeezed him with all her might until the force of it flung her bodily, to burn amongst the stars.

Sophia woke with a start, panting, confused…

Mired in that *feeling* again. She rarely experienced it, and only after Geoffrey had kissed her with more than his usual enthusiasm. A feeling so wonderful and luscious and exhausting and energizing all at once. And tonight so much more splendid. If there was only a way she could control it.

She heaved an exhale then laughed softly to herself. She would blush terribly the next time she saw Mr. Joseph Phillips.

CHAPTER TWO

From the wingback in his study, Arthur peeked over the afternoon paper at Geoffrey, who sat behind the grand desk shuffling documents and muttering to himself.

"My sister said she barely got in a dance with you at her birthday. And never got the thorough tonguing she was hoping for."

Geoffrey stopped cold and stared at him. "She said nothing of the sort."

"I really should be defending her honor."

"You're not supposed to know."

"Henny thinks it's marvelous."

"Ah." Geoffrey shook his head and resumed sorting the piles on the desk.

"Anyway, apparently when she couldn't find you she ended up on my terrace with Joseph."

That got a rise out of him. "Who?"

"Phillips. The American. You might have some competition."

"Well, he'll be sorry as neither one of us can win that game."

A tentative knock sounded at the door.

"Speak of the devil," Arthur murmured. "Come."

Joseph entered, his hair slightly disheveled, his rumpled jacket stretched a tad tightly on his bulky form. "Sorry. I guess I didn't realize how exhausted I was from the voyage."

As always, his accent was simply charming.

Geoffrey stood, unfolding his lanky height from behind the desk. "You must be Joseph Phillips."

Surprise flickered briefly on Joseph's face as he took in Geoffrey's stature. "I am."

Geoffrey strode forward, ably covering the length of the carpet with only a few steps. He held out his hand. "A pleasure to finally meet you, Phillips. Geoffrey Peel."

"My solicitor," Arthur said, getting up from the wingback.

The two men shook hands. Geoffrey returned to the desk while Arthur motioned to the other wingback.

"There's still some tea left. Unless you want sherry. It *is* after four," Arthur said.

"I think I'm supposed to get used to tea." Joseph sat heavily in the chair.

"It's very good. Next time think twice before you dump a shipload into the harbor."

He laughed—a hearty, genuine, *American* laugh. Arthur handed him a cup and Joseph relaxed into the cushioned upholstery.

"Right," Geoffrey announced as he patted three stacks of paper on the desk. He picked up two stacks, handed one to Arthur and the other to Joseph.

"What's this?" Joseph put the tea down on the side table and took the sheaf of papers.

"Lord Petersham's contract," Geoffrey said with a flourish. "The initial private partnership."

"That which binds us together," Arthur said. "Like a marriage."

"Except," said Geoffrey, "you can sever the ties that bind when the relationship is no longer profitable. You don't need an Act of Parliament."

"And there will be three of us," Arthur chuckled.

Joseph grinned then flipped through the pages. "I've already read it, haven't I?"

"Yes, yes, it's the same document." Geoffrey paced before the desk, crossing the distance in only two strides. "I had official copies made. That's yours. We should go ahead and sign them now."

"I can trust him, right?" Joseph jested as Geoffrey laid out the signature pages.

"I do," said Arthur. "Even with my sister."

Joseph colored slightly. "Are congratulations in order, Peel?"

Geoffrey let out a sharp laugh. "Ah, no. But I've known the family so long, I'm allowed certain liberties." He winked.

The three gathered along the desk, each signing his name in turn as partners in *Harwell & Co.*

"Now what?" Joseph sank into the wingback.

"Arthur and I will draw up a list of potential investors, get an idea of interest." Geoffrey leaned against the desk. "That sort of thing."

Arthur took the seat opposite. "We already have a short list of initial backers."

"I'll draw up a separate contract establishing the joint-stock company. Eventually, we'll have to conform to your American laws as well."

Arthur turned to Joseph. "I've set up a studio for you, away from the house. Very private. There should be everything you need for drawing preliminaries. We'll present drafts of the plans to the investors, show off your talents so they'll have more confidence in the scheme. We'll have official plans made up for manufacturing purposes later." He angled forward, his elbows on his knees. "If you need anything, *anything*, do not hesitate to ask. I have no idea what sort of materials engineers need."

Joseph looked a bit stunned. Perhaps overwhelmed. "Thank you, Peel. Thank you, Arthur."

Geoffrey started at that. "'Arthur'?"

Joseph flushed. "I just made a faux pas, didn't I?"

Arthur shook his head. "We agreed in New York that titles didn't matter between us." He sighed. "But Geoff's right. In company, especially when business is at stake, you should probably be a bit more formal. Definitely call my parents by their titles. I insist on it, really."

Joseph turned to Geoffrey. "Do you have one?"

"Not yet. I have to wait for my father to die." He chuckled. "He's rather hale and hearty so I don't expect it to be anytime soon." All of a sudden he snapped his fingers. "I almost forgot." He opened a tooled leather portfolio and searched the documents. "Ah. Here it is." He placed a document on the table and offered the pen to Joseph.

Joseph furrowed his brow. "Something else for me to sign?"

Arthur slapped his hands on his thighs and stood. "Of course. I almost forgot as well. Thank you, Geoff." He grabbed the pen and dipped it in the inkwell and signed. "I'm selling my property in Lamberton to you. To give you a foothold here. Well Scotland actually, just over the border. It's a small cottage, no great tract of land. But it's the only land I own that's not entailed in some manner."

Joseph blushed. "But I don't have any money." He took the pen gingerly.

"I'm loaning you the money or rather the corporation is loaning you the money. Anyway I don't need the property. You'll like it up there I'm sure. Green and rural. Near the coast. Take the Great Northern to York then the North Eastern. Lovely ride."

Joseph signed and handed the pen back to Geoffrey. "So if you don't need it, why did you buy the house in the first place?"

Geoffrey laughed. "Arthur thought he might secure an irregular marriage when he first met Henny."

Arthur flushed at his foolhardy impulse. "You can marry whomever you choose in Scotland with the simple act of living there for twenty-one days. Henny was not of age when we first met."

"And not properly yours," Geoffrey added.

Arthur flashed him a chiding look. "Visit whenever you want," he said to Joseph. "I keep a steward and a housekeeper. Briggs is an old widower and Mrs. Reed is his sister. Endearing pair. You should keep them."

"By all means," Joseph chortled.

Geoffrey held his pen over the inkwell, more documents spread before him. "As your New York address legally belongs to your landlord, we'll establish the Lamberton house as your place of residence on the corporation contract. Once we have you set up with an office in New York we'll amend the paperwork."

Arthur returned to his teacup. "By the way, are you staying for dinner, Geoff?"

"Absolutely. Any chance to see your delightful sister, Petersham."

Arthur grinned. "Don't get your hopes up. Royston's still here."

"Of course he is." Geoffrey laughed. "Free meals and endless coal. Anything to economize on his own expenses. Does your father send over his tailor while he's here as well?"

Geoffrey's assessment was too cutting but he merely said aloud what they both felt about the man.

"Who's this Royston fellow anyway?" Joseph asked. "You mentioned him the other night. Your sister did not look pleased."

"Friend of the family. He stays here an awful lot, presumably to court Sophia but Geoff's not half wrong either. He may be a duke but he's practically in the poorhouse."

"He simply ill-manages what's left of his estate," Geoffrey said.

"And he's a bad investor," Arthur muttered into his teacup.

"That as well."

"You'll meet him tonight, Joseph. You're coming with me to dinner at the main house."

Joseph grinned. "Am I also allowed to say 'any chance to see your delightful sister'?"

Geoffrey guffawed.

"Both of you will have to behave. There's a houseful of guests." He eyed Joseph. "You do have dinner dress, do you not?"

"I think I might have something slightly surpassing what I have on."

"Bollocks." They were about the same height but Joseph was wide in the shoulders, with thick arms and chest. Geoffrey was taller and thinner than either of them.

"Unacceptable, huh?" Joseph crinkled his brow.

"Stand up, Phillips." Geoffrey circled thoughtfully around a mystified Joseph. "Right. I have to go home to dress anyway. I'll bring you something of my father's. You look to be about the same build."

"Hale and hearty?"

Geoffrey chuckled. "Similar sense of humor as well. He's got more around the middle though."

"Thank you, Geoff. We'll make do. I'll have to set you up with my tailor soon, Joseph."

"You make me feel like a duke, my lord."

Arthur's jaw dropped and Geoffrey roared with laughter. A shared private joke was the perfect beginning to their partnership.

Dining every so often with the marquess and marchioness would be necessary, Arthur had said, and Joseph had agreed to comply with his wishes, albeit with a little reluctance. Insipid, polite chatter while liveried servants watched and listened was disconcerting. But he would have to get used to such surroundings and mingling with the aristocracy if he and Arthur were to have any success. Besides, Lady Sophia would be in attendance. The opportunity to gaze at her would be a pleasant diversion.

A long oak table, its thick legs carved in twisted spirals, dominated the linen-fold-paneled dining room. Joseph was placed on the left of the Marchioness of Richmond, a place of honor Arthur had said. The Duke of Royston sat directly across from him, Lady Sophia at the duke's right, which meant the duke could not leer at her without being conspicuous. Disgust bristled the nape of Joseph's neck. A wrinkled, portly man ogling a girl who looked as if she could be his granddaughter was just grotesque. Not only was the duke presumably lacking in wealth, he most definitely lacked manners. Why Lady Sophia allowed his suit was beyond comprehension.

For the moment though, Joseph had the advantage. Unlike Royston's sidelong glances with slivered gray eyes, Joseph had a full view of her stunningly low neckline, the pale skin of her bosom flushing a delicate rose whenever she dared meet his gaze.

Peel sat next to Joseph and it seemed when Lady Sophia wasn't glancing at him she was glancing at Peel. Her gaze was more confident when turned on the lanky solicitor, the flush mellowing to a creamy ivory, the curl of the lip knowing. There was definitely something between them.

The marquess, his face lined too deeply for a man probably only in his forties, occupied the far end of the table. Arthur sat on his left, Lady Henrietta across from her fiancé in the place of honor. A flicker of joy brightened Arthur's face every time he looked at his beloved, a sight wonderfully sweet to behold.

Of the other men and women present, Joseph had only a passing acquaintance. A few were potential investors Arthur had said. But most were friends of the marquess and marchioness who had stayed on after Lady Sophia's birthday ball and who now eyed him with the same curiosity reserved for the creatures in a zoo. The marchioness, at least, tried to engage him, probably at Arthur's behest.

"Did you say your father *owns* the docks in New York, Mr. Phillips?" Lady Richmond's voice dripped with honeyed hauteur.

Joseph looked up from cutting the succulent spring lamb on the gold-rimmed porcelain dinner plate set before him. "No, ma'am. I said he works on the docks in New York City. These days he takes care of the books—the accounts—for a few companies."

"Oh, my word." She gasped in obvious shock, her hand covering her mouth, her eyes clouding with incredulity. She glanced around at the guests, whose own conversations had paused at her outburst. "Then how is it you seem so well-educated and refined?"

Joseph ignored the condescension in her voice. Maintaining a veneer of civility took a lot of fucking effort around the half-witted upper crust. "One meets quite a number of interesting people growing up around the port. I ingratiated myself to the best among them, worked hard and gained their trust and respect. In the mornings, I was tutored with the children of New York society. In the afternoons and evenings, I worked. Nights I studied. I had to scrounge in the trash heaps for enough candles."

"Goodness. When did you have time to sleep?" Lady Henrietta blurted.

Joseph chuckled. "Sleep is a luxury for the laboring classes, my lady."

He caught the butler's eye. The old man looked away in horror. Even the servants of England's aristocracy felt themselves above him.

"I apologize," Lady Henrietta said ingenuously. "I hope I did not cause offense."

"No offense, my lady." He smiled at her. He really liked Lady Henrietta, liked that she said what she thought.

"Might we know any of these families of New York society, Mr. Phillips?" The marchioness seemed hopeful, perhaps a tad desperate for her son's reputation.

"I sincerely doubt it, ma'am. Not unless you know the Stuyvesants, Coopers, Schermerhorns, and Astors."

"Those sound like foreign names," the duke snorted.

"I would assume so, Your Grace," Peel said. "America is known for its surfeit of immigrants building a new country as opportunity is lacking in their own."

Joseph hid a smile as he resumed eating his dinner. The conversation quickly turned to more pleasant, vacuous topics, which suited him just fine. It gave him a chance to observe the marquess and marchioness. Lady Richmond wore a striped dress of emerald and rust, the green matching her eyes, the rust-red a reminder of the former vivid color of her graying tresses. Lord Richmond's formerly brown hair was now graying in a frame around his face, his green-brown eyes almost the twin of Arthur's but with the sadness of regret. The couple looked weary and seemed to merely tolerate each other despite their having been wed for what must have been nigh on thirty years. So unlike his parents. Mother and Father acted more like Arthur and Lady Henrietta.

He glanced at Lady Sophia and caught her looking at him. Her guilty blush sent an inappropriate shiver down his back. That morning he had masturbated to a fantasy of her, to a remembrance of her body trapped by his against the balustrade. But that fleeting moment of intimacy would be all he would have with her, especially as her supposed fiancé was fawning possessively at her side.

The Duke of Royston was a dour man and utterly unsuitable for the captivating innocent that was Lady Sophia. But marriage amongst the upper classes was not for love and passion. Such unions were for wealth and connections. Joseph had seen some of the daughters of American society married off at far too young an age to men old enough to be their fathers. Probably their fathers' friends and business associates. The practice was despicable.

Inwardly Joseph sighed. Men such as the duke and the marquess were mired in history, in tenaciously preserving the past instead of exploring new opportunities, planning new adventures. There would be more evenings like this one. Joseph would just have to brace himself.

Geoffrey carefully negotiated the warren of dim, oak-paneled passageways in Harwell Hall on his way to the drawing room. He did appreciate that the Richmonds were modern enough to have indoor plumbing in their Tudor manor but the journey from the dining room to the water closet was a bit circuitous. Of course he might have taken a wrong turn at some point. Perhaps he needed to visit the main house more often to get to know the place.

He chuckled. Royston probably knew every blasted nook and cranny in the estate for all the time he spent there.

The next corridor should lead him back to the drawing room, which was next to the dining room. The men would have finished their port by now. He turned the corner—

"Oof." Geoffrey grunted as he crashed into a woman, instinctively grasping her shoulders to steady them both.

Her yelp of surprise lingered in midair as her book fell to the floor, just missing his foot.

Anna. Wonderfully kissable Anna. He flushed. He should not think of such things in mixed company.

"Mr. Peel."

He continued to hold her at the shoulders. The only thing preventing him from pulling her against him was his damnable honor and an accursed sewing basket she clutched before her.

"Miss…Miss…"

"I'm Anna, sir." Her gaze fell to the basket.

"I thought to give you the same courtesy of using your surname."

She smiled a sweet, sweet smile with her kissable lips. "Colney, sir. Anna Colney."

"Well, Miss Colney, will you accept an apology from an ungraceful clod?" His hands tingled from the lingering touch. He drew them down her arms adroitly.

She looked up at him. Her brown eyes matched the rich oak of the wainscoting and her cheeks were accentuated with a rosy flush. He had never noticed until that moment how much she resembled Sophia. If not for the severe servant's uniform, one might mistake her for a cousin. Perhaps a cousin in mourning.

"You're not a clod, sir. It's a hazard of the ground floor. Such accidents happen more often than not amongst the servants."

"Ah." He should leave but he couldn't. "So what are you doing down here on the ground floor?"

"Lady Sophia called. She needed a quick repair to her bodice."

Hence the sewing basket. "You're wearing a different dress," he blurted.

"Sir?" She blushed.

Bollocks. "From the other night. This one is black. And is it silk?"

"It is last year's mourning gown from my lady." She nibbled on her lower lip. "When guests are lodging we're to dress for dinner as well, sir. I need to be presentable in case I am called upon."

He could not take his eyes off her now-moistened lip. "You would think my house barbaric then. I'm certain we do no such thing."

She smiled the loveliest of smiles. "I'm sure the lady of your house sees to it, sir."

"My mother."

"Sir?"

"My mother. Lady Bucknall. There is no Mrs. Peel."

She blushed. "I had gathered that, sir."

Of course. His kissing Sophia. Or Anna, rather.

She curtsied. "I'll take my leave, if you don't mind, sir."

She bent to pick up her book, almost crashing into him again as he thought to do the same.

He straightened and glanced at the gilded letters on the cover. "*North and South*. I've not read that one. Is it good?"

"I am enjoying it, sir."

"It's about industrialization, is it not? I should probably read it."

She laughed softly. "Yes, I suppose Mrs. Gaskell does touch on similar themes to what you and Lord Petersham are about to embark upon." Her hand flew to her mouth. "I'm dreadfully sorry, sir. My lady has spoken a little about your scheme. I have not been indiscreet with the knowledge."

"You have already proved your penchant for discretion with your silence concerning my relationship with Lady Sophia." He handed her the book.

She looked away as she tucked it inside her basket. "Thank you, sir." She curtsied and started in the direction from where he had just come.

"Wait."

She hesitated. "Sir?"

He had to say something. Really he just wanted to kiss her but such a move would reek of power and privilege, making him yet another aristocrat abusing a servant. He did not want such a base relationship with her. He wanted something more. But such a thing could never be managed.

"I just wanted…I mean to say that…I think you look lovely tonight."

She blushed. "Thank you, sir."

"Last time I saw you it was practically pitch dark, otherwise I would have told you then." *Blast*. That sounded stupid.

"And you were otherwise occupied. Good night, sir." She turned and left.

Otherwise occupied, indeed. Geoffrey chuckled to himself. Anna Colney was simply magnificent.

* * * * *

Arthur gritted his teeth and clenched his fists as he crossed from the dining room into the drawing room to join the women. Henny furrowed her brow briefly then offered a comforting expression as she took his arm.

"Was the port that bad, darling?" she said.

"They excoriated him and by default, excoriated me."

"Who, darling?"

"Father for one."

"You and the marquess have never really got on. It's a shame."

That was, unfortunately, too true. Relations between father and son had always been rather formal, even when Arthur was a boy. He watched as more of the men filed leisurely into the drawing room. "And him."

Arthur eyed Royston cautiously as the duke approached. He not only abhorred Royston's cutting remarks regarding Joseph's background, he was wary of Royston's continued fascination with Henny. The duke practically leered at her.

"Henny, my darling—"

Arthur buried his fury. The man had no right to call her anything but Lady Henrietta.

"You look absolutely ravishing this evening."

"Thank you, Your Grace. My engagement to the most fascinating of men has heightened my complexion and my spirits."

God he loved her. She was fabulously clever. And he had to agree, absolutely ravishing in a blue and gold striped, ruffled confection that matched her coloring to perfection.

"Fascinating is right, my dear, what with his unusual choice of a business partner."

Arthur seethed.

Father joined them. "Yes, I must agree with that, Royston." He scowled at Arthur. "Where on earth did you find him?"

"In New York," Arthur shot back, searching the room for Joseph, catching his eye as he conversed with Geoffrey and Sophia. Arthur raised a brow in invitation.

"Unusual, Your Grace?" Henny responded coolly. "Why, the Americans are a most enterprising lot. Arthur is poised to make millions, if you ask me." She smiled sweetly.

Arthur squelched a grin. Royston had just lost quite a bundle in his last investment. Something involving whale oil, as Arthur understood it.

"Why would I ever seek the opinion of a woman, my dear?" Royston asked derisively.

Father chuckled.

"Because she's got a point, Your Grace," Geoffrey retorted as he approached them.

Joseph and Sophia followed close behind, Sophia's blush a little too deep. Really, his sister's dalliance with Geoffrey had gone too far. He would have to scold her about her behavior later. She needed to maintain her reputation, for God's sake.

"Really, Peel? And what is that?" Royston's tone reflected his annoyance. He moved next to Sophia as if he owned her.

"Well, the scheme is absolutely brilliant," Geoffrey effused. "There's talk of building a railway all the way from the east coast of America to California. That's three thousand miles. That's a lot of railway carriages *and* that's a lot of railway parts. Phillips here has a plan to supply all those carriages with parts. I mean no offense, Your Grace, but only a fool would eschew such an investment."

"An investment in a scheme that merely supports a fantastical future is not my idea of a sound investment." Royston's lips thinned disdainfully. "You boys go ahead and spend your money on outlandish propositions. But don't gripe about it when you end up in the poorhouse." He shifted his attention to Henny, placing a hand on her shoulder. "I do hope, for your sake, that profits are more than a mere trifle so as to keep you in such splendid gowns." He let his hand slide down her arm to her hand. "My dear." He bowed his head over her hand and made his exit to the other side of the room.

Father followed at his heels.

Arthur's blood boiled too hot for him to speak and Joseph clearly struggled to keep a lid on his own fumes. Luckily Geoffrey had a cool head.

"Don't pay him any mind, Phillips. Petersham has shown me some of your preliminary sketches and really, I think they're brilliant. However we must be reasonable and keep in mind men of Royston's generation will be skeptical. We must make it presentable to them. We can add some interest, something unique for the younger investors, but for his lot we need to balance that with the practicalities. You know…a sound investment in the future."

Arthur shook his head in amazement. Geoffrey was a lifesaver. So maybe Arthur wouldn't scold his sister so much. She should have her fun while she could.

Sophia turned her attention from Geoffrey to Joseph. "I'd love to see your sketches, Mr. Phillips." She looked at Arthur. "If I'm allowed that is."

"I suppose." He sought confirmation from Joseph.

He nodded with a quirk of his lips.

"But it's a secret, Sophie, so you can't tell anyone," Arthur chided.

"Who am I going to tell?"

Henny laughed. "And who would believe a mere woman anyway, Arthur, darling?"

Arthur grunted in annoyance. "Tomorrow. Come by the studio tomorrow."

Sophia clapped her hands. "Oh, what fun," she chirped. She boldly took Geoffrey's arm. "Now you two gentlemen can tell me all about railways while Arthur and Henny coo."

Joseph offered his arm for her other side. She blushed as she took it and bit her lip with a grin as they sauntered away.

A pang of regret gripped Arthur's heart. Such a shame that after one year of marriage to Royston she'd have lost all that girlish exuberance.

CHAPTER THREE

Sophia huffed and puffed in laughter and exhaustion as she ran across the estate with Henny, her exertions warming her against the chill of early spring.

"C'mon, Sophie, the studio is just there." Henny was glowing. She wanted to see Arthur as much as Sophia wanted to see Mr. Phillips.

Henny was far too encouraging an ally when it came to matters regarding Mr. Phillips. She confessed she knew Sophia was utterly smitten but counseled a connection with Mr. Phillips would be dangerous. Yet Henny acknowledged she trusted Sophia could be discreet when she put her mind to it, as her liaison with Geoffrey proved.

The folly finally came into view, its exuberance of wrought iron a testament to an earlier time when a fascination for the material indicated modernity and progress. That such a harsh material could be shaped and cast into delicate columns and curlicue capitals supporting roofs and frames filled with expanses of glass had been a symbol of the new industrial age. The Marquesses of Richmond had prided themselves as forward thinkers. Alas, Papa seemed to have forgotten such a sentiment, although Arthur was taking up the standard of their forebears with alacrity.

Inside the glazed outbuilding Mr. Phillips sat hunched over a writing desk, his pen moving over paper, while Arthur paced about, waving his hands. Mr. Phillips worked steadily, intent on whatever it was he was doing, not at all distracted by Arthur's dramatic gestures. Such focus was so very…*attractive.*

Henny grabbed her hand and they skulked closer.

"Let's not go in just yet," Henny whispered. "It looks as if they're mired in something important."

Indeed. Arthur had pulled up a chair alongside the desk and seemed to be listening intently, nodding as Mr. Phillips pointed then traced his finger around the document before him. While Mr. Phillips continued to talk Arthur stared at him, examining him, his face cast by a queer expression, something akin to how he regarded Henny sometimes. Mr. Phillips finished talking and met Arthur's gaze and for a moment the two men remained in that position, until Arthur shook his head, got up and flopped down in a stuffed armchair.

"Now's our chance." Henny bounced up and skipped toward the studio.

A rush of insecurity overwhelmed her but Sophia found the courage to follow. She caught a glimpse of Mr. Phillips through the tall window, flushed at a recollection of what she had done while dreaming about him the night before then began to giggle uncontrollably.

Arthur greeted them with a mixture of relief and annoyance, the latter directed mostly at Sophia's girlish foolishness.

"Henny, darling." He kissed her cheek and squeezed her hand.

Mr. Phillips stood. "Ladies," he greeted with a bow.

"Please, Mr. Phillips, don't let us girls disturb you." Henny motioned for him to sit.

He smiled at her then flashed an even bigger grin at Sophia. Her face grew hot.

Henny wandered around the small space, made more intimate by stacks of discarded furniture covered with sheets. She lifted a corner of a sheet and examined the pile beneath it. "Where's that infamous bed, Arthur?"

Sophia swallowed hard. Mr. Phillips threw a look of astonishment at Henny.

"Bed?" inquired Arthur.

"Oh, darling, didn't you say this is where all the marquesses used to take their mistresses? It's a lovely space. I can see having a tryst here."

Arthur chuckled.

"The light is very good for drawing, Lady Henrietta," remarked Joseph.

"'Henny'. Please you *must* call me 'Henny' when we are alone like this."

"O.K., Henny."

Mr. Phillips' lips curled exquisitely. Sophia regretted not kissing him the other night.

"So show me your work, Mr. Phillips." Henny strolled over to the desk.

"Joseph." He turned to Sophia. "You too, my lady. I'm not quite comfortable with all this aristocratic politeness."

To be so intimate as to say his Christian name aloud sparked a naughty thrill. She was already practiced with whispering it in the dark.

"Sophie, you must look at this," Henny exclaimed.

Sophia joined them at the desk, her heart thumping a bit too rapidly as she stood next to Mr. Phillips—Joseph. On the desk before her lay a drawing of what looked like the exterior of a railway passenger car, every piece of it precisely delineated with the greatest attention paid to the workings underneath.

Joseph pulled out another drawing from under the stack of papers, a more detailed view of all the mechanical elements of the car.

"All these undercarriage components are made from metal. The rest of the car," he said, pointing to the full view, "is made from wood. Operating from the principle of specialization in manufacturing, I want to set up factories that create only the undercarriage components."

"So that's what you two are up to." Henny sounded impressed.

Arthur wrapped his arm around her waist. "The idea of a railway across the American continent is…well…I cringe to say, picking up steam—"

Joseph chuckled.

"And Joseph has the idea of being at the ready with parts for railway carriages once the thing is finally built."

"But won't thousands of miles of railway take a long time to build?" Sophia asked.

"You mean won't we have parts sitting in warehouses during all that time?" Joseph's eyes twinkled at her.

"Well, yes, I suppose. Something like that."

"The proposition is for us to start small. Fulfill existing need. But look toward the longer term and be ready for expansion, my lady."

"Sophia," she said softly. "You should call me Sophia, Joseph."

She could have sworn he blushed slightly at the sign of intimacy.

He cleared his throat. "But we don't want to show our cards just yet. We want our competitors to think we're not their competition. We want the element of surprise."

"Which is another reason why we're looking for multiple backers," added Arthur. "We're hoping more names attached to more companies might confuse competition."

"Geoffrey," Sophia said.

"Yes," Joseph replied. "Incorporation contracts seem to be Peel's specialty."

Henny sat in the armchair with a laugh. "Oh, Royston is going to hate the lot of you."

"He already does, Henny, darling."

"If you don't mind my asking," Joseph began circumspectly, "why is that?"

Henny flicked her gaze toward Arthur. "Arthur's less than half his age and has far better luck with his investments."

"It's not luck, Henny," Sophia countered. "Arthur takes great care and consideration with financial matters. The duke seems old-fashioned with his money."

"And I stole Henny from him," Arthur added sullenly.

Joseph glanced between Henny and Arthur, appearing a little stunned. "Really?"

Henny got up. "Arthur, you know it wasn't like that at all." She paced nervously.

"Well, that's how Royston sees it."

Joseph looked at Sophia in supplication.

"The Duke of Royston is a cousin of Henny's mother—" Sophia began.

"Distant cousin," Henny corrected.

"So Henny had been…well…sort of promised to him—"

"Since I was an adolescent," Henny added with disgust.

"But she and Arthur met at her coming out and I suppose," Sophia glanced at her brother, "they fell in love."

Arthur took Henny's hand. "That was three years ago."

Henny smiled up at him.

"But," Sophia continued, "then the duke lost a great deal of money on an absolutely foolish investment—"

"Wig powder," Arthur joked.

Henny laughed sharply.

"And Henny's father had second thoughts."

"Thank God," Henny breathed.

"At the same time Arthur had made a fortune in his transatlantic telegraph cable investment and he asked Henny's father for her hand in marriage."

"Dad jumped at the chance to marry his daughter to someone with intelligence and fabulous good looks." Henny glowed with love.

"Ah," Joseph said. He raised a brow at Sophia. "And how does Lady, uh, Sophia fit into all of this? With Royston I mean."

Arthur shuffled his feet. "My father is not as radical as Henny's father is. He sees an alliance with the duke as benefiting the legacy of the Marquessate of Richmond."

Sophia's heart fell. She knew all too well marriage to the duke was her fate but to hear the words spoken aloud in front of a man who inhabited her dreams was absolutely depressing.

"And how do you feel about this, Sophia?" Joseph's voice conveyed concern.

"It does not matter how I feel. It is my duty."

"Well, I for one think it does matter how you feel," he responded. "What about this Peel fellow?"

"You mean marry Geoffrey?" she exclaimed. "I can't. He's only an heir to a viscountcy. Papa says he wants more for me."

Joseph turned to her brother. "Arthur?"

"There's really nothing I can do. I've told Father I don't think the match is a good idea. He says young people today have foolish romantic notions. I'm not even entirely certain he approves of Henny."

A bleak silence descended upon the group until Henny puffed a sigh.

"Sophie, we promised your mother we would be back for tea. We'll have to change first."

"Yes, Henny."

Henny gave Arthur a peck on the cheek. "Right. We'll see you boys later." She grabbed Sophia's hand.

As she left, Sophia caught Joseph's sympathetic look, spurring her heart to beat a little faster.

Henny waited until almost midnight before she wended her way through darkened corridors to Arthur's apartments in the sprawling Harwell Hall. Servants clung to shadows, keeping silent as she traversed the lengths of hallways, crossed courtyards, climbed stairs. They would know the Earl of Petersham and his fiancée were desperately in love and deserved their privacy.

Light streamed into the hall from under Arthur's library door, flickering and wavering but bright. The faint scent of pipe tobacco hung in the air. She hesitated a moment, wondering if she should knock, knowing he wouldn't expect her to. She turned the knob, opened the door and stepped through.

Arthur started then stared at her with a guilty expression, the same expression he got when he had been thinking of her in a rather naughty way. He stood with his back to the fire, his hands behind him flexing in the warmth.

Before him sat Joseph, a book opened in his hand, one leg crossed over the other, dressed, as was Arthur, in a smoking jacket. Joseph, too, stared at her until realization washed over his features. He said nothing as he stood and walked toward the door, merely nodding politely at her, although she could swear there was a measure of amused approbation in his countenance. He closed the door quietly behind him.

"Henny, is something wrong?" Arthur came toward her, his gaze searching her face. "You look a bit worried."

"I do?" She touched her fingers to her cheek.

He held out his hands and she took them. "Come to the fire. Tell me."

He knew… Arthur *always* knew when her mind weighed heavily with cares and concerns. But this one was difficult to put into words.

"I'm leaving tomorrow."

"Yes. I knew it would be soon, darling," he responded softly.

"My parents are expected home from the Continent this week. Mama and I need to start planning the wedding but once we have a few things settled we'll both return here, you know, so Sophie and your mother can help too. Maybe in a few weeks or so."

He tenderly brushed a fallen curl from her face. She took his hand and pressed it to her cheek.

"I'm so lucky." She could not stop the tears from falling.

"Darling Henny, what's the matter? Please tell me."

"It's Sophie. I feel for Sophie." Young, beautiful, virginal Sophie. "Royston is remaining here, presumably to woo her." She looked up at him. "Arthur, it is a terrible match."

"I know." He wrapped his arms around her. "There's just nothing I can do."

His voice held frustration and a measure of disquietude. He might be willing to try to stop the match.

"Poor Geoffrey." She sighed. "They would make a good pair." She hesitated, knowing her next thought was daring to the point of impropriety. "And then there's Mr. Phillips."

Arthur pulled back with a furrowed brow. "What about Joseph?"

"Your sister obviously has a case on him." *Maybe you could encourage it?*

"She's eighteen. Girls her age get a 'case' on young men all the time. Besides, such a match would be preposterous, Henny."

"Sadly, yes. I just wish Sophie could have one romance before she's fettered to Royston for life." *And if she did, he might set his sights elsewhere.*

"She'll have to content herself with Geoffrey."

Henny sighed. Geoffrey was too much of a gentleman to do anything but kiss Sophia senseless. Certainly he would never deflower her without marrying her. "I suppose so."

Arthur eyed her intensely. "There's something else, isn't there?"

Her lungs constricted in dread. "It's just that," she said, trying to steady her voice, "I don't want to have to go back to that predicament ever again."

"What predicament? Henny, what are you talking about?"

"Royston," she blurted, tears streaming down her face. "I don't ever want to be considered a match for Royston."

"What?" he exclaimed incredulously. "Darling, that's never going to happen. You're engaged to me. We have a settlement, remember?"

"But what if you died?"

His incredulity sharpened. "What if I *died*?" He searched her face. "Henny, what is this about?"

She closed her eyes as she gathered her courage. "In the drawing room tonight, before Royston walked away he touched my arm." She hesitated.

Arthur gave her a gentle squeeze. "Go on."

She looked up at him, finding her strength in his eyes. "You didn't see it, I know you didn't, but I felt it. He touched me." She could not hold back the tears. "His thumb scraped along the side of my breast."

Arthur paled. "My God. No," he said hoarsely. "I'll call him out."

"Oh, no you won't," she sobbed. "I won't stand for such foolishness."

His brow twisted. "Henny, I can't let this go. He has no right." He folded her in his arms and rocked her gently, imbuing her with warm safety.

"No," she sniffled. "I know you can't. But there is another way to defeat the villain." She looked into Arthur's eyes. "Make me yours."

The incredulity returned, this time tinged with hope. "Henny?"

"I'm ready, Arthur. I want to leave here already your wife."

"But darling—"

"He won't touch me if I am spoiled. He has a letch for innocence."

He gaped in horror. "Henny—"

"Please don't ask me how I know. Please."

He enfolded her in his arms. "No. I won't."

The fire popped and sputtered, the only accompaniment to the uneasiness that hung in the air. Arthur held her tightly, gently swaying to some unheard tune.

"Kiss me," she whispered.

He bent and kissed her mouth slowly, succulently, his tongue gently probing, tantalizing her. She wrapped her hands about his neck, clinging to him for dear life. Her life.

He pulled back, his face a little flushed, his green-brown eyes dark with arousal.

"Make love to me, Arthur. Now."

"Oh, darling." His lips quirked up in a smile. "Let's go to my room."

"What about here?"

"In the library?"

"It's lovely in here. The room is warm. There's light." She cupped his cheek. "I want to see you and I want you to see me."

With an enthusiasm she had never witnessed he tore off his jacket and laid it down on the rug before the fire then divested himself of the rest of his clothes, inviting her to do the same, helping her with buttons and ties. He made a comfortable nest with the pile of garments then knelt and held out his hand, grinning broadly.

She knelt next to him, panic and desire coursing through her at the sight of his nude body rampant and ready. He motioned for her to lie down, preceding her in the act, patting the space next to him. She stretched herself out at his side, shivering despite the fire.

He traced curves from her breasts to her belly with his finger. "Relax, darling."

But she couldn't. Because of excitement? Or nerves?

"Perhaps if we play one of our games," he murmured in her ear. He cupped a breast, weighing it.

Her nipples crinkled at his touch. "Yes."

"My desert flower." He kissed the crook of her neck. "So soft, so shy. One would not expect such fragility from one sullied and hardened by nomadic life."

She closed her eyes, breathing out her trepidation, breathing in the fantasy of the exotic East, the fire like the desert sun streaming through the flaps of their tent, their clothing a bed of silken pillows. "I was kept locked away, my master—"

He drew the tip of his tongue along her neck to suck lightly on the delicate pulse point.

"For your pleasure." She surrendered to the wet heat like the dunes yielding to the relentless sirocco.

"You will make a fine addition to my seraglio." He caressed her waist, continuing down her hip to her thigh. "Your radiant beauty belies your experience."

His warmth imbued her with confidence. "But no man has touched me, my sultan."

"No man has breached the walls of your innocence?" He dragged his fingernails up her thigh, tickling the flesh at her hip until she squirmed.

"None, sire."

"Then you are the jewel in my crown of pleasures." He smoothed his hand across her belly, continuing lower until he reached the thatch of hair at her mons. "You inflame me, my odalisque." He threaded his fingers through the strands, dallying a moment before reaching for his intended target. "I am rendered incautious in your arms. I cannot wait to pluck your rose in my garden of delights." He parted her wetness and slid a finger through to touch her clit. "I must have you now."

He rubbed in a slow, circular motion, murmuring praise as she softened under his touch. She exhaled a moan.

"You cannot deny nature's ways, my gem." He stroked and twisted his finger mercilessly, willing her to climb to her peak. "Give in to your lustful desires."

She writhed as sensuous waves ebbed and flowed within.

He inserted a finger inside her. Her eyes flew open. He had never done that before. He held her gaze with his, libidinous, dreamy, his pupils full and dark as he moved his finger, then two, in and out. She had expected such intimacy to hurt, had even been told it would. Instead Arthur's ministrations were wonderfully exhilarating. And she wanted more.

"Arthur?" she said beseechingly.

He flashed a gentle smile and moved to lie between her legs, parting her thighs with his knees and positioning himself at her opening. He watched her face as he pressed in tentatively.

There was a pinch, slightly painful. She gulped a mouthful of air.

His forehead furrowed and he pushed in a little more. He was huge and exquisite all at once.

He looked down at her questioningly. She nodded. Slowly he pushed in fully and then pulled out.

She sighed in ecstasy and he continued his motions. She rode the waves of pleasure, closing her eyes briefly before realizing she wanted to see him, needed to see him, to see what he felt, to know what he experienced was the same for her. His eyes were black with desire, his expression lost in a fog of lubriciousness. He increased his pace then slowed, raising an eyebrow for her consent. She nodded again.

With every thrust he plunged deeper, picked up speed, his breaths puffing to the beat of his exertions. The need for his touch at her core overwhelmed her. She tilted her hips to goad him. The depths of his penetration surprised her, propelling her to exhort him even further.

His sweat-sheened forehead wrinkled in splendid agony above his blank eyes, his lips parted and rounded. She knew the signs of his crisis. Unexpectedly her own burgeoned, matching his, until her body clenched around him, drawing a wail from her lungs. He jerked and held himself against her in one final thrust, groaning his ecstasy.

He gently collapsed on top of her, pressing his face into the crook of her neck. "Henny, Henny," he whispered reverently. "Darling. My wife."

She stared at the shadowed ceiling, astounded at the sensation of pure joy. Tears threatened her eyes then fell in an uncontrollable flood down her cheeks.

He wrapped his arms around her and pulled her close, kissing her hair, her face. His hardness waned and he slipped from her body. He rolled to her side, still touching her, still murmuring in awe of their love.

"Come to my bed," he said, wiping damp strands from her forehead. "Stay part of the night with me."

"Oh, Arthur, that was simply extraordinary." The flush of satiation still suffused her skin. "We should have done that a long time ago."

He chuckled. "Yes, we should have." He cupped her breast.

"Now whenever I'm in this room I'll think of what we did," she said, biting her lip playfully.

He laughed then stood and extended his hand. "Up. And gather your clothes, my sinful mistress."

"Rakehell," she laughed.

As they fussed with the pile of clothing, Henny breathed a sigh of relief that she was out of the clutches of truly evil sin.

Sophia stopped on the vast lawn of the Harwell estate to toss her head back and look at the threatening clouds.

She grinned at her own audaciousness. The past few days and nights spent dreaming of Mr. Phillips—*Joseph*—had emboldened her.

Before Henny left she had told Sophia to make the most of her freedom while it lasted, to be as a carefree young girl but to pepper that girlish exuberance with a bit of womanly flirtation. Sophia understood the covert meaning of Henny's advice. Royston loomed large in Sophia's fate and if she actually did marry him, every scrap of freedom she once enjoyed would be buried forever in a horrid existence.

Sophia presumed Henny had meant a flirtation with Geoffrey but Geoffrey only came to the estate occasionally. Their relationship wasn't so much flirtation anymore—it was more like *arrangement*, planning when they could both get away and meet. Their rendezvous were still daring and fun but Geoffrey had said he wouldn't go any further than necking and a bit of touching on top of their clothes.

And Sophia wanted more than that. She had wanted more than that the minute she had seen Joseph in the billiard room with his shirt undone, smelling of cigars and brandy, tempting and tantalizing her with gallantry and masculinity.

Now she practically swooned whenever she saw him. And she really liked how she felt around him, the warmth in her belly, the tingle up her spine, the swollen dampness between her legs.

She even liked the nerve-racking thrill she got as she walked— skipped, really—across the rolling lawn to the wrought iron folly. She had to slow down as the studio came into view. Its occupant would be able to see her approaching and would wonder what she was doing skipping on the lawn in the middle of the estate. She paused. She hadn't yet thought of an excuse. Of course it could simply be that she was out for a walk and saw the studio and thought she'd pop in for a chat with her brother. She wouldn't tell Joseph she knew Arthur had gone to Little Bytham to check on a tenant's ill mother.

The front windows framed Joseph standing by the stove, pouring water from the kettle into a teapot. He placed the teapot on a table nestled between two stuffed armchairs, a wonderfully domestic act in such a cozy setting, which for some reason inspired all sorts of naughty thoughts. She was futilely trying to dismiss those thoughts when Joseph caught sight of her. He stood by the drapes at the front window and waved a welcome. She inhaled a fortifying breath and went inside.

The studio was pleasantly warm from a fire crackling in the corner hearth opposite the stove. Some of the discarded furniture had been grouped into a seating arrangement, giving the space a homier feel. Books had been stacked neatly on the floor and on a chair. Joseph pulled the front curtains closed then motioned for her to sit.

"All this glass," he explained. "The drapes will keep the heat in. I've tea enough for two if you'd like to join me."

"I'd love to." She placed her bonnet on a table and sat.

"Are you out for a walk on this dreary day?" His tone suggested it was a slightly ridiculous notion.

"Well, it's not raining."

"Yet."

He smiled at her and she could swear his eyes twinkled. He often got such a look where his eyes revealed he knew a lot more about a situation than was being said, but he always held his tongue. Sophia liked that about him, although he seemed to be implying now that she had chosen a time of day when it might start pouring rain and she and he would be trapped together for hours upon hours.

A wonderful thought…

He poured out two cups of tea then added milk from a little jug into one cup. He held out the jug and raised a brow at her.

"Yes please."

"There's sugar in the cooling cupboard, if you like."

"No, thank you."

Not only was this the first time they had been alone together, they were engaged in one of the most mundane acts of the day. And she loved every minute of it. His every move fascinated her—so careful, deliberate, measured. Like his drawings of railway carriages.

"Are you drawing today?" she asked, sipping her tea.

"Yes. I've just finished some preliminary designs. I always like to take a break afterward then go back and look things over. Taking a break can stir up new ideas." He moved a stack of books from a chair onto the floor then relaxed into the seat with his teacup.

She glanced at the books. On the top was a well-read copy of *The Odyssey*. Impulsively she picked it up and flipped through the pages.

He chuckled. "A rather appropriate story for a traveler like me. Have you read it?"

"Not thoroughly, I admit. Is it good?"

"Lately I've been reading literature whether I enjoy it or not. I'm trying to gain an understanding of the literary references in upper-class society. I don't want to appear uneducated in such company. My accent is unsophisticated enough."

That he felt comfortable enough to reveal such an insecurity moved her deeply. "I can't see anyone thinking that about you," she said, subdued. "You're very confident, you know the railway business and your accent is exotic." *And ridiculously seductive.* She could listen to him reading railway schedules and be riveted.

He sipped his tea. "Thank you," he said. "Still, I have to mingle with the Cambridge and Oxford set to get investors. There's only so much ignorance I can attribute to cultural difference."

"I admire that very much. Does Arthur know you put in all this extra effort?"

"He does. He says I shouldn't worry."

Sophia stood. "Well you shouldn't. Would you want to take money from someone who minds if you don't know your Homer from your Shakespeare? I'd rather my investors cared that I knew about railway parts."

He smirked. "That's what your brother said."

"Well, it's true," she said, her hands on her hips. She went to the writing desk. "May I see what you've done today?"

"Of course." He got up and joined her.

Before them were multiple pages of drawings of machines. Some of the drawings appeared to be of the same machine, as if Joseph was trying to get it just right but didn't quite know what was missing. The mechanical pieces were just that—mechanical. Nothing special. Nothing spectacular. Nothing that would incite a man with money to lay it down very readily.

"They're so precise, so perfect. So…lifeless."

"They're machines. They're supposed to be lifeless."

"Well, yes, but…" The drawings lacked *something* but what? She looked around the studio at the ornate metal rafters, the disused furniture of forgotten eras, the stacks of books… One very large book stuck out in the middle of one of the stacks. A folio.

The Grammar of Ornament by Owen Jones. Perfect.

She grabbed the pasteboard folder and opened it on the floor, spreading out the plates. "What if you put some decoration on your machines?"

He pursed his lips as his gaze followed her finger tracing a curling tendril of Greek design. "They go under the carriage—one really does not see them."

"But a railway carriage is big. You have to step up onto it. So you might see all these bits?" She waved over at his drawings on the desk. "Like if you were a passenger and walked by it on the platform."

"You might." He eyed her with a smirk.

"And what about the men who build the carriage?"

"What about them?" His challenge was tinged with enthusiasm.

"They'll see all these parts, won't they?"

"Yes," he admitted, "they will."

"And the investors. They'll see all your drawings, won't they?"

"Many of them, yes."

"So make it beautiful for them."

He crinkled his forehead. "For whom exactly?"

"For all of them."

"But the passengers—surely they won't even notice," he countered.

"The women will notice. And the children. The parts will be at their eye level."

"And the laborers—they're just workers. Surely they do not matter?" he said with playful antagonism.

"How will they ever be elevated from their base and horrid state unless they are exposed to beauty?" she said in a teasingly condescending tone.

"And the investors?" A quiver at the corner of his mouth revealed he fought to quell a grin.

"What better way to appeal to the classically educated investors from Cambridge and Oxford than to make the designs more classical in form?"

Joseph beamed. "You have a point."

"And you could convince my brother such elegance will be good for the business. Surely the wealthier railroad men could be enticed by their vanity into having the most beautiful machines? You would simply charge them more for the privilege."

"Sophia, you're a genius." He put his arm around her shoulders and kissed her hair.

Her breath hitched, her head tingled where his lips had touched her. She drew back slightly and looked up at him. He gazed down at her with a grin until a faraway gleam flashed in his eyes and his expression softened. His face moved toward hers almost imperceptibly. Every muscle in her body tensed in anticipation as her heart thudded in hope.

Suddenly he pulled back. "God, what am I thinking?" he muttered.

"Joseph?"

He took her hands in his. "Sophia, you're brilliant. And I thank you." He gazed at her with something akin to joy then shook his head and looked away, releasing his hold.

She searched his face. "You were going to kiss me," she said boldly. "Weren't you?"

His gaze met hers, a tiny crease deepening between his lovely gray eyes. "Look…I apologize if I caused any distress."

"Distress? I *want* you to kiss me. Don't you see?"

He stared blankly at her, sucking in his lower lip, biting it. "Sophia, that cannot happen."

"And why not?"

"Because you are Lady Sophia Harwell, engaged to marry a duke. And I am a poor American commoner. That's why."

"I don't care who you are. I like you. I like spending time with you. And besides, I'm not engaged actually. It hasn't been settled."

"It's been settled as far as your father is concerned."

He was right. Still… "I don't see why we can't, well, pursue something."

"Such as me ravishing you in this studio?"

"Well, yes." Her words came out far too sharply.

"That is not going to happen. Royston would discover you're not a virgin on your wedding night and attempt to find the ravisher."

"But it might not be you."

"I would at the very least be among the accused and both your brother and I would be ruined as far as our business was concerned."

"How do you know I'm a virgin anyway?" A foolish question only an annoyed virgin would ask.

He quirked an eyebrow. "Because you're the eighteen-year-old daughter of a marquess. That's how."

She flopped down into the armchair and pouted. He knelt beside her and took her hand.

"Sophia, I'm flattered. Believe me I am. And if the circumstances were different, I would be willing, oh so very willing…"

Every nerve in her body sparked with desire, utterly at odds with the tears that threatened to fall.

"I've thought about you ever since the night we met as strangers," he said gently. "I would have kissed you then if Arthur hadn't appeared."

"I've thought of nothing but you since that night, Joseph." The tears welled and trickled down her cheeks.

"God, don't do this to me," he murmured with a rasp.

He placed his fingers under her chin and steadied her as he drew his face nearer. He closed his eyes and tenderly touched his lips to hers.

The desire flared, flushing her skin, rushing to her head, enthralling her. The kiss lasted but a few fleeting seconds, seconds that left her astounded and wanting more.

He pulled back, a dreamy look in his eyes. She touched her fingers to her still-tingling lips.

He smiled. "Let me think about your proposition. But right now you ought to leave. Not only because rain is imminent but because I need you to. Before I really do ravish you."

CHAPTER FOUR

Joseph speared his fingers through his hair and stared blankly through the glass walls of the studio at the well-tended lawn. Over a week had passed since he dared kiss Sophia and he could not stop thinking about her. Well, when he wasn't engrossed in new drawings for railway parts…but even as he added little flourishes here and there he was reminded that it had been Sophia's idea to do so. Then drawing was forgotten and she filled his thoughts all over again—what he wanted to do to her, knowing she wanted him to do all those things to her…

He needed to take a swim in a cold lake or a long walk to Little Bytham and back again with nothing but farms and woods and strangers, alone with his thoughts…his thoughts about Sophia. His very salacious thoughts about Sophia. Even the long journey to Lamberton to visit his new home for a few days didn't help, vistas of England's gray-green coast only heightening the romanticism of lust denied flesh.

Upon his return to Harwell Hall, Arthur noticed Joseph's funk and suggested an outing to Stamford to explore the bookstore there.

Jacobs Books had anything and everything, and if Mr. Jacobs did not have a particular title, he could get it for you through his vast connections with booksellers around the world. Joseph just wanted some transportation engineering studies to spark his creative spirit, which had, of late, been dreaming up all sorts of creative things to do with a virgin…

He shook his head. He simply had to stop thinking about her. A railway trip to Stamford would be just the thing.

The bookstore fronted on High Street, an elegant Georgian façade rising three stories, its golden stone capturing the remains of the morning light. Inside, the store was filled with books, stacks upon stacks of books, on tables, on library ladders and of course on shelves lining the walls. A sign on a staircase indicated the upper floor was similarly inundated with books. The short, wiry, middle-aged man who greeted Joseph with a wave turned out to be Mr. Jacobs himself, a consummate businessman who, when he wasn't fawning over one customer, was running about retrieving tomes to place before another.

He knew Joseph by reputation—how many American guests of earls could there possibly be in Lincolnshire?—and directed him to the engineering section, a bookcase in the back corner obscured by a disused ladder piled with the overflow of architectural and medical treatises. From his vantage point Joseph could see most of the store. Two young women tittered together by the novels, an older woman and her charge leafed through fashion plates, a young man stood engrossed with a law book, his lips moving as his gaze scanned across the page. Except for the occasional squeal from the novels section the store was wonderfully quiet, perfect for a contemplative discussion with one's muse.

The section on engineering did indeed have everything, and in several languages. Until that moment Joseph hadn't really ever thought to peruse a book in another language. Mathematical models were in the universal language of equations and the drawings were comprehensible to anyone who knew what they were looking at. A volume on Ottoman ships proved quite illuminating in putting into practice Sophia's idea of decoration.

Sophia. Damn. Even staring at Arabic script couldn't distract him.

Mr. Jacobs' jovial "good afternoon" to the Earl of Thuxton jolted Joseph back to reality. Lord Thuxton was fabulously wealthy and a notorious rake with mistresses ensconced—and apparently kept satisfied—at his Lincolnshire estate, at his home in London, and at his coastal cottage near Penzance. Arthur had been wooing the earl as he enjoyed investing in modern schemes. Joseph had met the man only once but knew him immediately, his shock of close-clipped gray hair, striking Roman profile and sportsman physique singular among the ruddy-faced and paunch-bellied visitors to Harwell Hall. Joseph was certain it would not be correct to present oneself to a potential investor in a bookstore and Arthur had said he would take care of all such contact anyway. From deep in the agricultural section, Mr. Jacobs waved the earl over and handed him a nondescript tome. Mr. Jacobs then made his customary bow and left the man alone. The earl seemed happy, a smile creeping over his lips as he leafed through the volume. Joseph resumed his own perusal of the suddenly more fascinating Ottoman study.

The bell on the entrance door drew his attention once again away from his musings. He looked up just in time to see Lord Thuxton exit and chase after a woman in a billowing blue skirt. Another mistress perhaps? Joseph chuckled to himself. Ah the life of the aristocracy—words and women.

But his amusement soon dissipated. Sophia entered in the wake of the earl's exit, accompanied by her maid Anna. She waved and smiled at Mr. Jacobs, who held up a finger indicating she should wait a moment. She nodded and unfastened her coat as the bookseller disappeared into one of his storerooms. She was stunning in her high-collared dress trimmed with lace and plaid, the bodice clinging tightly to her breasts and waist like a second skin. Joseph ducked a little farther behind the library ladder. He wanted to simply observe for a moment.

She and Anna conversed briefly before Anna joined the young women by the novels. He hadn't noticed until that moment how much Anna resembled her mistress. The color of hair, the proportions, they could be considered sisters except Sophia had that upturn in her nose so prevalent among the aristocracy and of course, her dress was the utmost in fashion. Anna wore a severe frock of pale green completely devoid of frills and trim under her plain brown coat.

Sophia wandered around the store until she came to the agricultural section where she aimlessly picked up volumes, browsing covers and spines, then happened upon the book Lord Thuxton had left in his pursuit of the woman in blue. She glanced at the spine, opened the cover and turned a few pages. Then quite suddenly, her eyes widened, she blushed crimson, raised her head and looked around furtively. Apparently satisfied no one in the bookstore was watching her, she resumed her attention to the book, peeking up occasionally and checking over her shoulder in the direction Mr. Jacobs had gone. She kept her head lowered so her bonnet obscured her features but whatever was in the book clearly held her rapt attention. One more glance up revealed an agitated expression on her flushed face. Mr. Jacobs returned from the storeroom and she moved away from the engrossing volume. She reviewed the book retrieved by the bookseller, thanked him while he wrapped it in brown paper, then left with a bit of a skip in her step.

His interest thoroughly piqued, Joseph forgot about the Ottomans and etchings of their ships and moved to investigate the intriguing volume left among the agricultural treatises. He opened to the title page and had to choke back a guffaw.

It was a first edition of *The Lustful Turk; or, Scenes in the Harem of an Eastern Potentate*, the title of which he vaguely knew as it had recently been reprinted by a notorious London publisher by the name of Dugdale. What he had neglected to tell Sophia the other day was that this was also the sort of book he had been reading to keep up with the habits and tastes of aristocratic British men—his instincts now confirmed after witnessing the scene involving Lord Thuxton. Joseph had garnered a few titles for himself in New York and upon seeing Arthur's vast library, had pestered Arthur mercilessly about what he had. Finally Arthur dug out a couple of gems well-hidden in his shelves. Each story proved to be a fascinating read of prurient sexual escapades, some of which Joseph had himself performed in the past. From his quick perusal, the adventures of the eponymous Turk included the defloration of a young British maid. Joseph grabbed the book then several of the engineering tomes and went to Mr. Jacobs to settle his account.

"Please wrap that one separately," Joseph requested, pointing to the salacious tome.

"Of course." Mr. Jacobs picked up the book as if he were inured of such content. He busied himself with the rest of the stack, pausing momentarily over the Ottoman ships book. "Ah, I see you are interested in things Turkish, young man," the bookseller said with not a hint of prejudice.

"Actually I suspect I have all the technical books I need. I am, however, looking to start a collection of books of an erotic nature."

Mr. Jacobs smiled. "Any particular specifications? First editions? A certain letch?"

The man was shrewd. "That which is of interest to the Cambridge and Oxford lot."

The bookseller grinned widely. "Very good."

Joseph left his details and a deposit. Then he too exited with a bit of a skip in his step.

After the farce that was her birthday party, Sophia was looking forward to the Fosdykes' annual pre-Season ball, which was bound to include plenty of men she hadn't yet met. She would make mental note of those whose attentions she wanted to enjoy in London. Best of all, Joseph would be there. Arthur was making him go and now she had an excuse to be in his arms, even if it was just for a waltz.

Nothing had happened since the afternoon in the studio. A few longing looks on her part, with meaning-laden smiles returned by him, furtive exchanges that were maddening and exciting all at once. He didn't avoid her or tell her to go away as he could have—instead they talked a great deal, becoming friends, their interchanges almost as thrilling as what she did with Geoffrey.

She took the carriage with Mama and Papa to the Fosdyke estate, Arthur and Joseph riding behind. Royston was expected to be there so she had agonized over what she should wear—a neckline low and revealing for all the promising men or something a bit more modest for when she had to dance with the duke. He always stared at her bosom in a most disgusting way. She settled on low and revealing with a delicate lace shawl collar that she would put on just before her dance with Royston.

Upon arrival, Arthur and Joseph immediately ran off to the smoking room. To chat up potential investors, Arthur said, but Sophia knew it was to drink spirits, smoke cigars and gamble. She didn't mind too much. Joseph would return with the fragrance of fine tobacco lingering on his jacket, evoking a seductive memory.

The first few dances were pleasant enough and she got the requisite waltz with Royston out of the way as soon as she could. After that, Mama was too distracted by her gossiping friends to care which men Sophia danced with. Two or three young men were agreeable and as they parted, she said she hoped she would see them often during the Season. Such banter rendered them overly talkative, which meant they liked her too. So she pushed out her chest just a little as they chatted on.

The most wondrous and unexpected event was the arrival of Henny. "My mother purchased loads of Romanian lace during her trip and she promised Lady Fosdyke a few yards. The rest is to decorate my wedding dress," she chirped with glee.

From then on, Mama allowed Henny to chaperon and what a wonderful chaperon she was. She knew how to read men, which ones were bores, which ones were romantic, which ones were good dancers. Her witty assessments made for quite a diverting time between dances and for plenty of suppressed giggles on the ballroom floor.

"Let's get some punch, Sophie," Henny said, entwining their arms. "I want to hear about what you've been doing. How's Joseph?" she teased.

After they had their glasses of punch and had tucked themselves off in a corner of the refreshment room Sophia let loose her secret.

"He kissed me," she said behind her fan.

"He kissed you?" Henny squealed and fanned herself. "In the way Geoffrey kisses?"

"No, nothing like that and yet so much more exciting."

"Oh, Sophie, you're in love. I'm so happy for you. I just wish…" She trailed off.

"What? Wish what?"

"Sophie, has there been anybody here tonight, *anybody* who could rival Royston in the eyes of your father?"

"I don't know, Henny."

"Maybe not necessarily an heir to a dukedom—there aren't many of those. What about an earl with gobs of money and loads of political connections?"

"I haven't really paid much mind to all of that. Arthur would know."

"Yes, of course, dear. Arthur and I will have to think about all that. It's just, well you see, I don't want you with Royston and it looks as if your father won't back down. The duke is a horrid man, Sophie. And if they insist you marry a peer, I'm certain we could find you someone far more palatable. Someone who eventually wouldn't mind if you took a lover."

"Henny," Sophia exclaimed.

But Henny just smirked suggestively.

Sophia stepped closer to her friend. "Henny, what did he do to you that was so awful?"

Henny paled but quickly recovered. "I won't talk about it here, darling. I'll tell you later."

Sophia squeezed her hand. Henny smiled and squeezed back.

"Come…let's find my Arthur and your Joseph. Surely they must have smoked all the cigars in Cuba by now."

They found them deep in conversation in the lobby next to the grand staircase. Joseph barely got in a greeting before Arthur grabbed Henny's hands and kissed her cheeks.

"Darling, why didn't you write me you'd be here?"

"It was rather sudden. That's why I'm wearing this old rag of a dress—"

The shimmering, gold silk gown exquisitely set off her blonde locks and fit fabulously on her perfect figure.

"But I knew you'd be here. I knew I'd see you."

They were lost in each other's eyes. Sophia glanced up at Joseph. He appeared to be trying hard not to grin at the moony couple.

"Sweetheart," Henny said with a bat of her lashes, "there's something I'd like to talk to you about. Alone. But I've been charged by your mother with watching over Sophie. Do you think Mr. Phillips is up to the task? There shouldn't be any impropriety with the arrangement. He is your business partner, after all."

Sophia couldn't believe her ears. Joseph seemed to be quite amused by Henny's machinations.

Arthur was quick to accept. "Of course, darling."

Henny grabbed his arm and sidled up to him, beaming. He turned to Joseph.

"You don't mind, do you?"

"Not at all."

The touch of eagerness in Joseph's response sent a little flutter to Sophia's belly.

After a nod Arthur and Henny mounted the stairs with an enthusiastic flourish.

Joseph shook his head, a wry curl on his lips.

"You're laughing, aren't you? Why?"

"The bedrooms are upstairs, my lady," he murmured closely in her ear. He placed her arm around his and proceeded to the ballroom.

Heat flushed her face. Arthur and Henny? But only scandalous couples did such things. She glanced over at Joseph. Yes, but only scandalous women tried to seduce men in estate follies on rainy days.

"Shall we dance?" she asked, now thoroughly flustered.

"I think I'm supposed to ask you that," he countered teasingly.

"Yes. Of course."

The music had already started, the ballroom bustling with a polka. Joseph steered her to a spot on the edge of the room next to a decorative column and a potted palm. They were tucked away, obscured by the leafy fronds but with a view of the dancers. He positioned himself behind her, so close he crushed her skirts. The heat of his body radiated into hers. His breath warmed her bare shoulders. Yet he did not touch her in any way.

Geoffrey's tall, lanky form bobbed noticeably above the crowd on the dance floor. He was a good dancer and especially enjoyed the liveliness of polkas. His partner was beautiful, her golden curls swaying in time to their movements, her face glowing from his attentions, her tightly bound bosom rising and falling as she flashed demure glances his way. Did he hold this beauty a little more closely than he would hold her? Sophia tried to remember the last time she and Geoffrey danced and how far apart their bodies were—

"Is he thinking of you as he moves with his partner?"

Joseph's voice thrummed low and intimate from behind, startling her from her thoughts.

"Imagining it is you in his arms, your palm against his as his fingers press into the back of your hand? He holds you tight at your waist, his grasp strong and demanding, controlling you, commanding your body to move with his."

Sophia swayed to the music, swayed to Geoffrey's steadying strength.

"But it is not a dance he imagines when you are in his arms. He craves a deeper connection. Are you willing to surrender?"

Sophia gasped. Joseph's words sparked an unexplored yearning.

"The heat of his arousal penetrates the space between your bodies. The burn of his gaze on your décolletage stirs the peaks of your breasts to harden against their prison of stays."

Her flesh prickled to excitement.

"You hunger for the passion of his lips against yours, the warm wetness of his mouth on your neck, his kiss grazing lower to your now-heaving bosom. His hands slide up your waist to cup your perfect breasts—his thumbs tantalize the tips as his breath lies hot against your cleavage."

Sophia flexed her fingers, needing to grip, to clutch something, anything, desperately wanting Geoffrey's touch in return. Desire dampened her drawers. Her breasts ached in her corset, chafing for freedom, for his hands, his mouth. Her breath came in agitated, hurried puffs as the lusciousness she could never control welled within, her disobedient body rushing toward release as if she were alone, lying in the dark, her hand between her legs, and not standing on the fringes of a crowded ballroom.

"Will you submit to his need as he presses against you, his hips thrust into you, as he grabs you where he's never ventured before…your arse, your thighs, drawing you so close your bodies meld together—"

She had never allowed him such liberties yet she would let him do anything to her now. The lusciousness consumed her, dizzied her, the ballroom and its occupants falling away as lust propelled her to soar above them, above the chandelier to absorb the brilliance of the lights until she shattered into a million droplets of crystal, twinkling in their descent.

She exhaled a mewling whimper. Lightheaded yet exhilarated, she stared blankly at the golden glow of the gas chandelier hanging above the dancers in the center of the room.

Joseph remained behind her, his body mere inches away, frustratingly close yet still not touching.

The music ended. The hustle and bustle of the party-goers reminded her of where she was—not in the embrace of a potent man but standing solitary in a crowd. Geoffrey waved. She barely saw him. Then he was right in front of her, still breathing excitedly from his exertions.

"I say, Sophia. We haven't had our dance yet tonight." His smile was charming, honest. "Phillips? May I?"

Joseph must have indicated his assent. As if he owned her. The thought only inflamed her further.

"Sophia? What say you?"

She struggled to find her voice. "Yes," she answered throatily.

Geoffrey was wonderful as always on the dance floor. But this time she noticed every move, every touch, every urging of his body against hers. She let go, allowing him to take control of her, to take her body where he wanted. The surrender was freeing, liberating in a new way. And when the dance ended she was left wanting more.

"Sophia, I don't know about you but I've been dancing practically all night. I'd like to take a turn on the terrace, if you don't mind."

He would suggest we go for a walk. "That would be lovely, Geoffrey."

They followed other couples seeking the comfort of the cool night air. Their footsteps clicked in unison quietly on the flagstones. He led her as far as the balustrade next to the steps going down into the darkened garden.

"Sophia," he said quietly, "have I told you how stunning you look tonight?"

He would flatter me. "No, Geoffrey, you have not." She tried to convey surprise at his pretty words.

He turned to her. "Well you do. A man would be a fool not to notice your charms. I'm lucky to garner your indulgence."

His tone conveyed his sincerity. She always liked that about him. If he weren't just the heir to a damn viscountcy, she'd be engaged to him by now.

I think I should like him to kiss me. "Geoffrey, I'd like to go into the garden now."

"Yes, Sophia. That would be nice."

Shit.

Shielded by a palm frond, Joseph adjusted the crowding in his crotch. *Amazing.* Sophia had climaxed from just his words—and the memory continued to bedevil his cock. He'd never been so damn hard in his life.

Watching her dance with Peel, watching her move rhythmically with him, their bodies in concert, hers under his command, had aroused Joseph even further. With him or with another man, Sophia's partner mattered not—he just wanted to be a witness to her passion.

When Sophia and Peel left the dance floor, Joseph followed surreptitiously, clinging to the shadows. They stood on the terrace for a minute before descending into the garden. The pitch-dark garden.

He kept an eye on them, trying to be stealthy. But no one paid him mind. All the others were lovers looking for a spot of their own in the dark.

He slowly rounded a thick trunk and almost fell into Sophia and Peel. He pulled back in awe and admiration. Peel had her pressed up against a tree, crushing her skirts as he rolled his hips between her legs, his hands roaming frantically. He kissed her mouth, her neck, her cleavage, his groans and growls muffled against her skin. Sophia responded with sighs, moaning entreaties, undulating beneath him to match his sensual rhythm.

Joseph palmed his cock, wanting very much to frig himself right then and there.

She would let him do everything Peel was doing to her. She'd probably let him join them in a sensual triad. But he wanted her just for himself the first time. He watched Peel's hands, imagining them as his own, flexing his fingers with every grasp and clutch…watched Peel's mouth, flicking his own tongue as if dueling with hers. Her sharp cry brought him back into his own body. He was deliriously aroused.

He closed his eyes and grabbed his crotch, seeking release. But he would not find it at that moment, in that place. If he were back on the docks, he would find a willing woman in seconds, would have his satisfaction, pay her and be done. Contemptible, yes, but no different than what others were doing at that moment in upstairs bedrooms, and a damn sight better than abusing servants in back stairwells. At least the women on Water Street knew what they were getting into.

He left Sophia and Peel to continue unwitnessed and walked back to the house. The ballroom held little appeal at the moment. A touch of the reality of his old world was what he needed. He walked around the back of the mansion, toward the ground-floor service entrance, knowing his attire would allow him privileges of polite interactions with the staff. A life of service was a life he—by pure chance—had dodged. He hardly knew what position he would have held anyway. Jack-of-all-trades? He snorted. He would have had a romance with one of the parlor maids or possibly the governess. Perhaps she would have discovered his talent for sketching, for drawing, for mechanics and engineering. She would have told their master, who would have—

The muffled cries of a girl caught his attention. Cries of distress, uneven sobs, timid pleading. He quickened his pace then slowed immediately when the scene came into view. He pulled back to hide in the shadows. The dim light of the upper floors illuminated the space below, where a large man crushed a slip of a girl against the wall of the mansion, his hand clamped against her mouth, berating her as she cried. His tone was gruff, brutal, his words indistinct but understood. He shoved her harshly then turned and stomped away. The girl collapsed to the ground.

Joseph stared as the man strode back to the terrace, passing right in front of him but not taking notice.

Royston. Unmistakably Royston.

Joseph ran to the girl and knelt beside her. She sobbed uncontrollably.

"I'm here. I'm a friend. Let me help you," he said softly.

His accent must have disconcerted her. The sobbing stopped and she stared at him.

The apron of her housemaid's uniform clung to one shoulder, the other strap drooped to her waist, torn and ragged. Her cap had fallen, still pinned to her hair, which hung in a rat's nest at her nape.

Her cheeks, streaked with tears and blood, retained the smooth plumpness of adolescence.

Good God Almighty, she's younger than Sophia.

Joseph pinched his lips tightly to smother a curse. Royston was the worst kind of villain.

"You need to be inside, my lady," he said, flattering her. He had found he could say such things and be considered merely an ignorant but charming American.

It worked. Courtly deference always worked.

She allowed him to help her to the garden entrance, into the service area and to the servant's common room. He sat her down by the fire.

"What is your name?" He grabbed a shawl and covered her.

"Sarah, sir." Her eyes were vacant.

"Who is your housekeeper? What is her name?"

"Mrs. Fitch." Her voice was subdued, her face disbelieving.

"Where will she be during such an event as this?"

"In the kitchen I should think. I really don't know." She shook her head without conviction.

By that time they had attracted a few onlookers amongst the staff. "Watch her, please," he said to a seemingly sympathetic maid. "She's had an accident outside."

He left to find Mrs. Fitch.

He found her in the hall near the kitchen, giving direction to a handsome pair in livery. Footmen. They dispersed according to their orders. She caught sight of Joseph and looked as if she was about to reprimand him when he approached.

"Mrs. Fitch. Madam, I am Joseph Phillips, a guest at this affair. I discovered your charge, Sarah, after she had been molested by another guest. I have brought her here."

The housekeeper looked at him dubiously. "Very well, sir. Show me to her." No doubt she had to clean up after her masters far too often.

He led the way and when Mrs. Fitch saw the wretch she went to her, kneeling and taking her hand.

"Sarah?" she said with motherly affection.

The girl flicked her eyes toward Joseph. "He helped me," she whispered.

The situation was out of his hands after that. Still, responsibility compelled him to stay. After brief words Sarah was taken away by another maid. Mrs. Fitch stood, defeat and anger coloring her expression.

He fished a sovereign from his coin purse then pressed it into her palm.

"Please, madam, fetch a doctor as soon as you can. She has been abused and will need medical care. And if I may be so bold, if there is a douching syringe and vinegar, she will require that as well. Please send word to me at Harwell Hall near Little Bytham about her care."

Mrs. Fitch held her hand against her mouth, nodding her assent to his advice, tears pooling on her lashes. "Why, oh why?" she gasped. "Such an innocent."

Joseph left to seethe in the depths of the garden. *Innocent no longer.*

CHAPTER FIVE

Sophia hadn't seen Joseph since he had left her alone with Geoffrey the night before. Well, not in real life, anyway. He incessantly filled her thoughts and dreams.

He had left her in such a state, excited beyond measure and with only Geoffrey to satisfy her. But Geoffrey was so willing, so malleable to her wishes, going further than he had ever gone before, stroking, massaging, nipping until she had reached a crisis and exhausted herself. Eventually they walked back to the ballroom where Geoffrey left her with Mama and excused himself, his face flushed, his hands quivering. Mama had commented that the poor fellow needed a doctor.

But in the morning, frustration still roiled within. She needed to be with Joseph.

She walked briskly across the estate, a present for him in her pocket. As the little iron studio came into view, puffy clouds skirted the blue sky above. There would be no hope of a sudden storm preventing her from leaving.

She walked in, looked around as casually as she could manage while she took off her coat and bonnet. "Arthur's not here?" she inquired as she warmed her hands by the fire.

Joseph did not get up from his drawing table. "He's with your tenant, Mr. Cogges, as you well know." He clipped his words with an acerbic edge.

She flushed from his revelation and turned back to the fire. "You left without saying goodbye last night."

He fell silent for a minute. "There was an incident with a servant girl," he said quietly. "I helped take care of her. I left after that." He sighed. "I was no longer in a party mood."

A curious statement. "A servant girl? What happened?"

"A guest abused her, injured her."

She faced him, horror-stricken. "But that's terrible. The party should have ended after such an incident."

"Servants are the playthings of the aristocracy, my lady," he bit out caustically.

His words stung, his gaze burned, stifling any comment she might have had. Surely he did not think her or her family capable of such a heinous act? They treated their servants very well. Why, she thought of her Anna as a friend.

But Joseph never had servants, had in fact grown up thinking he might be one himself. She swallowed hard.

"Joseph, I didn't mean to offend."

"No." His voice was tinged with regret. "I know you did not."

She held out her hand to him. "I missed you, that's all."

"Is that why you were kissing Peel last night?" he snapped.

His vituperation was unexpected. That he knew about Geoffrey was mortifying. "I kissed him because you inflamed me. And then you left me." She stepped forward. "Joseph, I thought of you the whole time."

He paled, his brow twisted, his expression distraught and lost. "Sophie, forgive me. I'm…I…"

In two strides he was before her, swooping her into his arms, taking her by surprise. His mouth descended upon hers, hungry, fervent, a passion that wasn't merely physical but pulsed with a deep emotional need. She wrapped her arms around his neck, pressed her body against his, melting into his warmth and strength, letting him take command.

His tongue sought hers, entangling in a sensual dance, a dance that should have been theirs the night before. She moaned into his mouth and he returned a growl of approbation. He clutched her to him more tightly, pulling her off her feet, swinging her legs into his arms. He gazed at her in admiration as he carried her across the room, tossed her onto a bed, then left to draw the studio drapes.

She looked around in surprise. She lay on a large, canopied, four-poster bed, the wood carved in the Chinese fashion to emulate bamboo, the spaces between the posts draped with faded silk curtains all around.

Joseph grinned at her curiosity as he flopped beside her. "It's the bed your ancestors the marquesses used with their mistresses," he explained. "The parts were all here. I set it up and managed to coax one of Arthur's maids into helping me furnish it with draperies and linens."

One of Arthur's maids? "Jenny?"

He chuckled. "How on earth did you know that?"

"She stares at you when she thinks no one is watching."

"So that explains it. She was easily persuaded with just a kiss."

A pang of jealousy shot through her. "And how did you kiss her?"

"Like this."

It was a nice kiss and if the girl was enamored of Joseph as much as Sophia was, it was certainly enough for her to do anything for him. But it was nothing to be jealous about.

He pulled back and looked at her longingly. "You don't know how much I've dreamed of this."

She smiled. "Oh, yes I do."

Hunger cast his countenance as he delved in again, attacking her mouth with such a fervor she giggled. She had never kissed Geoffrey lying down before. They had always been standing, sometimes up against a tree, which was sort of like lying down. But lying side by side with Joseph was heavenly, his body next to hers, melding into all her curves as she relaxed on the mattress.

His hands wandered freely about her, stroking and cupping, at times squeezing with an energetic intensity. He gathered her skirts, lifting them to explore what lay underneath, then stopped, feeling something in her pocket.

His present.

"What's this?" he asked.

Sophia pulled out the gift and handed it to him. "A present. For you."

He turned it over and over in his hands, surely knowing it was a book from its rectangular shape, but not which one, his narrowed eyes hinting he was considering the possibilities. He carefully opened the brown wrapping paper, revealing the cover, and slid his hand slowly across the buttery leather then traced the gilded title tentatively as if in awe.

"*The Iliad*," he murmured with a touch of reverence.

"I thought because you were reading *The Odyssey* you might like this one as well. It's Alexander Pope's translation with Flaxman's illustrations. It's rather lovely."

He opened the book and perused each page, his eyes widening as he skimmed the text, a smile playing on his lips as he studied the plates. "Yes it is," he said softly, not looking up, seemingly lost to her in a moment of contemplation.

He started, gazing at her with a twinkle in his eyes. "I have a present for you," he said and clambered off the bed. He returned holding a very similar object in the same brown wrapping paper.

She opened it and stared, equally awe-struck but with a little embarrassment.

Before her lay the copy of *The Lustful Turk* she had flipped through at Mr. Jacobs' bookstore. Her mind pulsed with scenarios as to how Joseph could have possibly known, *if* he could possibly know about how she had seen the book and thought it invigorating. She must have blushed for he covered her hand in his.

"I saw you that day at Jacobs'. The book had been left by the Earl of Thuxton. I saw you examine it with great interest."

"And you didn't say good afternoon?" She was mortified.

He chuckled. "Not after I saw you blushing over it. I had to get it for you. I had to get it for us."

Sophia was perplexed. "Us?" she asked hopefully. She and he…such a notion was too sublime.

He kissed her once again, his lips soft and seductive against her mouth.

"Us." He pulled back just a little. "Sophie," he began in a serious tone, "if you and I are to embark upon an affair, these are the rules—"

"Rules? You make it sound like a game."

"Ah, but my love, an aristocratic English lady and an American commoner engaging in bed sport can only be a game."

She had hoped that might not be the case but prudence forced her to accept the notion. "All right, what are the rules?"

He drew a finger down her neck to her shoulder. "No marks of any kind in any area that can be seen when fully dressed." His finger traced across her bosom where the deep neckline of her ball gown had been the night before then circled around her wrists, one at a time.

A touch of fright fringed her curiosity. "Marks?"

He rolled her onto her side, swiftly unbuttoning the top of her dress, then moved her back to face him and tugged down the bodice. "No penetration in your privates." His hand skated down to cup between her legs. "That rule includes tongue, finger, and prick. No matter how much you demand it."

Tongue? How thoroughly intriguing. "And?"

He removed her bodice with the expertise of a man who had done such an act many times. Her heart beat furiously at his touch, so eager was she to be naked before him. Her bodice removed, he began tugging on the sleeves of her chemise. "We're not allowed to fall in love."

Certainly she had already broken that rule, if love made her pulse rush and her breaths uneven, if love made her want to be with him every single minute of every single day.

Her chemise off her shoulders, he worked steadily at the fastenings of her corset then pulled the garment open and slid the chemise over her breasts, exposing her utterly.

She gasped. He licked his lips as he stared at her bared chest rising and falling rapidly. Her nipples crinkled from the chill of the room, the anticipation of his touch sparking pleasure to coil in her belly.

He cupped her tentatively, his hand warm, trembling ever so slightly. "Sophie…so…exquisite."

He caressed her slowly, his gentle touch discordant with her pounding heart. He hovered over her, his hot breath teasing her tender peaks before he dipped his head and wrapped his lips around a nipple.

Arousal shot straight to her sex. She arched up in reflex, holding the position, trying to comprehend the glorious sensation.

He sucked the sensitive peak, teasing it with quick flicks of his tongue then bathing the areola with the warm wetness of his entire mouth. He massaged the other breast, pinching and stroking the tip, adding a tortuous confusion to the assault of pleasure.

She melted back into the mattress, his mouth, his hand tormenting her, his body pressing into hers. She relented to his command, letting him take her on the sensual journey, new in its path but familiar in its goal. He knew how to control the lusciousness she found so elusive. He had already mastered its course the night before in the ballroom.

She grabbed his head, holding him against her, not letting him sever their connection as the sensual stirrings grew, warming her core, flushing her skin, building to her climax in such a wondrous way.

She cried out her ecstasy, bucking up, wrapping her arms around him as he slid up to kiss her neck, her cheeks, her lips.

She laughed, surprised, exhausted but rejuvenated. "Joseph, darling, that was wonderful."

He rolled to her side and pulled her to him to nuzzle in the crook of his arm. "That is to tempt you, darling. You may find other acts that pique your curiosity in that book. When we can find time we'll do more exploration."

Sophia could not wait.

Arthur placed the pen on the blotter and stared at the letter before him. *My darling Henny.* Whenever he wrote to her he felt nostalgia and hope all at once. And when he wrote letters such as these he ended up incredibly hard.

He had begun writing erotic stories to her, tales of what they had done, fantasies of what he wanted to do next time he saw her. Last night at the Fosdyke ball she told him she loved the stories, read them in bed at night, that they inflamed her so much she would touch herself and cry out his name at her climax.

They had made love twice last night, the first time quickly in his overexcited state, the second time after he had collected himself. That second time he had drawn out the act as long as he could, savoring every moment, watching her expression slacken with lust, feeling her throb and clench around him, her hips rocking urgently until she gripped with such force she sent him over the edge.

He did not regret that every time they made love he spent inside her. One day she would carry his child. That summer, he hoped. They would be married in June, only three months away. If she were pregnant, she would barely show, especially with today's exuberantly full fashions.

Joseph had scolded him about not taking precautions with Henny after their first night, the night she had come to the library, and had even given Arthur some advice on prophylactic measures. Joseph was surprisingly worldly for such a young man but he had seen and experienced a great deal in his hard life. He was full of amusing stories and ready with practical information, conveyed with a rough directness that eschewed niceties and pleasantries, getting right down to basics. Arthur found that very attractive in the man.

Perhaps a little too attractive.

It had been disconcerting at first when they were together in New York, the easy rapport that sparked a deeper chemistry, the continued magnetic draw, the flush of attraction. But Joseph was powerfully charismatic. Anyone would feel as such when they were in his presence.

Surely the distraction was temporary. Joseph would return to America, then he and Henny would live in wedded bliss, awaiting the birth of their first child.

Except he would eventually join Joseph across the Atlantic. But he would bring Henny and their child to counter whatever hold Joseph had over him.

He chuckled. Joseph would probably insist Henny join them.

The click of the library door startled him to the present. Joseph entered, greeted him distractedly then sat in an easy chair to the side of the fire with a sullen sigh.

Joseph hated small talk and they could simply exist in the same room without conversing but his sigh was laden with something akin to anguish.

"What's wrong? You left earlier today in quite a funk."

Joseph lifted his head to look at Arthur. "If it hadn't been for a brief, somewhat cheering visit by your sister this afternoon, I think I would be worse."

Arthur leaned back in his chair. "What happened?"

"Last night while I was taking a walk in the garden, I saw something I simply cannot get out of my head."

He stopped as if to collect his thoughts. Arthur knew better than to disturb him.

"I got lost in the garden and ended up by the service entrance on the ground floor. I heard a noise. The light from the upper floors was just enough to see what was going on. Against the side of the house a man, a party guest, a peer, was abusing one of the housemaids. Her cries were pathetic—pleading and resigned all at once. He hit her then left her crumpled on the ground."

Arthur had heard of such things but had never himself been a witness or known of someone personally who had bragged of such a conquest.

"I helped the girl as much as I could and left her in the care of the head housekeeper. I received a note today from the housekeeper, which raised my spirits some. The girl was seen by a doctor. She is still marred by cuts and bruises but will recover."

"It is unfortunate some men of the aristocracy feel they can do whatever they wish with servants."

Joseph glared at him. "She was sixteen years old, Arthur, a complete innocent. There is absolutely no reasoning behind such a heinous act."

Arthur's gut twisted. They shared the room in silence, Joseph trembling and boiling about something still left unsaid.

"You know who the man was, don't you?"

"I do."

"I fear there is nothing we can do. Such acts are often not considered crimes."

"And if I told you the man was Royston?"

Arthur's gut twisted further and he stared at his friend in momentary disbelief, realizing in a flash that Joseph was telling him what he had always suspected about the duke. "I can't say that I am surprised."

Joseph stood and leaned against the hearth, staring into the fire. "And your sister? You would allow her to marry such a villain?"

"I have no say in the matter."

"Of course you do," Joseph growled.

"The marquess pays me no mind."

"'The marquess'?" he cried. "You mean your father?"

"Yes." He had never called the man Papa.

"Then why don't you refer to him as such?"

Arthur joined him at the fire. "We're not close. We've never been close. He listens to his friends and considers me a foolish boy."

Joseph placed his hand on Arthur's shoulder. A strong, warm, comforting hand.

"Arthur," he said softly, "Sophie is a beautiful innocent who does not deserve such a horrible fate. If she is married to him, she will be abused and you can do nothing. He will own her, body and soul. She is still her father's daughter while she remains unmarried. You must stop this marriage."

"What can I possibly do?"

"You can talk to your father. Tell him my story."

"I'll try."

Joseph exhaled long and hard. "Look, even Henny is against this marriage and she was once considered a possible wife for the man.

Surely she knows something. Allow her opinions on this matter to guide your own."

Joseph was absolutely right.

"Very well, I'll tell my father what you told me," Arthur said, certain his opinion would have no merit.

CHAPTER SIX

Joseph thought about Sophia far too much. He relied on her to give him solace far too much. His mood had been black of late, driven by hatred of how men like Royston got away with far too much.

To keep his emotions in check, he needed to see her every damn day.

She didn't come every day, though. She had her own obligations—visitors, letters, shadowing her mother in the management of the house. Besides, Arthur was with Joseph in the studio at times, going over plans, discussing investors—not the most conducive situation for an affair. One afternoon Sophia had visited only briefly, apologizing for disturbing them before leaving. Another time he had seen her through the windows but the moment she spied her brother she turned and went the other way.

Finally one day, she arrived when he was alone, thinking of her so intently he'd looked down to find his pencil sketching her likeness. She entered and he quickly tucked the page under the blotter. She caught his eye and blushed, as if she had been thinking of him in a salacious way.

He could only hope.

She hung up her coat and bonnet and pulled off her gloves, then walked over to his desk. "May I see?"

"Of course, I trust you implicitly with our business confidences," he teased.

She colored once more, heightening the rose on her cheeks already flushed from her walk, a flush he imagined she would have after more erotic exertions.

She stood next to him, the heat of her body and her delicious fragrance magnifying his burgeoning arousal. She placed a hand casually on the desk, her slender, delicate fingers careful not to touch the paper but, he hoped, unafraid to stroke and tame his unruly cock.

"Have I seen this before?" she asked with interest, perusing the document from beneath long lashes.

"Yes. It's a copy. We have to have several at our disposal."

"Oh. Of course. I hadn't thought of that, I suppose." She met his gaze, her lips curving unrestrained into a gentle smile, one tinged with a secret. She left the desk, ambled around to the window then the hearth, and finally sat in the armchair. She looked at him. "I finished the book you gave me."

He grinned. "And?"

"Why would a whip arouse a woman to desire?" she asked, obviously perplexed.

Oh, God, yes. Joseph closed his eyes and let out a sigh.

"And what does it mean to press a kiss between a woman's legs?"

His heart thrummed faster. "Would you like to know these things?"

She stood and flicked her eyes away briefly. "Yes."

"Undress to your underclothes," he said as he surreptitiously unfastened the buttons at her back, his voice and fingers trembling in anticipation. He left her side to close the drapes and lock the door.

And when she stood before him half-dressed and willing he held out his hand. She took it and he led her before the four-poster bed. He wrapped one arm around her waist and drew her to him, kissing her slowly, deliberately, reaching between the slit in her drawers to stroke her sex.

She was not ready.

She stared up at him, her eyes cast with apprehension. "Joseph, I'm scared."

"What do you fear?"

"I don't know." Her brow furrowed. "The unknown. The forbidden."

"I won't hurt you," he murmured urgently. "I need you to trust me."

She nodded her assent.

He bent her over the side of the bed. "Stretch your arms out against the mattress."

She did so obediently. He drew his hand down her back to her behind, rucked up her chemise, reached around to untie her drawers then pulled them down to her ankles.

Before him were the most exquisite buttocks he had ever seen, shapely firm flesh, enticingly pale. He gave his cock a squeeze, quelling his lust for a more forbidden adventure. He smoothed a palm over each mound to find the well-cushioned spot he wanted, rubbing it gently with a circular motion.

He swung his arm and swatted her sharply.

Sophia yelped with a hop toward the mattress, tripping on the drawers wrapped around her feet. Joseph pulled her back into position and caressed the faint pink spot, fighting the urge to frig himself and jet his emission on her bum.

He swatted her again. And again. She did not yelp quite so loudly.

He pulled one of her feet free from the restraint of the drawers to separate her legs then softly swirled his palm across her reddened skin. With the next swat his fingers flicked against her now-swollen labia.

She moaned and pressed her hips into the mattress. Ever so slightly she wriggled her behind. His prick ached with need.

He delivered a final swat, the hardest, his hand falling against the fleshiest part of her butt.

She gasped sharply.

Her quim glistened. He drew a finger along the plumped labia, through the sticky wetness, then bent over her as he explored, carefully avoiding her clitoris. "Do you see how a woman can become inflamed by a whip?" he asked gently.

"Yes," she breathed.

"Tell me what you feel."

"The pain dissolved into…heat between my legs. I'm aroused, but unfulfilled. I want something more but I don't know what it is."

Joseph picked her up, disentangling her from the fallen drawers, and moved her onto the bed facing him. He studied her features as he shucked off his jacket and waistcoat, pulled off his tie and loosened his collar.

A smile spread on her lips. "You're preparing for something."

He closed the drapes around the bed then met her gaze with a raised brow. "What was the other curiosity you mentioned?" He slid his hands down her thighs and urged her legs open.

"A kiss."

"Ah…" He held a finger to her lips. "Not just any kiss. I've kissed you before."

He bent over and touched his lips to hers, slowly deepening the union, reminding her of the familiar depths of their passion. He pulled back despite her yearning protest then moved lower and knelt between her legs.

He sighed at the sight of her virgin flesh, plump and moist. He slid down the mattress and placed his hands under her butt to lift her, a sigh escaping once again.

"Sophie," he murmured reverently then pressed his mouth to her sex.

She gasped and bucked up against him, only to be met with his now-determined tongue, stroking her wetness, exploring the delicate folds. Her gasps turned to muttered oaths as she thrashed under him. He cradled her in his hands, following her with his mouth until she found her sensual cadence, until she gently stroked his head in rhythm with her moans. He wanted her subdued before his next assault of pleasure.

He pulled her open with his thumbs, revealing the sensitive pearl of her clit. He flicked the tip of his tongue on the delicious nub.

She jerked up with a cry.

He gripped her hips, steadying her, and then began his relentless assault with lips and tongue.

She sucked in air, let loose a wail, tried to pull back until desire overtook her and she thrust up once again. He drew her into his mouth, sucking and licking ceaselessly.

She grabbed fistfuls of his hair as she writhed frantically, uttering senseless words, her breaths puffing, building until she inhaled sharply. She lifted her hips and held herself aloft in the stillness of anticipation.

Then with a roaring groan she crashed back down to the mattress, her body shuddering in exhaustion. He followed her with his mouth, slowing his tongue and lips, calming her once again.

She exhaled loudly and looked down at him still between her legs. "Joseph, I barely understand…I… That was wonderful."

He pulled himself alongside her and drew her body to his, breathing in his relief at her pleasure. She gingerly pecked his still-wet lips then slid her tongue along the seam of his mouth.

"Do you like how I taste?"

He squeezed her. "You are ambrosia, an elixir to my spirits."

She nuzzled against him. "How did you know?"

A curious question. "Know what, love?"

"How to make me feel that way."

He had to tread lightly. "I suppose it's pretty much the same for most women. I confess you are not my first. I hope that does not make me despicable in your eyes."

"No. But that's not what I meant. I mean what did you do to make me feel that way."

Could she possibly be innocent of her own body? "Have you not touched yourself?"

"No. Well, I have. Just not in *that* way. The way you did."

"You don't touch your clitoris?"

She looked up at him. "I'm not sure."

He chuckled. "I think you would know if you had."

"Would you teach me?"

"Of course." He kissed her hair. "But not today. We've had enough amorous lessons."

She hummed in agreement while she skimmed her hand over his torso, over his hip to his thigh. She hesitated, bit her upper lip then rested her hand over the bulge still prominent under his trousers.

He groaned in encouragement.

"There must be something I can do for you," she said quietly. "Like what you did for me. I think I can imagine, although the book did not mention such an act."

He grew even harder. But despite her precocious charms she was still an innocent. "Sophie, have you ever seen a man, seen his cock?"

"I've seen statues and paintings," she admitted shyly.

"But not the flesh?"

"No."

He held her hand against him, moving it up and down the length. "Do you want to see me?"

"Yes. Please." Her voice held awe.

"O.K. One more lesson."

Sophia tried to still her excited breaths as Joseph knelt before her on the mattress, pulled off his braces then unbuttoned his trousers and drawers. He gazed at her as he reached under his shirt and freed himself.

She stared, thoroughly stunned, not having known what to expect. Joseph's cock was simply magnificent.

It jutted proudly with a little bounce, red-purple skin pulled taut at the tip, gleaming as if polished. She touched tentatively, finding him as smooth as glass, as soft as velvet. She curled her fingers around the shaft, surprised by its hardness and warmth.

Joseph's chest rose and fell steadily. "Do you want to learn how to pleasure me?"

"Yes." She could barely get the word out.

"Loosen your grip a little. Yes, like that. Now slide your hand up and down the length."

She did as bidden.

Joseph jerked forward slightly, emitting a clipped groan. "Yes. Like that," he breathed. "Exactly like that."

A droplet of fluid formed at the eye of the tip. Sophia licked her lips then bent and ran her tongue across the opening. He tasted...*masculine*.

Joseph pulled back. "Sophie, darling, is that what you want?"

She smiled sweetly. "Is that what *you* want?"

"I would be in heaven if you put me in your mouth."

She bent over in answer, wrapping her lips around him, then slowly slid her mouth and tongue along his shaft.

He rewarded her with a new drop of his emission, salty and pungent. She wanted more, wanted to drink from him as he had from her.

"Suck me harder."

She did so, empowered by his sensual groan.

"Use your hands to help." His tone was urgent.

But she wanted to take all of him in her mouth. Her eyes watered, her throat tensed and she had to release him.

He smiled at her efforts. "Try breathing in at the same moment you take me deeper."

She made attempt after attempt, his groans of satisfaction and oaths of encouragement goading her to succeed until finally she discovered the right rhythm. She sucked him to the back of her throat, held him but a moment—as long as she could stand—before she released him to begin again.

"Oh, God."

His fingers gripped her hair, tightening and releasing, flexing to the rhythm of her mouth and tongue. His breathing quickened to racing puffs.

"Darling, you have to stop," he exclaimed without conviction.

A sensual groan followed the meek plea. She increased her efforts.

"Sweet, I'm going to spend."

She hardly knew what that meant but he said it as if it was something he wanted to do.

"God, Sophie, if you keep that up, I'm going to spend in your damn mouth!"

She kept it up.

He grabbed her head and held her steady as he jerked against her. The spurt of hot liquid against the back of her throat shocked her into recoiling but he would not let her go. He pumped his seed and she had no recourse but to swallow every drop.

He pulled out and lifted her, clasping her to him, his body trembling. "Darling, oh my darling," he murmured, kissing her hair. "I didn't mean for that to happen. I'm sorry, I'm so sorry. I couldn't control myself at the end. Please forgive me." He looked down at her then kissed her forehead. "Are you all right?"

She licked her lips and swallowed again, the taste of him invigorating her, filling her with an understanding of their intimate connection. "That was fun, Joseph." She hugged him back. "But I think I should like a drop of tea now. Or possibly brandy."

He laughed a joyful laugh. "Get dressed." He gave her bottom a gentle swat. "We've been far too long behind these curtains. And I need to get those copies made." His eyes twinkled with an unspoken sentiment.

At least they had both broken the rule of not falling in love.

Arthur paced in the vestibule outside the door to the Harwell Hall estate office. Having to make an appointment with one's own father was damned inconvenient but the marquess preferred it that way. Planned consultations relieved Father of messy familial encounters involving emotions. Arthur was determined that life with Henny and their children would be the complete opposite. His children would call him "Papa" and they would be the most important thing in his life.

Well, after Henny, of course. She had arrived the day before with her mother to begin wedding arrangements with the marchioness—*Mother*, Arthur reminded himself with a scowl—who had insisted she be involved "so I can be a better friend to my daughter during her special time," which seemed like a preposterous notion since the marchioness was practically a stranger to Sophia now.

No, that wasn't true. Sophie and Mother had a congenial relationship, not as close as Henny and her mother but nothing like the chasm that separated him and the marquess—*Father, damn it.*

Arthur drew in a fortifying breath. He knew he had to discuss the Royston business with Father, not only because the duke was expected any day but because Joseph would eventually question him about it and Henny had insisted he do so. She had come to his room the night before and after a blissful reunion they had talked for hours, eventually touching upon the topic of Royston and Sophia.

"He doesn't love her one whit, darling, and he'll discard her once he feels she's been used up. He'll make sure she has children to keep up appearances really, but he'll do it on his own terms. Sophie will be reduced to nerves living with that man." Henny had snuggled up to him at that point, probably realizing how lucky the two of them were. "Sophie's a treasure, darling. She deserves more."

Henny was right. Sophia was a dear little sister and as her brother, he should look after her.

The door to the estate office creaked open, jolting him to the present.

Father's secretary regarded him with a dour expression. "My lord, the marquess will see you now."

"Thank you, Billings."

The secretary held the door while Arthur stepped inside then closed the door behind him and took a seat.

"Arthur," Father greeted pleasantly. "To what do I owe the honor?"

Arthur glanced over at Billings. "It's a family matter."

Father seemed about to protest then merely waved to his secretary, who exited. He invited Arthur to sit.

"What is the problem?" he asked in a voice trying to convey fatherly concern. "Is it Henny?"

"No, Father. Henny is very well, thank you. It is rather Sophia I am concerned about."

"Ah."

Father surely had an idea what was coming so Arthur went straight to the point. "The Duke of Royston was seen attacking a servant girl at the Fosdyke ball."

That got a rise out of Father's eyebrows at least. "Oh?"

"The girl was raped and beaten. Royston left her outside the kitchen."

Father cleared his throat. "And where did you hear this, son?"

He had debated whether or not to reveal the source of information then had decided to leave that part of the story vague. There had been several men there that night with whom Arthur and Joseph had discussed their scheme. Any one of them could have pulled Arthur aside and confided in him. "One of my business associates saw the completion of the incident."

"Did the man approach the duke?"

"No, Father. He thought that ill-advised as the duke had just injured the girl. He did not know Royston's state of mind and did not want to incite more violence."

"I see." Father leaned back in his chair and steepled his fingers. "Why do you think this man told you?"

"He knows you and the duke are good friends and that my sister is being considered for him."

"Hmm. This girl was a servant, you say?"

"Yes, Father."

"A servant girl who has no qualms following a man she does not know out into the kitchen garden?"

He should have seen that coming. "I don't know the girl, Father."

"Ah, yes, but we all understand the lower classes are of a much more passionate nature than we are."

Speak for yourself, old man. "Yes, sir."

Father sighed. "Son, it is a man's natural inclination to accept a flirtatious invitation from a young girl, especially at Royston's age. It's rather flattering really. I don't think you should concern yourself any further with the incident."

Arthur tempered the rage welling within. "I was only thinking of Sophia, Father."

"Sophia? How does she fit into all of this?"

"I was concerned the duke might be of a violent nature. I don't want to see her hurt. The servant girl had cuts and bruises."

"Oh, pshaw. Men don't act so fervently toward their own wives. It's all rather staid and unenthusiastic. You'll see after you get married."

If you please, sir, no I will not.

"It's not quite settled yet with Royston anyway. He has some debts he's promised to clear. I want Sophia starting off managing a well-financed household. And your mother and I want Sophia to have her first Season after coming out. It's what every girl dreams about, I suppose."

Arthur cleared his throat. "What if she meets a suitor during the summer, then? At one of the many soirées? A peer with good accounts?"

"I suppose such a match is possible. Your mother and I haven't discussed it. There may be someone we overlooked."

Luckily he and Henny had made up a list of all the marriageable, financially stable, good-natured peers above the rank of viscount. They would make damn sure Sophia met every single one of them.

"Thank you, Father. I appreciate your taking the time to talk with me."

"Very good." His father shuffled some papers on his desk then looked up. "Arthur?"

He hesitated, perhaps a bit too hopeful. "Yes, Father?"

"Send Billings back in as you leave, will you?"

"Yes, Father."

CHAPTER SEVEN

It was her duty, Sophia reminded herself, to spend time with the Duke of Royston, to have him court her. Gone were her carefree days of meandering on the estate, always ending up at the little iron-and-glass folly where Joseph spent much of his time. She smiled to herself. Her meanderings were really fully cognizant endeavors to seek out the handsome American, although she did devise circuitous routes so as not to be so obvious.

Now with Royston returned for a visit at Harwell Hall, she had to be far more clever in devising diversions from his attentions. Wedding planning with Henny was always a standby. Exercising to relieve vague "women's complaints" could only be stretched so far. Then there were the one-time-only excuses—going into the village to the dressmaker's or the milliner's, helping Mama with her charity, wanting to finish a chapter of an exciting novel—and there were just not enough of those. Eventually she had to give in to a request for a drive and a picnic. Mama was beside herself imagining the romantic possibilities.

"Oh, my Sophia, all grown up," she had effused, clapping her hands. "Out for a ride with Giles."

"Giles?"

"That's his Christian name, dear."

She didn't inquire further. Mama and Papa had known Royston a long time, since before he was a duke. Maybe they called him that when they were younger. Whatever their past Sophia was adamant *she* would never call him anything but his title so as to maintain an emotional distance.

The day came and what a lovely day it was. What a shame such fair weather would be wasted on a dull man. But Sophia loved the countryside and she would eventually need to eat lunch so it was not to be a total loss. Anna was to act as chaperon, which seemed irregular. Weren't chaperons dowdy old servants or spinster relations? She and Anna got on rather well so her company would definitely alleviate the expected boredom.

The duke arrived promptly at lunchtime, driving a borrowed carriage—her father's phaeton—and protested Anna's presence with a grimace and a comment that had he known, he would have brought along his valet Jasper to keep her company. But after helping Anna into the boot, purring pleasantries as he tucked her in beside the baskets and blankets, he seemed resigned to the arrangement.

"My lady," he said with exaggerated gallantry, holding out his hand to help Sophia up to the seat.

Sophia was glad her crocheted gloves were thicker than her kid gloves. It meant her hand was that much farther from his when she was compelled to take it. Once seated she had to endure his attentions and pretty words as he tucked a blanket around her, spending too much time fussing about. Then, with an unexpected agility counter to his stocky build, he swung himself up next to her, took the reins, and they were off.

The drive was tedious—fraught with awkward small talk—and frightening, given that the duke seemed more interested in looking at her—and sometimes at Anna—than watching the road. The horses—a sleek, matched pair of Papa's—seemed confused at times from his muddled handling of the reins. They reached their destination and jerked to a stop with such a jolt poor Anna exclaimed her discomfort out loud.

The duke helped Sophia down and stood staring at her until Anna appeared with a basket and a blanket, probably having decided she was not going to have him manhandle her again upon her descent.

"Ah, my dear, I promised a picnic but I suggest a stroll first. How does that sound?"

Sophia turned to Anna. "Are your shoes adequate for a walk?"

The duke winced. "No, no, no, my dear," he said, shaking his head. "Your maid will be preoccupied with setting up our luncheon. If you are concerned about propriety, we will only be going as far as the creek. I'm sure your maid will be able to keep an eye on us from here." He leaned in a bit. "There are trees aplenty for us to accidentally step behind should our passions take us in that direction."

Horror prickled along the back of her neck. She flashed Anna a helpless look as she took the duke's proffered arm.

He walked as erratically as he drove, occasionally bumping into her, his forearm brushing her breast followed by apologies in a low, husky snigger. Once or twice she was able to turn to see if Anna was still within sight and to Sophia's relief her maid stood watching them.

The creek burbled from recent rain, the banks green and damp. Sophia breathed in the spring air and, for a moment, forgot whom she was with and how she got there.

But only for a moment.

The duke turned to her with such a sudden movement she jumped back. "Sophia, my love," he said urgently, grabbing her arms. "Your beauty inflames my passions. I am convulsed with desire when I am around you."

She froze in panic. "Your Grace, please, I am not used to being wooed with such extravagant words."

"I cannot help myself. My body trembles in your presence." One hand released her arm only to wend its way around her waist. "I am greatly aroused." He pulled her toward him with a jerk.

His wheezing breaths huffed wet and heavy against her forehead. She turned her face away. "Your Grace, sir, please let me go."

The arm at her waist tightened. "I will, my darling, in exchange for one little kiss."

Disgust shivered up her spine to break out in a sweat on her brow. "Please, Your Grace, don't ask of me that which I cannot give freely."

"Ah such virginal coyness is utterly delightful." He cupped her cheek, pushing her head to face him.

"No," she whimpered.

"Relax, my darling, you'll enjoy it."

Never. She would never kiss him. There could be nothing more foul than kissing the Duke of Royston. She placed her palms against his chest and pushed with all her might.

He didn't budge. Instead he let her go. Sophia fell backward with a thud, slipping on mud as she tried to right herself then tumbling down the creek bank.

Instantly he was on top of her in a feigned attempt at rescue. His body weighed her down, his weathered face hovered above her. He licked his lips.

"Sophia, I only want what will eventually be mine." His hot, moist breath wet her cheek. "Don't think you'll be able to put me off our wedding bed. You should avail yourself of the fruits of my experience." His hips pressed slightly into her. "You'll grow to crave my presence."

No. She tried to push him off. He gripped her wrists with one hand.

"Please leave me be." She closed her eyes, wringing tears to fall down the sides of her face.

He pawed at her skirts. "I promise the pain will be momentary and if you're a good girl, the pleasure will be endless."

"My lady?" Anna's anxious cry rang above her. "Are you injured?"

The duke barked an expletive then stood and helped Sophia up.

Anna stared at her like a frightened rabbit.

"I'm fine, Anna," she assured, brushing her skirt, righting her bonnet.

Anna smiled in relief before staring at Sophia's dress. "My lady, you're terrifically muddy."

Sophia had purposely worn an old dress, something she was never going to wear again so she wouldn't be reminded of the occasion. However, she had planned to give it to Anna. Now the dress was ruined.

"Ah," said the duke, looking too long at her backside, "but it hasn't soaked through. You'll not catch a cold."

Anna curtsied and apologized as if she had interrupted a planned event. "My lady, I've prepared the luncheon, if you are so inclined," she said politely.

"Yes, Lady Sophia, we mustn't let a little misstep upset our whole outing." The duke's smile was sickeningly sweet.

Sophia *was* hungry. She pursed her lips and readied herself for the rest of the afternoon.

Anna brushed out Lady Sophia's hair, the long tresses still damp from her evening bath but finally clean. They had both been surprised at how insidious the mud had been at the base of her chignon.

When she first saw her lady fallen on the creek bank—her bonnet askew, her skirts crumpled at her knees—Anna was certain what had happened wasn't a simple accident, that she had been *made* to fall in some way. By the time they finished luncheon, Lady Sophia's mood was in such a state that the wickedness of the situation was fully apparent—to Anna at least, as she knew her lady's moods. The duke continued to chatter away as if Lady Sophia wasn't sullenly picking at her food in a muddy dress.

The dress was from Lady Sophia's autumn wardrobe, a lovely violet silk with green and cream stripes, pagoda sleeves with cream lace lining. Anna had admired it during a hunting luncheon and her lady had said she could certainly have the dress the following year. The day's events left the fabric quite stained and her lady had offered her profound regrets for its condition when Anna undressed her. Anna decided to take it anyway. Her mother would clean it, alter it, and give it to one of her sisters. The dress would not go unused.

Lady Sophia followed her reflection in the mirror. "Thank you, Anna, for coming when you did, when I had fallen. I think the duke was of a mind to do something most monstrous."

Anna slid the silver brush through a handful of silken strands. "I had thought as much, my lady."

"You see, he was about to kiss me. I do not want to be kissed by him. Ever."

"Oh." It wasn't as if her lady had never been kissed before. At the very least there was the rather dashing and handsome Mr. Peel. His kisses were truly seductive. Anna's insides flipped every time she thought of the night of her lady's birthday party. She would love a chance for such an opportunity to arise again.

Really, Lady Sophia should be engaged to him by now. Yet for some reason, Mr. Peel was not considered a proper suitor. And while there had not been an official announcement, the duke's successive invitations to Harwell Hall implied *something*. A something that made him think he had the right to kiss her.

Anna shuddered. Lady Sophia wed to the Duke of Royston? The idea was appalling.

Practically every female servant at Harwell Hall had been groped, leered at, or inelegantly flattered by the man. That morning she had bristled as he tucked the blankets around her skirts, squeezing her thighs in the process. Everything about the duke was thoroughly disgusting.

Anna placed her hands on her lady's shoulders, the sign she was finished. "Whatever I can do to help you, Lady Sophia, please let me know." Anna met her mistress' gaze in the mirror.

Lady Sophia clasped her hands with trembling fingers. "Thank you, Anna."

After making sure her lady was comfortable in her bed, Anna said her good night and left for her own bed upstairs.

The hall clock chimed the early morning hour. The family and their guests had stayed up very late talking, playing games and having a bit too much brandy. She could not stifle a yawn and almost tripped on the stairs, righting herself drowsily…

Someone grabbed her from behind, lifted her bodily. A hand clamped over her mouth as her candle was snuffed out.

She struggled, tried to scream, but the man carrying her was too strong and too determined.

He carried her to his room, told her to shut up, that if she did not shut up he would hit her…if she did not let him do what he was going to do to her, he would hit her harder…if she told anyone about any of this, he would do so much worse than merely hit her…

An hour later, when she stumbled into her bedroom, shaking with hatred and fear, she understood completely why her lady did not want to be kissed by the Duke of Royston.

Arthur leaned against the mantel in his library then swirled the brandy in his snifter. The amber liquor reflected the flames from the hearth as if it were liquid fire in the bowl of the crystal. He smiled. He was satisfied. And happy. Every aspect of his life was falling into place, and at a mere twenty-four years old. Most men of his class were whoring and gambling at his age, getting it out of their systems before the day came when they would have to assume the responsibilities of a peerage, an estate—most likely sprawling and poorly maintained— and spend endless hours in Parliament, debating the price of grain. But Arthur wasn't the whoring and gambling type.

And neither, it seemed, was Joseph. As business partners, they were perfect for each other—Joseph had the ideas and technical know-how, Arthur had access to money and investors. He was rather lucky to have been introduced to Joseph during the one time he allowed himself the opportunity to sow his wild oats in that exciting upstart of a country, the United States.

"Now what?" Joseph asked languidly from the leather wingback.

The day had been a busy one of answering correspondence, of compiling lists, of checking financial accounts. Arthur hadn't been able to talk much to Henny since breakfast but she had been busy with wedding plans anyway. He wasn't even sure she was coming to his room that night since she had excused herself early at dinner. He had been far too tired to join his family in the drawing room afterward so he and Joseph had decided to have a quiet evening alone.

"Well, now that we have loads of interest in the scheme, the idea is to meet with small groups when we get to London. Show them the plans, answer any questions." He sipped his brandy. "I expect there'll be lots of questions about America in general that I simply will not be able to answer."

Joseph chuckled. "It's a country that spans three thousand miles and is full of all sorts of people from all sorts of places. I wonder if I will be able to adequately respond myself."

Arthur flashed a grin. "Then you'll have to make something up. Something that makes America seem exciting enough to be a high-yield investment but not so thrilling that they'll fear they'll lose all their money."

"Ha." Joseph downed his brandy then rose to pour himself another. "I've been out West. I've got some exciting stories. I'll try to temper them."

Joseph went to the liquor cabinet, decanted some brandy carefully as if it were a precious liquid, swirled it in his glass, then upended the snifter and swallowed every drop. He moved gracefully but with a roughness that reflected his background, giving him a distinctive appeal Arthur hoped investors would find enticing and encouraging. It was certainly enticing and encouraging to him.

Joseph poured himself another and joined Arthur at the hearth.

"When do we go to London?" Joseph placed his glass on the mantel then yawned and ran his fingers through his hair.

That Joseph acted with such familiarity was gratifying. Their relationship had become as intimate as Arthur's with Henny. Almost. "Next week. It's the beginning of the Season."

"I've heard of your Seasons. Lots of parties." He raised a suggestive brow. "Rather decadent."

"Yes, like Rome I'm sure." Arthur chuckled.

"Not really my milieu. I'll be out of my element. I'm nervous about all this."

Another endearing quality was his bald honesty.

Arthur placed a reassuring hand on Joseph's arm. "You don't have to attend every event, just the more strategic ones. I'll introduce you around at my club as you might be spending a lot of time there. Also, I want you to see my tailor once we get to town."

Joseph crinkled his forehead. "Oh?"

"You'll need the latest fashion in evening dress, plus a morning suit. And there's my wedding in June."

"Ah yes." He sighed with a touch of melancholy.

"Trust me…my tailor will make you look so smart my distant cousins will just assume you're another distant cousin."

Joseph stared into the fire. "You're doing an awful lot for me, Arthur."

"If you don't want to accept my generosity as a token of my esteem and friendship, consider my support as part of my investment." He patted his shoulder. "Don't feel beholden to me, Joseph. I'll take my cut when the time comes."

"O.K." He squeezed Arthur's hand. "What about after the wedding?"

"What do you mean?"

"Well, am I to continue staying with you? I could go to a hotel."

"Joseph, the house is huge. Don't worry—you won't hear me and Henny."

Joseph grinned, and when Joseph grinned ingenuously, he was quite handsome. Too handsome.

"What about a honeymoon?" he asked, possibly with a hint of envy.

Was he so important in Joseph's life? The thought was flattering.

"We won't go anywhere until the business is settled and you're back home across the pond."

"Hmm…" Joseph snorted, holding Arthur's gaze. "You have your life all planned out, don't you?" His tone conveyed only comment, not judgment.

Arthur smirked. "I like living that way."

Joseph glanced at his brandy. "What if it doesn't turn out as planned?"

"Well," Arthur started, suddenly self-conscious, "I think we can figure something out between the two of us. We make a great team, don't you think?"

Joseph smiled. "Yes, I do."

A moment of stillness hovered in the air. Perhaps it was just the liquor mingling with the heat from the fire but a giddiness riled Arthur to the notion that he could do anything. The world was full of possibilities.

He cupped the back of Joseph's head then leaned in and kissed him full on the mouth.

Joseph recoiled for a split second before giving in, letting Arthur explore him, their lips grazing, their tongues tangling, rough skin against rough skin. It was absolutely marvelous.

It was positively wrong.

Arthur pulled back, panting. "Christ, Joseph, you must forgive me. I cannot think what I was doing." *Good God*, he was mortified.

Joseph stared at him stunned but not horrified. "And have you ever done such a thing?"

"No, never." Arthur closed his eyes briefly. "I mean not that I haven't ever thought… I just haven't."

"Oh." Joseph seemed befuddled.

"And you?" he dared ask.

"Yes. But never of my own volition. I was always—" He sighed heavily. "It's different for me. I'm always the prey. When one is the mere courier boy of the wealthy, one must endure a great deal—"

"Oh, Christ, Joseph, I'm so sorry—"

"I've never been with a man because I wanted to, I mean, sometimes I wanted to but it simply was not my choice and I was doing it anyway."

Arthur searched his face. "Then make it your choice. Don't let men like me bully you around."

Joseph's gaze was deep, grateful. "Yeah…O.K."

Arthur turned away. "It's late. I'm going to my room."

In an instant, Joseph had Arthur in his arms, his mouth pressed against Arthur's, assaulting him with passion. Arthur submitted willingly, reveling in the powerful embrace, his cock springing to life as it rubbed against Joseph's crotch.

Joseph let him go. "I'll have you know I like women very much."

Arthur chuckled in relief. "Obviously I like them quite a bit too."

"I've had enough of you, Lord Petersham."

The use of his title cut but was probably Joseph's way of establishing a modicum of control.

"Thank you, Joseph. I'll see you in the morning."

CHAPTER EIGHT

A tumult of emotions racked Joseph to the core. The scheme had been progressing smoothly then Arthur had to go muck things up by kissing him. Joseph would have taken Arthur to bed except Henny might have come looking for her fiancé in the middle of the night. Discovering him in Joseph's bed, in Joseph's arms, would have been an utter and complete disaster.

He and Arthur cleared things up in the morning, Arthur apologizing profusely, endearingly heartfelt, Joseph finding himself with the upper hand, as the one to offer solace. They both agreed that while their brief intimacy had been diverting, it should never happen again, chiefly out of consideration for Henny, even though, Arthur insisted, she might find the idea intriguing.

"She could join us," Joseph had joked.

"You'll touch her over my dead body, Mr. Phillips," Arthur had retorted with a laugh.

And then the incident had blown over. Except Joseph remained agitated in such a way solitary gratification was unsatisfying. He needed something more.

He needed Sophia.

As always, he had difficulty pinning her down. She was either with Henny and their mothers, discussing wedding plans, or dodging—so it seemed as his presence was far too ubiquitous—the Duke of Royston's attentions. She did not come to the studio much and when she did, Henny often accompanied her.

Without her, frustration mounted and tore at his concentration.

He paced and wandered around the studio, poking the fire, twiddling his pencils, thinking of her, his cock aching with unrequited desire, his mind unable to focus on whatever it was he was supposed to be preparing for Arthur…

And then she walked in.

It was as if the gods had decided to smile upon him.

"Joseph?" she said, her gaze sweeping over him, assessing his state of discomposure.

"Sophie, my love." He held back. They were on display behind the wall of glass.

She flicked her gaze to the curtains then walked to the door and locked it.

Joseph casually strolled to draw the drapes and pulled the cords slowly.

With privacy secured they fell into each other's arms.

Their reunion had been too long delayed. Her mouth was an exquisite refuge into which he fell completely, her body a sanctuary for his lustful fantasies. He stroked and squeezed, deliriously murmuring endearments, licking and nipping, removing bits of his clothing, unfastening bits of hers, leading them both toward the bed, picking her up and placing her on the mattress, stretching himself alongside her.

"Darling, I've missed you," he murmured against her neck.

She wrapped her arms around him. "Oh, Joseph. It's been horrid. Mama made me go for a drive with him and then he tried to kiss me." She shuddered. "I'm always on my guard because he might suddenly appear and he usually does. He's gone into Little Bytham this afternoon. I headed here as soon as I could."

"I'm glad you came. I need you, Sophia." He kissed away the tears that dampened her lashes.

"I need you too." She propped herself up on an elbow. "It's just not the same when I touch myself alone." She plucked at the buttons of his shirt. "I think of you but it's nothing compared to what you did to me last week."

"Or what you did to me." The memory lingered vividly.

She hid a smile as she continued to play with his buttons. "You said you would teach me." She raised her gaze to meet his.

His cock stirred at the entreaty, seductive yet so innocent. "Of course." He kissed her tenderly. "Lie down."

She rolled onto her back, pulled up her skirts and gave him a wistful, encouraging smile. He slid his fingers through the split of her drawers, between the plump folds of her feminine flesh already wet for him. He spread the sticky moisture and when he reached her clit she yelped, staring at him wide-eyed.

"That, my love, is your clitoris. Your locus of pleasure."

She blushed. It was damned charming.

"When you are aroused as you are now, you create a natural wetness. Use that to stroke yourself." He flicked his finger back and forth, petting her, keeping in check his own desire in order to bring her to ecstasy.

She sucked in a mouthful of air and held it too long.

"Darling, breathe."

He stilled his finger against her and she exhaled.

"Good. Relax." He resumed his ministrations using a circular motion. "You can do whatever feels good—pressing, rubbing, pinching—"

"Pinching?"

He chuckled. "Give me your hand. I'll show you." He guided her finger to her sex. "It's that little nubbin. Do you feel it?"

"Oh!" She jerked her hand away.

He calmly reclaimed it and returned it between her legs.

"Touch yourself in the way that feels most pleasing to you. I'll be right here."

Arousal vexed his cock as her expression transitioned from surprise to curiosity to delight to bliss, her finger working steadily, rhythmically.

"Now increase the pace and you'll find the pleasure grows."

She worked furiously, lost to him, lolling her head, arching against the mattress, moaning distractedly. The magnificent display of sensuality taunted him to satisfy his own needs but he resisted and watched her, mesmerized, until she bucked up with a cry then landed on the mattress, panting and staring up at the canopy.

"Oh," she said. "I've always wondered how to capture that feeling. Sometimes I wake up from the most luscious dream. Now I can make it happen without dreaming." She smiled. "Thank you."

Joseph chuckled in amazement. This was a woman who could orgasm from a lover's spoken fantasy or, apparently, from a dream.

"How did you know how to do that?" The rasp of afterglow tinged her voice.

"I've had some experience."

"With women, you mean."

"Yes," he stammered. "A few."

One by one she opened the buttons of his trousers. "How many?"

Shit. He should not have said that. "Sophie…"

She untucked his shirt. "How many?"

Would the number seem high to her? Or surprisingly low?

She started to unbutton his drawers, a devious glint in her eye. "You know I could just look at you and not touch you."

Jesus, he'd probably come anyway. "Twelve."

She stared at him in astonishment.

"That's not what you were expecting."

"No."

He raised a brow in invitation for her to extend the thought.

"Three. I thought it would be three." She plopped down. "Did you love all of them?"

Shit. "Look, Sophie, darling, I wasn't in love with any of them." He inhaled deeply. "Do you really want to know?" He turned to face her.

She stared at the canopy with a dreamy expression. "I guess you really have had an exciting life. Arthur said so."

"Do you think me despicable? If you want to end our liaison—"

"No." She propped herself up on her elbow again. "I want to continue exploring. I want you to show me the ways of pleasure." She toyed with the buttons on his shirt.

"And I want to continue all of that too. But I need to know if you are comfortable with my past."

"Your past? Were you the Don Juan of New York?"

He laughed. "Nothing so romantic." He stroked her cheek. "You know how your virginity is a highly valued treasure and you are taught to keep it, and not to do anything like what we are doing or you'll be ruined?"

"Yes. My governess made sure I understood all of that. And Mama has admonished me about dancing too much with one man or taking walks with Geoffrey. And about how my husband wants me to be pure and unsullied and even the hint of impurity would be ruinous."

"Well, it's different for girls of my class. There are not the same strictures. For some of them the act of sex is just another pastime and for others, it is their profession."

"Oh. I suppose I did know about that. But that's awful, isn't it? And we should pity such women who have been led astray?"

Joseph composed his thoughts. "For some yes, it is a horrible necessity and life for them is brutish. For others, though, they choose that way of life and are very well compensated for it. Some are quite rich."

"Like mistresses and kept women? I've heard some men have those."

"Sort of like that. There are also women who employ other women. They give them a warm place to live, food to eat, pretty dresses, and in exchange the girls provide services to men."

Sophia stared at him, realization dawning on her face. "Is that who you were with?"

He dragged his fingers through his hair. He did not want to have this conversation with her. Not now, probably not ever. "Well, yes, some of them were. Do you despise me?"

"No. It's just so different than the men I know. Well…I think it is."

"More likely they're too polite to discuss such things with you." He pulled her against him. "My father had a business arrangement with a courtesan. He would treat her shipments with extra care and she would compensate him for the service. They eventually became good friends. When I turned eighteen he sent me to her to learn about women and their desires." He ran his hand slowly down her body to rest on her hip. "So I would know how to please them and especially—if I were to marry—so I would know how to please my wife. I had been with girls before but didn't really know what I was doing. She taught me."

"What you did for me the last time we were together."

"Yes…and what you did for me."

"You're tutoring me for my husband," she huffed with disappointment.

"That's certainly not my intention, love. I'm doing this for us. But your husband will be pleasantly surprised."

"Joseph," she began haltingly, "I don't want my virginity to be such a treasure."

His gut clenched. "Oh no, I'm not taking it, Sophia. I won't. You know I won't."

"I thought as much. I just wish it were the same for me as it is for those other girls."

"Their days are difficult, darling. They work themselves ragged. Their lives are short and their joys few."

"Our time together is short," she said with a melancholy smile. "What pleasure shall we share today?"

She was right. They might never find themselves alone ever again. He wanted to possess her, yet there was only one way a man like him could possess a girl of her class. He rolled on top of her and kissed her deeply.

"Do you feel my weight against you?" He trailed kisses down her neck, undulating his hips, his cock threatening to free itself from his only partially buttoned drawers. "My body's rhythm. That is the movement of carnal love."

Her respiration increased as she followed his lead, moving her body in time with his, her hands gripping his back.

He lifted his head to gaze upon her. Her cheeks flushed a sinfully alluring shade of pink. "I can't give you that pleasure, Sophia. But I can give you another. A similar pleasure, where I enter you, our bodies join, I bring you to orgasm, I fill you with my seed. Do you want this?"

Her eyes widened. "Yes."

Her reply rendered him rock-hard. Inwardly he cursed and thanked the clothing acting as a barrier between them. His wasn't just bald lust—*she* did something to him, made him want their coupling more than ever and made him want to give pleasure more than ever.

And they were about to do something rather unconventional. Whoever her husband would be, most likely he would never require it of her. This would be her first and last time. And Joseph wanted it to be the most wondrous sensual experience of her life.

"Darling, I want you to undress while I fetch something from the cupboard."

"Yes, Joseph." Her eyes flickered with unspoken inquisitiveness.

"And take off every stitch this time."

Sophia pulled her dress off her shoulders then fussed with her underclothes, trying to ignore the sounds of Joseph rummaging about on the other side of the studio as she stripped bare.

He returned with a butter dish and placed it on the bedside table. A bizarre accessory indeed, but the sight of him frantically removing what remained of his clothing diverted her attention from the curiosity.

He stood before her, stark naked and magnificent. She swallowed a gasp of surprise as she stared in aroused disbelief.

She had seen marble statues of Herakles and Zeus on the Continent, her governess explaining that such powerful muscularity was a representation of an ideal in Greek society, an ideal that good Christian British men were meant to aspire to in their virtuous living.

The lesson had not included a word about the raw, masculine sexuality that would make her blood pump harder, flushing her skin and swelling her sex, warming her despite her own nudity. For before her was the ideal made flesh, flexing and breathing and covered in fine, light-brown hair.

Joseph too was flushed and gawking, the wonder on his face softening the brutish strength suggested by his bulk. "Sophie. You are divine."

He pulled her into a passionate embrace, his mouth feasting like a hungry man's, his avaricious grasp claiming her down the length of her spine to grab her buttocks.

"Get on the bed." The brown flecks in his gray eyes darkened to a foreboding hue.

He jumped on the mattress after her, clutching her to him, delving in with a deep kiss, the new intimacy of skin on skin thrilling, warmth melding into warmth, blurring where her body ended and his began. He cupped a breast, pinched the nipple and growled a laugh when she jerked against him. He smoothed his hand down her curves to rest at the pleasure spot between her legs then rubbed gently, his strokes long and languorous, tantalizing her only enough to start that luscious climb to oblivion. His tongue in her mouth matched the slow cadence.

"God, Sophie," he rasped, "you don't know what you do to me. I'm trembling on the edge of desire."

She trembled too. His hand, his tongue held her captive in a heightened state of arousal, an erotic prison from which she clambered to burst free.

"Joseph," she moaned against his lips. "Please, I need you to…to release me. To let me have my crisis."

"No." He removed his hand, leaving her bereft. "Not yet."

And then he reached over and retrieved the butter dish.

"I found this among all the other discarded bric-a-brac here. I got quite a surprise when I cleaned it up." He held it out as if studying it. "Such a curious thing. Then I remembered this used to be where the marquesses of yore brought their mistresses and it made sense." He brought it before her view. "If you notice, there is an intriguing erotic scene on the cover, apparently indicating what one is to do with the butter stored inside."

A man, dressed in a style of clothing worn one hundred years ago, held his erect and frighteningly huge penis in his hand, aiming it at the exposed buttocks of what looked to be another man, who smiled.

Sophia had never seen anything like it. "Those are two men!"

Joseph chuckled. "Yes they are. But if one were to try to explain the act to one's mistress, it would be in this context—*this is how men take pleasure from each other so let's do it too*." He raised his brows provocatively.

Sophia's eyes widened. "You mean in my," she lowered her voice as if someone else might hear, "arse?"

Joseph grinned with excitement. "Yes, love." He placed the dish on the mattress.

She looked down at his jutting erection. He too was huge, although not so out of proportion as depicted on the porcelain cover.

"Will you fit?"

"I'll take that as a compliment to my manhood."

She giggled at his naughtiness. "Will you enjoy it?"

"Every damn second, darling. It is extraordinary." He kissed the tip of her nose. "You'll enjoy it, too. Trust me."

"All right." She nodded.

His expression of pure joy shot a shiver of excitement through her. He retraced the tracks of his touch with his mouth, pecking, licking, nipping from her neck to her mons, pausing at her breasts to suck her yearning nipples, turning anticipation into craving. Once at her excited clitoris, his tongue nimbly stroked, awakening her desires once again to that maddening point just before the climb to the peak. He fumbled with the butter dish then lifted her hips off the mattress, reaching under her.

He prodded her tight hole. She yelped.

"Shh, shh," he consoled. "Just let go and feel it." He recommenced his torment of her clit.

She relaxed as he lubricated his way into her most forbidden of places, one finger circling around the orifice, spreading the creamy butter. Then ever so slowly he pushed in and pulled out, one finger joined by a second then perhaps—but she wasn't quite sure—a third.

Because by that time she was absolutely lost in a new oblivion, a place where she relished being trapped in an unfulfilled state of arousal.

"Darling, do you want me?" His low, sultry voice rumbled up her core.

"Yes, Joseph."

He sat on the mattress on his knees, reached for another scoop of butter then massaged his formidable cock until it was glossy. He grabbed two pillows from the head of the bed. "Lift up," he directed, indicating her hips.

He put the pillows under her buttocks, raising her, then positioned himself at the entrance. "Darling, it will hurt for a moment. Take deep breaths when you feel pain. Let your body release the tension with every exhale."

And then he pushed in. Slowly.

A slight pinch was followed by a sensation of luscious fullness. She wanted more and tilted her hips to give him better access, thrusting forward in encouragement. He held her gaze as he advanced further.

A jolt of pain seared her core. She choked.

He paled. "Breathe, Sophie, breathe. Calmly, slowly."

She puffed breaths, releasing her grip with every exhale, enabling his further entry until he was deeply embedded. A wave of sensuality flooded over her. She gasped.

"Darling?" His forehead wrinkled.

She moved her hips. "Is there more?"

He chuckled and pulled out, only to push in again, steadily, gradually increasing his rhythm, his concerned gaze continuing to track her expression. Her hips undulated to his cadence and his lips curled in satisfaction. He reached down and caressed her clit.

The familiar torment began, now juxtaposed with a new pleasure, a pleasure tinged with pain, delicious pain, like the exquisite burn from the swats on her behind. He drove into her, his ragged breaths laden with groans and oaths, mingling with her moans of joy, her utterances encouraging him to give her more, for she was climbing, climbing to the peak again, and he with her, the exertions of their bodies synced to reach the goal together.

She was there a second before him, the sensuous assault too much for her virgin sensibilities. Her body tensed as she screamed a growl, thrusting her hips up and holding them in the air as she shook and continued to shatter.

He came with a barking cry, thrusting deeper, piercing a tight muscle, shooting a searing shock of pain to tear through her, a pain that only heightened the incredible climax to another level of orgiastic delight.

He dropped onto her, exhausted, his heart thudding against hers, his chest heaving from his exertions. His cock slackened as he calmed and he pulled out from the intimate connection.

"Sophie, my Sophie." He kissed her cheeks, clutching her to him. "Darling, please tell me you're all right."

She was more than all right. She was stunned into elation. "Joseph, that was simply amazing."

He chuckled softly. "Would you believe me if I told you the same. We're perfect together."

They *were* perfect. She had nothing to compare such intense intimacy to, but it was perfect. She wrapped her arms around him more tightly. "We are, aren't we?"

"Oh, my sweet—"

An insistent knock on the front door resounded through the studio. They froze.

"Sophie? Are you in there?"

"Henny." Sophia gaped at Joseph in panic.

He placed his finger over her lips to silence her then got up and put on enough clothes for propriety's sake and threw the rest on the bed. *Don't worry*, he mouthed, then closed the bed curtains.

CHAPTER NINE

Henny stood outside the door of the wrought iron folly, concerned her knock had yielded no response. The windows were shrouded by drapes as was usual to ward off the chill that burdened the space even in spring, but the door was locked. If someone was inside, there were few reasons why they would lock the door.

And if the occupants were Sophia and a certain handsome American, there could only be one reason.

She had looked everywhere for Sophia but couldn't find her in any of the usual places so headed for the studio. As she had approached the ornate structure, hope and fear had swelled her heart. She trusted Sophia but running off at midnight during a crowded ball was one thing. Disappearing in the middle of the day when sins could be too easily exposed was quite another.

She was about to leave when the door opened part way. Joseph poked his head out. "Henny? Come inside."

He seemed abashed, not his usual self. He was in a state of disheveled undress, much like the first night she met him only more so. His unbuttoned shirt hung outside his trousers, his cuffs flapped loosely around his wrists.

She flushed from embarrassment. "Joseph, if this is a bad time, I apologize. I'm looking for Sophia. Well, her mother is and I offered to help."

He remained before her, befuddled, shifting his weight. He raked his fingers through his hair. His very messy hair.

An acrid scent lingered in the air. She had intruded on a very private interlude indeed.

She flicked her gaze to the old curtained bed in the back of the space that Joseph had set up in part to humor her. He slid his hand down his face as he let out an exhale.

"Henny, please believe me, we haven't done anything we should not have done. I mean we have but look, see Sophie's still, well she's still—"

"Intact?"

He colored and nodded.

She had wanted Sophia to explore a bit. But to be starkly presented with the afterglow of a sensual scenario was rather shocking.

"Please don't tell Arthur, whatever you do." He looked at her pleadingly. "It would ruin everything."

She shook her head. "I have no intention of telling Arthur. I'm partly to blame here."

The curtains around the bed rustled and the mattress squeaked with movement. A moment later Sophia peeked out. She grinned.

"Henny." Sophia ran to her, dressed only in her drawers and chemise, and flung her arms around Henny's neck.

"Oh my dear, dear Sophie." Henny kissed Sophia's hair, put her hands on either side of her head and looked her in the eye. "Get dressed, darling. Since you really should not be here unchaperoned, say you were walking in the old birch copse. I'll tell your mother I couldn't find you."

"Thank you, Henny."

Sophia returned to the bed, stopping to grasp Joseph's hand, to gaze at him. He gazed back with a twinkle in his eye and a smile curving his lips. They were dangerously in love. And Henny was foolishly elated for them.

"I'll leave you two now," she said, turning to go.

"Henny, wait," Joseph called.

She stopped.

"Look, if you see Arthur, say you came here and found me just woken up. I was drawing and felt I needed a rest. That covers us both—you don't have to lie completely about coming here and I have an excuse why I'm a little tardy with the copies."

In their rumpled state, Joseph with his arm around Sophia's shoulders, she nestled comfortably against his chest, they appeared a perfect picture of young love. Her heart broke. There was no possible future for them.

"Yes, Joseph. If he asks, that's what I'll tell him." She smiled and left, her only cheering thought that if Sophia did have to marry Royston, eventually he'd tire of her. And Joseph would be waiting.

Arthur swirled his port, the liquor's sweet bouquet mingling perfectly with the intoxicating fragrance of Henny's perfume. She had come to his study that afternoon agitated and wanting the release only physical intimacy could bring. It was risky doing such a thing in the light of day but it was, oh, so wonderful.

She cleaved to his side in the drawing room after dinner. Dinners with his family could be pleasant respites from bachelor meals in his apartments but were more diverting when Henny and her mother came to stay. This time though, Royston was visiting as well and Arthur wanted to avoid the man. But Henny insisted Arthur attend every damn dinner while all three were visiting.

At least Henny had insisted the men take their port with the ladies in the drawing room—a modern arrangement to be sure. She knew he could not stand to be in such limited male company. The presence of the women would dull the sting of the duke's caustic remarks.

And the duke was always ready with a caustic remark.

"How is this little project of yours faring, Petersham?"

If anyone other than Royston had posed the question, Arthur would have felt compelled to answer politely with a hint of intrigue to spark the man's interest. Instead the purpose of the statement as a condescending jab was altogether apparent.

"It is faring quite smoothly, Your Grace," he responded noncommittally.

"I'm sure it is easy to sway the novice investor with fantastical stories of America, the land of plenty and possibilities."

"Really, Your Grace," countered Father, "I think Arthur has found some good men. I know Thuxton is very interested."

How unexpected that Father would show even a modicum of support.

"Thuxton? Well that's impressive," the duke responded rather indifferently.

"Indeed it is, Your Grace," said Henny. "It seems every scheme the earl involves himself in becomes a success."

Arthur smiled behind his port. Thuxton and Royston were rivals in business, Royston having lost a bundle far too many times just because he felt the need to be stubbornly contrary. Arthur could not understand such antagonism. If a scheme was good, it was good. Unfortunately Royston had become a barometer for bad investments, just as Thuxton had become the measure of good ones.

"By all means then, I should pay more attention to his habits," Royston responded acerbically. He turned to Arthur. "Perhaps I'll think about joining your little venture."

Arthur did not want a ha'penny from the man. "Initial investments are quite high to ensure complete commitment."

"Didn't I hear you recently sold your fleet of carriages, Your Grace?" Henny's honeyed voice dripped with scorn. "I'm sure you have something left over from whatever debts were paid with the proceeds from that."

"The carriages were worn and broken down and really only appropriate for a bachelor," Royston replied with a glance across the room at Sophia. "I'm in the market for something more family oriented." He downed his port with repressed annoyance.

The sound of Sophia's gleeful laughter turned all attention to her. Arthur was glad for the distraction.

Henny took his arm. "Let's join your sister, darling, to see what all the fuss is about."

"Yes, love," he responded. "Thank you," he said under his breath.

Sophia, Mother, and Henny's mother Lady Bloxholme surrounded Joseph while he drew at a writing desk.

"No, ma'am, I really do not know anyone who got rich off gold," Joseph said to Mother. "I've heard that most of the money was made by those selling shovels and pick-axes."

"Oh dear." Mother smiled. She had become less aggrieved by Joseph's habit of not calling her by the proper form of address.

"What's so funny, Sophia?" Henny asked.

"Mr. Phillips drew a picture of a cattleman in the wild West. He called him a 'cow-boy' and said I could have it." She held the drawing out for Henny. "Look at the wonderful cows."

"Ooh," Henny chirped. "And that precious calf."

Joseph had sketched a charming picture, something Arthur rarely saw from his friend since he spent much of his time drafting mechanical plans. The women were agog over his drawings of what looked like scenes and people from the western United States.

"And he said he could only draw a certain type of Indian," Sophia said to Henny, "because some of them walk around with barely a stitch of clothing."

Henny gasped and the two women giggled.

"Let's see what you got there, Phillips," Royston said, barging in.

The duke shuffled through the drawings, grunting and humming dismissively. "Not quite good enough for the Royal Academy but rather quaint." He placed them back on the desk. "Where did you learn to draw?"

"Here and there," Joseph responded politely.

"Didn't you say artists would come to one of the houses where you took lessons?" Sophia piped in then blushed.

"Yes, that's true, Lady Sophia. I was allowed to take such lessons with the other children of the house."

Royston sneered. "So you have no academic training?"

"Nothing as formal as that," Joseph agreed.

"Yes, I can tell," concluded the duke. "It definitely shows with some of this unpolished line work over here." He waved his hand casually over no particular part of a landscape.

"Oh, pshaw, Your Grace," Lady Bloxholme countered. "Mr. Phillips is quite skilled and you know it. The Royal Academy would be pleased to have him exhibit with them."

"Thank you, ma'am," Joseph said bashfully.

"You'll have your chance to compare, Your Grace, soon enough," Father rumbled.

Joseph raised a brow at Arthur.

"The Season opens with the Royal Academy Exhibition," he explained. "Next week."

"We'll take you to the Exhibition, Mr. Phillips." Henny smiled. "We'll make a young persons' outing of it, just the four of us."

"Four?" queried Royston.

"Why me and Arthur, and Mr. Phillips and Sophia."

"I'm sure Lady Sophia would rather go to the Exhibition with a proper escort." Royston scoffed. "Wouldn't you, my dear?"

Sophia remained silent and averted her eyes.

"Let the young people have their fun, Your Grace," Mother said. "Sophia will be beset upon by suitors at every occasion. She'll need a respite from all the attention. She can play tour guide one afternoon with our American guest."

Royston looked as if he would boil over. Clearly this was the first he had heard of Sophia having suitors other than him. He had probably assumed she would be hanging off his arm at every event that Season. For Arthur, that his parents had admitted Sophia could even have other suitors held the promise they were coming to their senses.

CHAPTER TEN

London, 4 May 1860

"So this is the famous London Season."

Joseph could barely maneuver in the crush of bodies at the Royal Academy Exhibition. He had never seen such a gathering of the rich and powerful in one single location. The galleries teemed with what seemed to be every fashionable lady and gentleman in the entire country. Only the stiff crinolines of the women's skirts kept breathing room between the patrons. And air was at a premium. The pungent odor of drying varnish clashed with French perfume and heady cologne.

"Rather more infamous, if you ask me," quipped Henny, clinging to Arthur for dear life.

Sophia hung on to her brother's other arm, staring in awe and admiration at the crowd. "It's magnificent."

"And we haven't even seen the art." Joseph winked at her and grinned at her blush.

Newcomers jostled the foursome, pushing Joseph right into Henny's bosom. He grinned again. Arthur glared.

"Let's start backward through the exhibit," she suggested. "Perhaps it won't be as stifling at the other end."

"Go with Joseph," Arthur said to his sister as he and Henny made their own path.

Joseph laughed. Sophia smiled and bit her lower lip then threaded her arm through his. They wended their way through the galleries, dodging voluminous skirts and protruding canes, gesticulating experts and dazzled amateurs. After a good ten minutes they joined Arthur and Henny in the East Room. The throng had indeed thinned considerably.

Arthur pulled him aside. "See that man over there? In the pale-green waistcoat?"

The waistcoat was the most unusual feature on the otherwise rather unremarkable, middle-aged man. "Yes."

"That's Prescott," he murmured. "Leonard Prescott. He's a good friend of Geoffrey's and he's expressed interest in our scheme."

Business, always business. Joseph had hoped he could concentrate on the art.

"And the man shaking his hand, that's Harland Moseby."

Another unremarkable gentleman. Striped waistcoat. "Shouldn't we introduce ourselves?"

"No. Geoffrey will make the introductions later. But remember you saw them here. Ask them about the art."

"Flatter them by pretending I value their opinions on such matters?"

Arthur nodded as a wry smile twisted his lips. "Something like that."

Sophia bounded up. "Mr. Phillips, I've just seen a picture you might find stimulating."

"Of course, Lady Sophia." Their veneer of formality was tiresome. He envied Arthur and Henny.

She led him to a spot on the wall near the door where hung a small but stunning canvas. A soldier dressed in a black uniform gazed down on a woman not quite in his arms but who had been perhaps a moment before. A dog—fidelity—sat at attention for his master. On the wall behind the pair hung an etching of Jacques-Louis David's *Napoleon Crossing the Alps*, hinting at the soldier's battle destination. The sheen on the woman's white satin gown was rendered expertly, challenging one to touch her skirts to prove it was merely a painting.

"It's called *The Black Brunswicker* by J.E. Millais." A giddiness rippled through Sophia's voice.

"It's exquisite."

She sidled up more closely to him. "It's like us," she whispered in his ear.

Joseph smiled. *Indeed.*

The coloring of the young man and woman were off, his hair was too dark, her eyes too blue. But the emotion conveyed was eerily accurate. Young lovers being ripped apart by duty, not wanting to give in to their respective fates, she trying to close the door, wanting to be with him one last time, he breathing her in to his memory before he sailed away and out of her life to certain death.

"I think they've just made love," she murmured daringly.

"Perhaps." He almost choked on the word as a pang of despair shot through him. While Sophia saw two beautiful lovers ending a tryst, all he could think about was how they would never be together again.

Shit. He wasn't supposed to fall in love.

"Ooh, that's a lovely one." Henny's voice at his side broke his thoughts.

He cleared his throat. "Yes, it is." He stared at the painting, blinking back emotions threatening to break.

Henny sought his gaze. "Arthur wants your opinion on some landscape on the other side of the room." Her smile conveyed empathy. "I'll watch Sophie."

"Thank you." He gave Sophia's hand a furtive squeeze and lost himself in the crowd.

* * * * *

Geoffrey sank into the sofa in Arthur's library and closed his eyes, ignoring the babel of Belgravia outside. The Season had opened with a grueling week of meetings with businessmen and bankers and peers with too much money, a week of stifling smoking rooms and an excess of spirits. A week assuring potential investors that indeed the Panic of '57 was very much in the past. A week of reiterating the scheme and gauging reactions to Phillips' designs. A week full of men, where the only female companion was his mother.

He slipped off his shoes and extended himself, his calves lying against the padded armrest. He was looking forward to the frivolity of the Wrexham ball that Saturday, women displaying their bosoms, enticing him with their finest perfumes, giggling at his insipid jokes. He sighed.

"Comfortable?"

He opened one eye. Phillips stood above him, holding two snifters of brandy.

"Very." He took a glass and swung his legs back to the floor, securing himself in a corner. Phillips sank into the other corner.

"We've got our twelve men." Arthur sat on the wingback opposite. "Each one of them very impressed with your elegant designs." He raised his snifter to Phillips.

"Is twelve a significant number?" Phillips inquired.

"No," Arthur said. "It's just enough. Not too many, not too few. A safeguard if someone drops out."

Geoffrey drained his glass. "I'll start drawing up the paperwork tomorrow." He leaned his head back to stare at the ceiling.

"You really put your heart and soul into this business, Peel. You look as beat out as a stevedore done landing cargo."

Geoffrey eyed Phillips with a scowl. "I'm sure that is a flattering description of my person."

Phillips laughed.

The more contact Geoffrey had with the man, the more he grew to like and respect him and the more he understood why Arthur called him by his Christian name. "Phillips" did not suit. He was "Joseph" through and through. It set him above the class distinctions he took pains to eschew.

"Just be well-rested for my wedding, Geoff. You're best man, remember?"

"Ah, the toast." Geoffrey lifted his head and raised his empty glass. "To Arthur, a man who knows how to make men and money work for him."

Arthur chuckled. "To the betterment of both, I would add."

A commotion in the lobby caused all to turn toward the door. A knock resounded, followed by Wittering's somber entrance, the open door augmenting the giggles and squeals emanating from the marble foyer.

"Lady Henrietta Langley and Lady Sophia to see you, sir. Shall I send them in?" the butler drawled.

A grin spread across Arthur's face. "Yes, Wittering. Please."

Henny entered and Arthur was at her side instantly, grabbing shopping boxes before grasping her hands, kissing her cheeks and calling her "darling".

That Arthur was so much in love instilled hope in Geoffrey's beleaguered heart.

Sophia followed in Henny's wake, swinging her wide skirts and her own purchases playfully. As she spied Joseph the color rose in her face. She met Geoffrey's gaze and smiled warmly. She greeted her brother with a peck.

The air was filled with their chatter and bustling as they piled up packages, their energy a distinct contrast to the men's enervation. Sophia sat on the sofa next to Joseph and took off her gloves then grabbed his snifter and took a sip. Joseph's face softened, the small act somehow laden with meaning.

"And what have the two of you been up to?" Arthur asked as he led Henny to an armchair.

"The seamstress'." Henny sighed. "For the Wrexham affair Saturday."

"It seems Henny's getting fat," Sophia teased.

A fleeting look of inquiry passed from Arthur to Henny. She looked away, busying herself with her reticule.

"I fear I'm not my usual abstemious self, what with the wedding nerves." She smiled at Arthur. "Are you going to offer us tea, dear?"

"Absolutely." Arthur tugged on the bell-pull.

For fifteen long minutes the women gabbed frenetically, stumbling over each other's words, telling stories of shopping and how their exertions left them as exhausted as the men. Relief came when the door opened.

And Anna walked in with the tea.

Geoffrey stood, exhilaration coursing straight up his spine. He went to her, took the heavy, well-laden tray, his fingers brushing hers in the process.

"Thank you, sir." She blushed. Her dress, a plaid of chestnut and copper, highlighted her brown eyes and auburn hair.

"Anna?" Arthur said with surprise. "What happened to Wittering?"

"Someone at the door, my lord. Mr. Wittering asked if I would bring in the tea."

Geoffrey put the tray down on a side table, his fingers still tingling where they had touched hers.

"Good," exclaimed Sophia. "Then you can pour and we can all be familiar." She glanced at Anna. "No sugar for Joseph, please."

While Sophia and Henny continued to regale the men with tales of shopping and gossip, Anna dutifully poured and passed out cups of tea. Geoffrey watched, riveted by the simple, domestic task performed with such polished elegance.

"And how do you take your tea, Mr. Peel?"

Preferably alone with you. "No sugar, Miss Colney."

"There's cake as well, sir."

"Ooh, Anna," Henny interjected. "If you please, cut me a slice. I'm famished."

"Henny, your waistline."

"Pshaw, Sophie. That's why I had my dress let out. I'm not passing up Mrs. Babcock's cake."

Joseph and Arthur sat in silent amusement. Geoffrey closed the space between him and Anna, shielding her from view of the others.

"Will you sit with us, Miss Colney, and take tea?" he asked softly.

She sucked in her lower lip and nibbled briefly. "That is not my place, sir." She lifted her gaze to meet his. "Mrs. Babcock will have tea and cake for me downstairs." Her eyes surveyed his face, slowly moving side to side, up and down, to his hair, his mouth, blushing at the last. "Shall I cut you a slice, sir?"

"Yes, please, Miss Colney."

He stood aside. Neither was it his place to upset the order of things.

"You're coming to the Wrexham ball, aren't you, Joseph?" Sophia asked. "Arthur will take you. I think as his official business partner you're even allowed a dance with me."

"Your mother has most likely already promised all your dances, dear," Henny said.

"But it will be Joseph's first London ball." Sophia clasped Henny's hand. "You must convince her to let me."

Anna handed Arthur his slice of cake. "If you're not needing me any longer, my lord, I'll take my leave."

"Yes, thank you, Anna."

Geoffrey's heart sank a little as she exited to take her place downstairs.

CHAPTER ELEVEN

Sophia shifted uncomfortably in her straight-backed chair and stared at her dance card. She had already endured over half of the dances at Lord and Lady Wrexham's annual May ball, each with a different partner, each partner with a different claim to the aristocracy. It must have been after one o'clock in the morning and she was exhausted, less from the dancing and more from the forced conversations about the exact same topics using the exact same words.

The Duke of Royston was partnering her next. She almost felt relieved. At least she didn't have to have the same mindless chitchat with him. He already knew who her parents were or how many siblings she had or even what she thought of the weather.

Henny and Arthur approached, flushed and giggling, probably having just availed themselves of a bedroom upstairs. She ruffled at the thought.

"Sophie," exclaimed Henny. "Not dancing?"

"I stood out this one. Mama said I could. My feet are killing me. And my head."

"How are the suitors?" Joseph asked, quietly appearing on her right.

She turned a smile to him. "Boring. What about you? Did you dance with anyone?"

"I did," he chuckled. "A lovely young lady put up with me for a polka. Unattached but no debutante."

"Oh, yes," said Henny. "Some of the girls are having their second seasons. Not everyone gets snatched up as quickly as I did."

She gazed at Arthur, who beamed lovingly.

Sophia gazed up at her own object of affection. "Arthur tells me you two had a busy afternoon, Mr. Phillips."

"We did, Lady Sophia." His eyes twinkled. "My accent enthralled the members of his club."

She giggled and inwardly sighed. All she really wanted was to laugh and dance with him, call him by his Christian name, bill and coo like Henny and Arthur. It was maddening.

"You look so pretty tonight, Sophie," Henny said. "Doesn't she, Arthur?" She squeezed his arm. "Compliment your sister on her new necklace, dear."

Sophia smiled. Henny had given her a gold locket with side-by-side miniature portraits of the two of them. She smoothed her thumb over the pendant.

"The splendid adornment is the perfect accompaniment to your captivating loveliness, Lady Sophia." Joseph winked at her.

Arthur rolled his eyes and flashed a smirk in Joseph's direction. Henny squealed with a clap.

The duke approached, his affected saunter spiked with urgency. "Lady Sophia, the next waltz is reserved for me."

"Yes, Your Grace." She tucked her card in her purse.

He glanced at the company and nodded his greetings all around, receiving mumbled courtesies in return.

"Mother tells me you escorted her to the Royal Academy Exhibition today, Your Grace," Henny said sweetly. "I must thank you for the distraction. She's been thinking of nothing but my wedding of late."

Henny was wicked to rub salt into the wound. So deliciously wicked.

Royston scowled. "Anything for my dear Cousin Edith."

"And which was your favorite?"

More cruelty. Henny knew the duke was not refined enough to have an opinion about art.

"I'm sure I don't know, they were all rather finely done." He turned to Arthur. "You, Petersham?"

"I liked Goodall's *Wilderness of Shur*. I rather fancy the exoticism of the Near East."

Henny giggled. Clearly a private joke. Another diversion Sophia was denied with Joseph.

"And what about Mr. Phillips?" Royston sneered. "You consider yourself something of an artist do you not?"

"I thought *The Black Brunswicker* by Millais to be exquisitely done."

"Dull and saccharine, if you ask me." The duke winced. "I'd think a man such as you would prefer a landscape or something involving industry."

"I feel it precisely depicts the emotion of true love, a sentiment, I would hope, understood by all men. Or perhaps it is a sentiment only understood by those still in the vigor of youth, my lord."

Royston turned a shade of red Sophia had not witnessed before. Joseph had, unwittingly or not, used an incorrect form of address and insulted the duke's manliness. She wanted to laugh but somehow managed to turn such jocularity into an expression of shock. Henny avoided her eyes, as she too seemed about to burst into guffaws.

The music started up in a waltz.

"Lady Sophia." The duke's tone verged on a growl. "Our dance." He held out his hand.

Sophia touched her glove to his and did not look at her companions. She simply could not.

And within a minute of dancing, she realized mundane conversation with young, awkward men was far more preferable than being whirled around the ballroom by a perturbed duke. He clutched at her more aggressively than a partner should and steered her with more insistence.

"You should find better company than American commoners, Sophia. Especially if you are to marry a man of status and prestige." His voice held a snarl.

"Yes, Your Grace," she said blandly.

"I'm sure there is no way you will ever be rid of the man if he is to persist as your brother's business partner. At least he'll be far away and you won't have intercourse with him too often. Or more likely the business will fail. Then you'll never have to see him again."

Sophia was not looking forward to the day Joseph would be far away. She wanted him as close to her as possible forever. And she certainly could not imagine never seeing him again. "Yes, Your Grace."

"You're rather dull tonight, my dear, aren't you?" he sniped.

"Please, Your Grace, I am tired. I've been dancing for hours. When you encountered me, it was the first I had sat all evening."

"Well then," he said with a keen glint in his eye, "we should find a bench for you to sit upon and catch your breath. Perhaps in the garden."

The last thing Sophia wanted to do was to stroll through a dark garden with the duke. If Joseph had asked her, she would have jumped at the chance. She pressed her lips together to stifle a smile.

"Ah, I see the idea intrigues you." He slowed as the music's *ritardando* signaled the *crescendo* of the finale. "I know a restful place. I'll take you there."

Sophia scanned the ballroom for someone familiar. She did not know her next dance partner—the son of a friend of her father's—and Henny, Arthur, and Mama were nowhere to be seen. Joseph neither, although even if she did spy him in the bustling crowd, she hardly knew how she could convince the duke to take her to him. Royston pulled her toward the French doors leading onto the terrace, conducting her rather emphatically through them and out into the frigid night air.

Instantly she chilled and not from the change in temperature. She tried to focus on how one might extricate oneself from such a situation. A need for a wrap? He would simply give her his jacket. A call of nature? He would wait nearby. She had no time to think of any other ruse, for he was being very insistent, guiding her forcefully, down the stone stairs, over the lawn, into the depths of the dark amongst the trees and arbors and gazebos that created shadows and enclosed spaces.

He had stopped chatting with her, instead was determined, adamant about getting somewhere in particular, gripping her arm tightly, unconcerned if she was scratched by a rosebush or tripped on a rut or snagged her voluminous skirt on a hedge. The light from lamps soon disappeared and party guests along with the lamps. They were utterly, completely alone in the moonless night.

And the duke was not in a good mood.

Soon they were at the back of the garden, a stone wall looming before them. Royston muttered an oath then yanked her to the right. He dragged her through a side door, cursing once again at the clank of the iron latch, and into the neighboring garden where a stand of trees, gnarled and ominous, clustered at the back. He pulled her inside amongst the twisted branches and slammed her up against a thick trunk and stripped off his gloves.

He held her against the coarse bark as he pressed his lips against hers, cold and clammy, his passion borne from anger. She struggled against him but he held her down firmly, resolutely, pulling her hands up over her head.

"You will learn that a fine lady does not keep company with such dogs. Once you are mine I will make sure of it." His hand tightened cruelly around her wrists.

"Please, Your Grace, you are hurting me," she said purposefully loudly.

He released her and slapped her face with such strength she doubled over. She cupped her stinging cheek, unsure if the wetness was blood or tears.

"I see you did not inherit your mother's fondness for pain. That is regrettable." He grabbed her by the hair, pulling back, forcing her to look at him. "You will keep your mouth shut while your better teaches you a lesson." He hauled her by the hair under a low branch, knocking her head against it as he yanked her to standing.

He placed his hands on the neckline of her dress and pulled outward, tearing the bodice in half. Sophia gasped a cry, clutching the ruined fabric to her bosom, her thumb reflexively reaching for her locket, finding nothing. Gone. Henny's precious gift was gone. She whimpered.

He slapped her hard across her face, his signet ring striking her cheekbone. "I told you to be silent."

He rent her dress viciously, shredding the skirt down the middle, grabbed her right hand and tore off her glove then crushed her forearm against the branch. He wrapped the length of fine kidskin around her wrist tightly, binding her to the tree.

Tears cascaded down her neck to her chest as he cruelly squeezed a breast, his tongue forcing its way into her mouth. He untied the tapes of her cage crinoline and petticoats then stomped them flat on the ground.

"No man will want damaged goods."

Sophia froze.

He tore open her drawers.

Her head spun, her stomach churned. Did she forget to breathe? Did she forget how to breathe? Her free hand lifted to touch her temple…

His fingers tightened on her wrist as he hastily unbuttoned his trousers and drawers. He kicked her legs apart.

She teetered and fell back against the trunk, her brain in a fog, not certain if what she was seeing in the dark was really happening…

Joseph berated himself for upsetting the duke just before the man partnered with Sophia. She had looked pained as Royston inelegantly moved her across the floor, dodging rather than floating among the other twirling bodies, their arbitrary path making it difficult to track them. Joseph had stepped forward to get a better view and practically crashed into a giggling, spinning couple, losing sight of Sophia for only a second. The music ended and he searched for her in the crowd.

Alarm stabbed up his spine. She was not there.

He searched the ballroom frantically, trying hard not to draw attention to himself. In the corner of his eye he saw a young man approach Henny and Arthur, showing them his dance card, questioning them, the pair shaking their heads and looking around as well, the young man shrugging and moving along.

Shit. Sophia had missed the next dance.

He espied the French doors leading out onto the terrace—the easiest way out of the ballroom—and moved as quickly as he could, still searching, glancing at every couple, noting sizes and shapes, the dresses of the women as he wound his way outside down the steps to the lawn spilling out into the garden. Couples milled about, most remaining close to the house, a few venturing off along lamp-lit paths to flirt and fondle in a romantic gazebo or arbor.

But if a man's motive was not romance, such a man would take his prey to the darkest corner of the garden.

Joseph drew in a breath and dived into the dark, allowing his eyes to adjust to the moonless night. He moved as swiftly and silently as possible, his senses on high alert, his ears competing with the worry and reprobation screaming in his head.

The screech of metal on metal and a throaty snarl stopped him cold.

He turned and sped toward the sounds, pushing through a side door in the garden wall, his way barely lit by the dim light glowing from the Wrexham's upper floors, his ears pounding at the sound of fabric tearing.

His eyes focused on the scene of his worst fear realized. Sophia captive and half-dressed, crying and exposed, sagging against a tree.

And the Duke of Royston with his prick in his hand.

He inhaled deeply to contain the fury balling within. He would not save Sophia by murdering the man, even though that was precisely what he wanted to do.

"Step away from Lady Sophia, Royston. If you know what's good for you."

The duke spun around, tucking and buttoning frenziedly. "This is not your concern, Phillips."

"The safety of Lord Petersham's sister is every bit my concern. Leave. Now."

Royston looked as if he were about to respond, thought better of it and ran off, away from the ball and the crowds.

Joseph flew to Sophia, gathering her in his arms, untying her wrist. She slumped down into a mass of undergarments and torn silk, her chemise wet with blood and tears.

She said nothing in her dazed state as he put her clothes back together as best he could, wrapping his jacket around her to hide her disarray. He carried her through the garden gate to the edge of the lawn then held her up as they walked along a narrow gardener's path to the front of the house.

He waved for a footman, who came instantly.

He gave the man a sovereign and his coat-room ticket. "The lady fell and injured herself. I need you to retrieve the Earl of Petersham and our hats."

Joseph held on to Sophia with all his might as they waited tucked behind a marble column, containing the anger, frustration and regret shaking him to his core.

If only he had not let her out of his sight.

S uspicion spiked through Arthur when a footman informed him he was required outside and requested he get his hat, his voice polite yet urgent. Suspicion turned to distress when he saw the footman retrieve Joseph's hat.

He grabbed the servant's arm "Where is this man?" He indicated the hat.

"He's out front with a woman, my lord. She has been injured."

Sophia. Something's happened to Sophia. She hadn't shown up for her dance with Viscount Welney.

"Get my carriage," he said to the footman. "The wrap of Lady Sophia Harwell," he called to the coat-room clerk. He jotted a note to Henny on the back of his ticket. "And please make sure the Lady Henrietta Langley gets this message."

Then he was out on the gravel.

Sophia looked barely alive.

"My God, what happened?" He held on to her as Joseph settled his hat on his head.

"Not here, my lord," Joseph said as the carriage pulled up.

The two men helped Sophia inside.

"Richmond residence," Joseph directed quietly to the coachman.

Arthur caught Joseph's eye as he took his seat opposite but his friend only shook his head. Joseph drew Sophia to him, wrapping an arm around her shoulders. Sophia roused then suddenly grabbed Joseph's arm. He whispered to her in soothing tones and she clung more desperately, crying softly all the way home.

Once parked in front of the house, Joseph lifted a crumpled Sophia into his arms and carried her inside.

"Get Anna," he said to the footman.

He motioned with his head to the staircase. "Which way to Sophia's room?"

"Follow me." Arthur led the way then opened the bedroom door and lit the bedside lamp.

Anna appeared directly. All color drained from her face the moment she saw her mistress.

Arthur chilled at the horror revealed in the glow of the light. Sophia's lip was swollen and cut, blood streaked down her chin and neck. Her left cheek was red, the eye above swollen. She hadn't met with an accident, someone had done this to her.

"Anna," Joseph said, distracting the maid from her astonishment, "I need you to get a sedative. Do you have such a thing in the house?"

Anna glanced at Arthur.

"Do what he says, Anna. Ask Cawston. He should have some laudanum in the butler's pantry. If not, bring brandy. Quickly."

Joseph removed the jacket covering Sophia. Arthur swallowed his shock at what was revealed underneath. His sister had been savagely attacked.

She livened, clutched at Joseph, sobbing uncontrollably.

"Shh, shh, darling, I'm here." He enveloped her shaking form in his arms and kissed her hair. "I'm here. You're safe now."

Darling?

"Arthur, help me." Joseph began removing the tattered dress from Sophia's body carefully, gently, coaxing her with soothing words.

Arthur held on to his sister as she followed Joseph's instructions to step out of her torn crinoline. Tears rolled down her cheeks as she grabbed her neck.

"My locket," she whispered.

Henny's gift. Arthur eased Sophia's hand down to her side. "I'll ask Lady Wrexham to report if it is found," he said calmly. The sight of her face twisted in too many emotions wrenched his gut.

Joseph moved away to place the rent garments on a chair. Sophia lurched and ran to him.

"*Don't leave me!*" she shrieked.

"No, no, darling. I'm not leaving." Joseph stroked her sagging, disheveled hair. He looked at Arthur. "Get a damp towel for the blood."

He wet a towel from the basin, returning to find Joseph removing Sophia's undergarments as if he had done such a thing before.

Joseph ignored his questioning look as he took the towel and proceeded to wipe the blood from Sophia's face, down her neck to her bosom, all the while cooing consolations.

Anna knocked then entered, registering brief surprise at the sight of Joseph and her mistress.

"Laudanum, Mr. Phillips." She held out a glass.

"Good. Thank you, Anna." Joseph took the glass. "Sophia, you need to drink this, love. It will help you forget."

He helped her with the glass as she drank the mixture. When she finished he held the glass out for Anna to take, separating his body from Sophia's ever so slightly.

"*Joseph, no!*" She grabbed at his waistcoat.

He wrapped his arms around her, patting her head against his chest. "I'll be here with you all night, darling." He glanced at Anna. "Make sure no one tells the Richmonds anything. Request silence from the staff who witnessed this tonight."

"Yes, sir." Anna curtsied and left.

"Lock the door," Joseph instructed Arthur. "You're staying the night in this room."

Joseph carried a weakened Sophia to the bed and tucked her in. Then he slipped off his shoes and climbed into bed alongside her, pulling her to him under the covers, kissing her hair, murmuring softly.

Arthur stared dumbfounded at the scene as he turned off the lamp. He grabbed Joseph's jacket and made himself comfortable on the day bed.

CHAPTER TWELVE

An incredible urge to piss woke Joseph. For a moment he forgot where he was until memories from the night before flooded his brain. He glanced at Sophia, safe in bed beside him, sound asleep.

As was Arthur, sprawled out on a day bed near the cheval glass.

He could relieve himself behind the dressing screen. He grabbed the pot from under the bed and was quick about it.

The room was cold and dark, the fire unlit, the curtains closed. The housemaid had not come in, under Anna's instruction he presumed. He lit the fire and went to the window, pulling aside the drapes just enough to see the cruel world waking up below.

Arthur sidled up next to him. "Tell me what happened," he said with quiet urgency.

"Royston had his trousers unbuttoned, his prick in his hand and was about to violate your sister before I intervened."

"Oh, God," Arthur muttered.

"From the look of it he beat her up as well."

"Jesus. I have to tell my father. He needs to know about this insult."

"He'll probably want to question her. She's in shock, Arthur. Be gentle with her."

"Yes, of course." Arthur shook his head. "How on earth could this have happened? There must have been hundreds of people there last night."

"Royston's no fool. He took her to the neighbor's garden. There's an adjoining gate."

"How is it were you there?" Arthur's voice was laced with incredulity.

"I followed them. I cannot abide that man and I cannot abide seeing Sophie with him."

Arthur remained silent for a moment. "Tell me about you and my sister."

Emotion welled in Joseph's chest. He knew the truth even though he swore it would not happen. "I'm in love with her," he said, staring blankly at the rug. "I didn't know until recently how deeply, how desperately in love with her I am."

Arthur placed a hand on his shoulder. "She seems to feel something very strongly for you as well."

"Arthur," he murmured gravely, "I of all men know this cannot, this *must* not be."

"How far has it gone?" he asked delicately. "Have you been intimate?"

Joseph met his gaze. "She's still a virgin, if that's what you mean. I would never—"

"I know you would not. You're the most honorable man I know."

"But, Arthur, listen, had I arrived a minute later last night, she would not still be. Royston will stop at nothing to make her his."

"Including violence, it seems." Arthur stared at his sister, tears misting his eyes. "They can't let him have her. They can't. Not after this."

"You must protect her. *We* must protect her. I would do anything to protect her from that man."

"As would I."

A tentative knock sounded at the door. Both men looked at each other in panic.

"It's probably just Anna." Arthur went to the door. "Yes?"

"I beg your pardon, my lord," said Anna meekly. "I brought a little breakfast and came to light the fire."

Arthur unlocked the door and quickly ushered the maid inside. Anna set down the tray then glanced over at Sophia.

"If I may, my lord, how is she?"

"Lady Sophia is sleeping," said Joseph. "She fell asleep soon after you brought the medicine last night. I think she will stay abed for most of the day."

"Thank you, sir." She glanced at the hearth. "Did Fanny light the fire?" she asked in surprise.

"No, I did." Joseph smiled at her.

"Thank you, sir." She curtsied with a blush. She turned to Arthur. "If I may, my lord, will my mistress need a doctor?"

Arthur puffed an exhale and scratched his head. "It's a rather delicate situation. I don't want to involve any of the family doctors just yet. But thank you, Anna, for thinking of that. We'll let you know."

She curtsied but hesitated.

"Is there anything else?" Arthur seemed a tad agitated.

She started to speak then stopped and cast her gaze to the carpet. She glanced at Joseph who smiled encouragingly.

"I know it is not my business, my lord, but was the Duke of Royston involved in the incident with my mistress?"

Arthur paled. "You are correct, Anna, it is not your business."

Joseph held up his hand. Something about her statement intrigued him. "Why would you ask such a question?"

"Because the duke insulted me one night during his last visit at Harwell Hall."

"Good God," muttered Arthur.

"Can you be sure it was Royston?"

Anna's eyes widened in shock.

"I mean no insult, Anna," Joseph said. "But a serious accusation will need evidence."

"Yes, sir." She drew in a breath. "He took me to his room. He threatened me. I know his voice." She wiped away a tear. "There was light from a lamp. I saw him clearly, sir."

Joseph wrapped his arm around her shoulders and led her to a chair by the fire. The man was an absolute animal to have attacked such a sweet, gentle girl.

Arthur held out his handkerchief.

"Thank you, my lord." She sniffled.

"He's a monster." Arthur paced then plopped in the opposite chair. "Anna, if I asked you to tell your story to the marquess, do you think you could?"

"I think so, sir." She looked at them. "If you or Mr. Phillips was there with me."

"If it ever comes to that, we will be right by your side," Joseph assured her.

"Thank you, sir." She got up and handed the handkerchief back to Arthur. "Please ring the bell, if you need me. I am at my lady's service at all times." She curtsied and turned to go.

"Anna," Joseph called. "Thank you for the breakfast."

She flashed a smile at him and left with a bit of color on her cheeks.

Later that morning Arthur called Anna back to stand guard over Sophia while he and Joseph went home to change. Before he left, though, as was proper protocol, Arthur made an appointment to see Father and requested Mother be there. When they returned to the Mayfair mansion, Joseph and Arthur's valet, Owens, relieved Anna of her duties.

Arthur greeted Mother and Father coolly once Billings showed him into the study. Mother sat in a straight-backed side chair against the wall, fretting with her skirts. The marquess sat at his desk, drumming his fingers against the mahogany.

"Well, Arthur? What is it?"

"A family matter, Father."

His mother squeaked a gasp. "It's Henrietta, isn't it?" She leaned forward in her chair.

Why were his parents so worried about Henny? "No, Mother. Everything is fine between Henny and me, if that's what you are asking."

"Oh dear," she apologized, "please excuse me."

"It's Sophia."

"What's wrong with Sophia, son?" Father asked indifferently.

"Last night at the Wrexham ball, Sophia was attacked—"

Mother gasped, her hands flying to her mouth. Father stared at him in shock.

"She was beaten and almost raped. Joseph Phillips discovered her and scared the man off."

Father stood. "Did he see him? Could he identify him?"

"Yes, Father." Arthur looked him in the eye, wanting to observe his reaction when he revealed the truth. "It was the Duke of Royston."

Mother screeched. Father met his eyes with a fixed stare. "Are you absolutely sure, Arthur?" he asked steadily.

"Yes, Father."

Father cleared his throat. "How do we know Phillips did not do this?"

Christ. He should have seen that coming. Arthur drew in a deep breath to tamp down the urge to lash out. "Because Sophia can attest to the fact that it was Royston," he said firmly.

"I must see her." Mother stood to go.

"Not yet, Mother." Arthur motioned for her to sit. "She's in good hands at the moment."

"How do you mean?" Father's tone was laden with suspicion.

"Joseph is guarding her while my valet Owens attends to her cuts and bruises. He served in a field hospital in the Crimea."

Mother whipped out her fan and began using it vigorously. Father uttered an oath.

"I thought it a good idea not to involve a family doctor who might be indiscreet."

"Thank you, Arthur." Father sighed as he sat back down. "We'll need to see Sophia, have a talk with her."

"Yes, Father. As soon as we are finished here."

Father gaped incredulously. "What more could there possibly be?"

Arthur stared back. "Royston."

"I'll have a talk with him. I'm sure it is all a misunderstanding."

Unbelievable. "The bruises on Sophia's face and wrists are not a misunderstanding."

Mother whimpered.

"Nothing has been promised to him," Father equivocated. "We'll keep him away from her until this cools down."

Christ. Was Father daft? That he would not simply write the man out of their lives was beyond comprehension. Arthur shook his head. "He should never see her again. And that's final."

Father's eyes narrowed. "That is my decision to make, Arthur. In the meantime I'll deny him access to any Richmond property, including our carriages and crest."

"Oh, at the very least," Arthur growled sardonically between his teeth.

Mother inhaled a sob. "Oh, my darling, dear child. And this was to be her first Season. We must not let on that anything is wrong. She must be presented at Court. She must appear at balls. She must…" She trailed off with a choking wail.

"Yes, Mother," Arthur bit back. "We must not reveal to polite society that one of their own savagely preys on young women and is a danger as long as he is able to walk freely among us."

Father slammed his fist on the desk. "Arthur! Enough! I want to see Sophia. Now."

"Yes, Father." None of this was the reaction he had hoped for. There was something very strange going on with his parents indeed.

Sophia rubbed her forehead in a vain attempt to dispel the dizzying fog. The light-headed daze persisted as if she were in a dream, but a dream that was far too real and seemingly endless. She had barely left the bed all day yet was somehow exhausted. She stared at the window, at the afternoon light fading into sunset behind the patterned sheers obscuring the view. Or were the curtains meant to hide the scene inside her bedroom?

Anna had attended her that morning, immediately rushing to Sophia's side when her eyes fluttered open. Anna held Sophia's hand as she inquired after her health and Sophia had to convince her maid she was sensible despite the effects of the laudanum. Then Anna pressed something cold into Sophia's palm.

Her locket.

"I found the chain of the necklace wrapped in the hoop of your crinoline."

Sophia traced the design of spiraling tendrils and delicate flowers engraved on the cover. She opened the compartment and instantly smiled at the tiny portraits of her and Henny.

"Thank you, Anna," she said, wiping a tear, marveling that such a fragile object had survived a harrowing ordeal. How a thing of beauty could be a reminder of an act so ugly.

"I'll return it to your jewelry box, my lady."

Anna left when Joseph and Owens arrived. Arthur's valet had been very efficient, asking Sophia pointed questions, seeking only the truth without judgment, saying the bruises were not serious and should disappear in a few days or maybe a week, the cuts perhaps longer. Occasionally she had glanced up at Joseph as he stood next to the bed, watching her and Owens, objecting when she yelped in pain, making sure she was comfortable, offering her a loving gaze. She was indebted to him for her life.

Then they had left and Papa, Mama, and Arthur had come in. Papa was relentless with his questions, implying she was to blame.

"Sophia, a girl of good breeding simply does not go into a garden alone at night with a man."

"Even with a man of good breeding, Papa?" she had asked innocently.

He had colored at that but never said anything about the duke no longer being considered a suitor. He couldn't possibly mean for her to still see him. She was determined never, ever to be in the same room with him again.

She wanted to scream that she had let Geoffrey take her into dark gardens and he had *never* done anything as horrible as what the duke had done. So why wasn't Geoffrey considered suitable for marriage?

And why wasn't Joseph, who had saved her?

Mama stayed after the men had left, her eyes bloodshot from tears.

"Sophie, sweet," she said, fussing with the coverlet, "we must put this incident behind us. You must proceed as if nothing untoward has happened. Do you think you can do that?"

Unbelievable. "I can try, Mama."

Mama, fretful by nature, seemed more nervous than usual. "There's the presentation at court we must prepare for. Since you cannot leave the house with those…those…marks on your face we'll bring the seamstress and the etiquette tutor here. We'll say you tripped and fell."

How strange that Mama had figured out how to handle the situation so cleverly and so quickly. "Yes, Mama."

"And we'll make sure all your ball gowns are absolutely de rigeur, à la mode, and all that." Mama patted her hand. "I should have sent you to Paris this week." Tears welled in her eyes.

"Mama, it's not your fault," she soothed. It wasn't anybody's fault but the duke's. Although Papa thought it was partly *her* fault.

"Yes, yes. I mean no. What's done is done." Her hands flew up to cover her mouth. "Oh, my Sophie. I'll make sure you meet many handsome young men." She fanned her face with her fingers. "Then there will be Henny and Arthur's wedding. You'll be as beautiful as the bride."

Sophia teared up at her mother's emotions. She squeezed her hands. "Thank you, Mama."

There was a light knock on the door. "My lady?"

"Yes, Anna?"

"Mr. Phillips is here to see you."

Sophia's heart leapt. "Please send him in."

"Oh, my dear, is that wise?" Mama queried quietly.

"Mama, Mr. Phillips saved me."

And then he entered, his face vibrant the moment their eyes met.

"Joseph." She could not stifle her grin, could not calm the thrum of her heart pounding in joy.

Mama stared at her in shock.

He did not take his eyes off her. "How are you this afternoon, my lady?"

His voice was a balm to every pain in her body.

Mama nodded her greeting. "Her spirits seem enlivened by your presence, Mr. Phillips."

"Thank you, ma'am. I am grateful I was able to prevent an insult to your daughter."

"And my family thanks you for that, Mr. Phillips. Pray tell, how is it that you came to be present at the moment when my daughter was in distress?"

"May I be frank, ma'am?"

"Yes."

"I followed Lady Sophia. I do not trust the Duke of Royston around your daughter. I never have since the first I met him."

"I see. And why is that?"

"I've met men like him before, ambitious men who seek spouses only to elevate themselves without concern for the woman in question. Whatever leverage they have they will use."

Mama paled briefly. "Surely that is an American proclivity."

"With all respect, ma'am, it is a proclivity anywhere power is at stake. I understand the duke has lost some money recently and is in great debt. He seeks power to regain his prestige and position in society. A marriage to Lady Sophia will bring him all that, along with financial gain. I only wonder what leverage he is using to obtain that which he seeks."

Mama folded her hands together and pursed her lips. "Your theories are very interesting, Mr. Phillips, and not without merit, I'm sure. Right now, though, we need to focus on Sophia's health. I thank you for your service to my family."

"Be assured, Lady Richmond, I would do it again but I hope I never have to." He bowed. "Lady Sophia, I will take my leave. I plan to visit every day until I am satisfied you are recovered."

She held her hand out to him. He kissed it tenderly, sending a tingling shiver to shoot straight to her heart.

He left. She smiled, hopeful she would recover swiftly and looking forward to seeing him every day.

CHAPTER THIRTEEN

Joseph lay in bed wide awake, unable to sleep, night bringing with it memories of Sophia's attack. A week had passed and he still jumped at what was probably just a servant slinking down the hall in Arthur's Belgravia house, pulling the sheets down as if that would augment his sense of hearing. He fretted as a carriage rolled by in the street, stopping briefly before rattling away. London was not as noisy as New York City but was more restless than bucolic Lincolnshire. He was irritated that every little thing out of the ordinary was setting him on edge.

He knew how to steady his nerves. A frig always worked. And seeing Sophia nude the other day—despite the circumstances—only made the urge more powerful. But anguish and anger had dulled his motivation. He couldn't get himself to begin. He just wanted to be spent already.

Perhaps he needed some inspiration.

He lit the oil lamp to a dim flame then fumbled through the books recently acquired from Mr. Jacobs. Sapphic schoolgirls? Maybe. Bondage? That would have to wait for recent memories to fade. A harem? Possibly. With virgins? Hmmm. Priests and nuns? Definitely not – why did he buy that one? Really anything would inspire him, but that would mean he would have to actually read the damn book to find the affecting scene and the impetus just wasn't there.

He paused at a sound. A woman's voice filtered briefly up the central stairwell then faded.

Henny was there.

To see Arthur.

And the wickedest notion to have ever occurred to him suddenly presented itself.

He doused the light. Quietly he opened the door to the hall, looked around and tiptoed out, listening intently. They must have gone to the library first. Joseph very carefully padded along the carpet to Arthur's bedroom. As quickly as he could he opened the door and slipped inside then closed the door behind him.

His heart raced at the daring recklessness of it all. But he had not thought the scheme through. He looked around the room and decided behind the curtains would be the best bet, provided of course, Arthur didn't decide to open the window. With a woman in his bedroom he probably wouldn't. Women were always cold at night.

Suddenly it seemed too easy. His heart sank. What if they decided to do it on the sofa in the library and Henny left after that? The best he could hope for was watching Arthur undress. This wouldn't necessarily be a bad thing but maybe not quite the hoped-for inspiration.

He stifled a chuckle. Arthur was randy as hell since he and Henny had breached the forced morality of their class. They wouldn't just stop at the library sofa. The two would be ready to go at it again the second they stepped through the bedroom door. Joseph tested various configurations of the curtains before settling upon the best view of the room and the bed.

The stairs creaked, the hall floorboards squeaked and the door to the bedroom opened quietly then clicked shut.

Henny giggled.

"It's nice to hear you laugh, darling," Arthur said sweetly as he lit the bedside lamp.

Henny flopped lazily in the slipper chair with a heavy sigh. "Seeing her today was heart-wrenching," she said, unlacing her shoes. "Your mother had covered her face in far too much powder and the seamstress tried not to notice." Her voice shook. "Apparently she's lost some weight. Her measurements have changed from only a few weeks ago." She inhaled a sob then covered her face with her hands.

"Shh, shh, love," Arthur consoled, removing her hands and pressing a kiss to her forehead. He knelt down next to her and reached under her skirts. "Let's not talk about it right now." He pulled off one stocking, then the other, then drew his hands up Henny's legs to rest on her thighs. He leaned in and kissed her mouth.

Joseph's cock livened in response.

Henny wrapped her arms around Arthur's neck and sounded a deep, yearning moan that resonated in Joseph's core.

The two were still practically fully dressed and he was already hard as a rock. *Shit*. He really did need the release.

Little by little buttons were unfastened and layers of clothes peeled away, Arthur teasing her about her crinolines as he shucked them to the carpet, she teasing him back about the distinct outline of his cock under his thin drawers.

"If you wore a crinoline, my lord, no one would see your monstrous machine."

At that he picked her up and threw her on the bed, pouncing on top and assailing her with nibbles and tickles. Within moments her giggles became sighs as his mouth sought hers, his hands deftly unpinning her hair.

He jumped off the bed and pulled off his drawers as she scrambled out of her remaining undergarments, her long hair shielding Joseph's view of her nudity. Arthur ripped off his shirt and held her gaze, the two of them naked and panting, their bodies youthful perfection.

Arthur was magnificent, lean and athletic, fine hair leading from his chest to his belly, growing thicker at his groin, from which bobbed a formidable cock. A monstrous machine indeed.

Henny angled her body as she reached for her lover, revealing her sleek curves and wondrously lush breasts. Arthur went to her, knelt before her on the bed, his mouth seeking a nipple, sucking, as Henny threw her head back with a sigh of encouragement.

Joseph's balls tightened. *Good move, my friend.*

And then she laid him back onto the mattress and bent over him, a curtain of her hair obscuring what the slow, rhythmic bobbing of her head implied.

"Oh, God, Henny."

Joseph's hands fisted, aching to grip himself.

Henny straightened, her body raised, straddling him, hovering. "Beg for it."

It took every ounce of effort for Joseph to keep still. He prayed he would not spontaneously come.

"Fuck me, Lady Henrietta, fuck me," Arthur pleaded. "I need to feel you, be inside you."

She stayed poised above him.

"Please."

She slammed down on his cock and he bucked up against her with a cry.

Joseph swallowed a gasp.

Henny rode Arthur gracefully, her cascading hair rippling in time to her undulating figure. Arthur reached for her and she grasped his hand for leverage. As she increased her pace he slid his other hand between her legs.

Watching the most intimate act between a couple deeply in love was wrong. But it was riveting, compelling and, oh, so very arousing. Joseph restrained himself from rocking to Henny's sensual cadence. He had half a notion to join them, bending Henny over, smoothing his palms over her ample behind, filling her arse, feeling Arthur's cock sliding against his inside her—

Henny yelped in ecstasy.

In one swift move, Arthur had her under him, plowing into her as she wrapped her legs around his hips, holding on. Her cries grew louder in rhythm to his huffing groans, the rhythm increasing, the thrust of his pelvis picking up speed until he drove into her one last time and held himself, jerking and growling, then collapsed against her with an exhausted chuckle.

She kissed him and stroked his hair. "I love you, Arthur. I love you beyond words."

"I know."

They chatted for a few minutes until they fell asleep, embraced in a tangle of limbs. When the respiration of slumber and Arthur's occasional snoring filled the room, Joseph noiselessly retreated to his own bedroom.

The erotic spectacle was the inspiration he had needed. He made quick work of himself, fantasizing about the future possibilities of himself with his handsome business partner and the man's luscious wife.

CHAPTER FOURTEEN

Henny brushed her hands over her body as she inspected herself in the mirror. Her figure was still perfect although her breasts were a little fuller. She reached for the ball gown that had just been delivered from the modiste's and held it against her. She was going to look absolutely divine. She loved the Season, loved London during the Season. The parties, the people, the gossip, the attention.

And her wedding was going to be *the* most talked about event of the Season of 1860.

She was even more excited that she wasn't showing yet—well…no one had remarked as such, not even Mother. She had confided in Sophie that wedding nerves were making her gain weight. She just had to make sure she did not eat too much and perhaps strolled rather than rode in the park…then she could keep her weight down.

She would worry about the baby after the wedding and tell Arthur on their wedding night. Any earlier and he would fuss and fret over her and he certainly did not need any more cares and concerns in his life.

She called for Adele to help her dress quickly. She wanted to see Sophia before going over ceremony details one last time, shopping for gloves and stockings, having tea with some friends of Mother's… The list of things to do was endless. She smiled. She was having so much fun doing them all.

Adele, in her pretty French accent, assured Henny that she looked perfect then curtsied and left to attend to the ironing.

Henny grabbed her gloves and a new bonnet and went to the landing. Mother's high-pitched laugh wafted up from below, counterpoint to a man's low rumble, perhaps coming from the morning room, which meant she was entertaining close friends. Which meant Henny had to avoid them if she was ever going to get to Sophia's. The servants' stairs were the best route under the circumstances and it wasn't as if she had never taken them before. She used the back stairs to sneak out to go see Arthur late at night.

She got halfway down the narrow stairwell when a male servant came running up, someone new, pudgy and balding. She stopped to let him pass. He lifted his head.

He wasn't a servant.

"What the hell are you doing here?" she hissed.

Royston smirked smugly, his eyes narrowed like a wild dog eying its prey. "I came to see you, my dear."

She backed up a step. "I do not ever want to see you again."

But he was too quick. He grabbed her arms and pinned her against the wall.

"Let go of me," she growled.

"Now my dear, it's because of your little friends I am no longer allowed to see my beloved."

"Your *beloved*?" He was despicable.

"Oh dear. Jealous? I know you were once going to be mine—"

"I was never going to be yours."

His face was too close to hers. "Ah, that's because I never had my chance to persuade you."

Henny's blood boiled. "You mean you never had the chance to rape me, like you almost did Sophia?"

He scrunched his face in disgust. "Such an ugly sentiment, my dear. And as I seem to recall you were not as reluctant as she."

"I was only a child. I was terrified, you bastard."

"Ah yes, I remember how scared you were. I tried to console you—"

"Get away from me!" She could endure his insults no more. She flailed her arms against him and slammed her knee into his crotch. He flinched, his face reddened.

"You little whore."

His hand came down hard against her cheek, the dizzying force destabilizing her. She slipped on the smooth wood of the stair, falling backward, her buttocks hitting first, skimming down the stairs, her skirts facilitating her slide, twisting her around until she crashed head first on a landing. She looked up to see Royston running up the stairs, escaping, her last vision before she swooned and blacked out.

"She's awake, my lord."

Arthur started, staring blankly at Henny's lady's maid bending over him, her hand on his shoulder, rousing him gently. He must have been asleep. But this was Henny's bedroom at the Bloxholme's London residence…

Then everything came back into focus.

Henny had fallen down the stairs, an accident they had said. The doctor had wanted to meet with Arthur privately. She had lost the child, the doctor had said. Henny had been pregnant and had lost the child. Their child.

And the doctor was not confident she would ever be able to have children again.

He had moved as if in a dream after that, sitting on the slipper chair, watching Lady Bloxholme and the servants putter around Henny's bedside, not hearing or understanding when they spoke to him. Letting the world slip away around him.

Jesus. First Sophia. Now Henny. What the hell was happening?

"Thank you, Adele." He got up, wobbling on his feet, Adele steadying him, helping him to Henny's bedside. Henny reached out her hand and smiled.

"Arthur." Her voice was weak.

"We'll leave the two of you alone, Arthur," Lady Bloxholme said.

He watched as they left then sat on the bed, sliding against the headboard, wrapping his arm around Henny's shoulders, her head resting in the crook of his arm.

He kissed her hair. "You knew, didn't you? About the baby."

"Yes. I wanted to tell you but it would have been too much of a distraction from your business."

He hugged her more closely. "More of a distraction than making love to you?"

"The doctor says I can't have another…" She began to cry.

"Henny, darling, shh, shh. We'll try again. We'll keep trying." The tears smarted in his eyes. He wiped them away. She mustn't see him cry. "We'll have fun trying," he joked weakly.

She giggled anyway. Then the flood of tears began again.

Arthur slid down until he lay alongside her and pulled her close. He could hide his tears no longer.

"Arthur," she sobbed, "it was horrible, he was there, he hit me."

He? "Who, darling? Who hit you?"

"Royston."

The name pierced him like a cold dagger. "Henny, darling, what do you mean?"

"Royston hit me."

She still wasn't making complete sense. "What happened exactly? They said you were on the back stairs. You slipped and fell."

"He came to see me. He was angry about being kept away from Sophia."

"Why on earth would he bother you about it?"

"To taunt me." She drew in a breath. "Arthur, I never told you. When I was fourteen he…he touched me. He insulted me. And I let him. I didn't want to but I didn't stop him." Her voice was weak. "I've carried the shame of it ever since."

His heart clenched. "Darling, that man is a monster. You should not carry the shame." He could not stop the tears. "He is responsible for his actions."

"And he made me believe that because he had…done that to me, I was to be his wife. I could think of no worse horror than to be married to that man. But Mama said I could be no man's wife until I had begun my courses."

"Did you tell your mother?"

"I've never told anyone." Her voice was but a whisper. "Until now."

He cradled her against him. "Henny, we must help Sophia. We must think of some young men to include at our wedding breakfast."

"Yes, we must save Sophie." She shifted against him, sinking lower. "Joseph. She's in love with Joseph."

Yes, she is. "How do you know this?"

"I saw them together," she said hoarsely. "In the studio at Harwell Hall. They had been intimate…"

So she knew all along.

"Joseph should be at our wedding."

"He will be, darling," he assured. But he couldn't possibly be considered a suitor.

She turned onto her side. "Arthur, I'm tired and my head hurts. I think I need to sleep now."

"Yes, darling. Of course." He got up, helping her settle back against the pillows.

Suddenly she flinched with a groan, squeezing her eyes shut. She curled her knees to her chest.

"My love?"

"Arthur, I think I need a doctor."

The fog of a dream engulfed him once again. Something was terribly wrong with Henny.

* * * * *

Arthur sat in the dark, the fire in his library long gone out. He reached for the decanter of brandy. Finding it empty, he moved on to the sherry.

There was to be no June wedding. Instead, in a lavish and well-attended event, Lady Henrietta Langley had her funeral at St. George's. She had been dressed in her wedding gown.

The doctor insisted there wasn't anything he could have done. He hadn't seen any sign of trauma to the mother after the fetus had been expelled. In fact, the patient had exhibited symptoms of recovery. The doctor had been surprised when Lady Henrietta had succumbed.

Expelled. What a horrid word.

She had carried his *child*, damn it! *Their* child. Their *first* child.

He downed his sherry. His last child.

He squeezed his lids shut, strangling back tears as he lifted the crystal decanter and drank deeply. But the flood of sorrow could not be banked. Tears cascaded down his cheeks as he croaked a sob-filled breath.

Henny. His Henny. Gone. *Shit*.

He would do more than just wear a black armband for the rest of his days. He would crush Royston.

There would never be an heir to the Marquessate of Richmond so long as Sophia was in the clutches of that villain. That much he could do. He would never marry—no one would replace Henny, no child would replace the one they had lost.

He would never perpetuate the horror of the peerage where the position and privilege of one man was deemed more important than the safety and security—and lives—of beautiful, sweet, intelligent young women. Women who were truly the future of the nation, far more so than tired old aristocrats clinging desperately to a past that disappeared faster than a landscape from a moving train.

His parents would be appalled, of course. Perhaps, however, they would be persuaded to see the error of their ways, to cede whatever claim Royston had over their precious daughter. The end to fifteen generations of Richmonds would be a powerful hold over them.

And if they refused to abandon Royston's suit, there were other ways of shielding Sophia.

CHAPTER FIFTEEN

Joseph surveyed the sympathetic expressions of the members gathered at the Merchants and Industry Club. Arthur was either admirable or daft to have called an evening meeting of investors. He needed to grieve. Henny had been dead and buried for less than a week.

As the men entered the club room, Arthur shook hands and accepted condolences but once everyone was settled he slumped into the curves of a leather chair and proceeded to drink too much brandy. Luckily Geoffrey was there to facilitate and answer questions, assuring the investors that indeed the scheme was proceeding as planned. Joseph did all he could to deflect scrutiny of Arthur's behavior—exhibiting new plans and drawings, explaining technical details, telling toned-down stories of the wild American West. Amidst the grins he received a handful of compliments on his sartorial choices, a few exclamations of delight on his accent and one offer of club nomination.

Meanwhile Arthur remained seated and silent, looking dapper and tipsy.

"Can you take him home?" Geoffrey asked. "He's looking more and more beleaguered."

Joseph offered a twisted smile at the diplomatic assessment of Arthur's state. "Can you handle questions about Indians and San Francisco?"

"Sometimes they wear clothes and there aren't enough women?"

Joseph chuckled. "All right. I'll see you tomorrow."

Arthur was not reluctant to go home. Once deposited in his foyer he headed straight for the library instead of his bed. He poured a snifter of brandy then held forth the decanter. "You?"

"Arthur, do you think you should have more?"

He downed his drink. "No. A Christian man is a temperate man." He poured two glasses, offering one to Joseph. "Of course, I stopped being a Christian man once I lost my wife to the devil."

Joseph took the proffered snifter. Arthur had told him everything about Henny and Royston past and present, details that just solidified Joseph's own belief that the man was pure evil.

He took a swig of his brandy. "Look, Arthur, the meeting went well. I'll see Geoffrey tomorrow to get further assessment. But right now you need to get to bed. You're drunk."

"Yes." Arthur snorted. "I am."

He took the glass from Arthur's hand. "I'm going to take you to your room and see that you are properly tucked in for the night."

"O.K." Arthur bit his lower lip as he smiled. His American accent was terrible.

He clung dramatically as Joseph hauled him up the stairs.

"You have your own legs, my lord," Joseph teased.

"Yes, but yours are so much stronger than mine at the moment."

Once in his bedroom Arthur stripped off his jacket and unbuttoned his waistcoat. He eyed Joseph with a raised brow, his lips curled in a sly smile. "Are you going to watch me undress?"

He hadn't considered it but the idea suddenly intrigued him. "Do you want me to?"

Arthur stepped forward until he was toe to toe with Joseph. He placed his hand at the back of Joseph's head and pulled him forward.

Then kissed him.

It was a slow, languorous kiss, their tongues tangling tentatively then twining with intention. Joseph held Arthur firmly, a hand on each shoulder. Arthur slowed to pull back slightly.

He leaned his forehead against Joseph's. "Stay the night in my room."

His cock throbbed in anticipation. "Arthur, you're vulnerable."

"I'm also randy as hell."

The offer was damn tempting. "Look, I—"

But Arthur was on his knees before Joseph, unbuttoning his trousers, his drawers, ignoring his flailing hands, his weak protestations, freeing his aroused cock, wrapping insistent lips around him.

"Christ!"

He could not remember the last time a man had done that to him. The last time anyone had done it was Sophia and that had been her first time, made apparent by her overzealousness and her gagging, attributes repeated by Arthur at that very moment.

He grabbed Arthur's hair, pulling him off. "This is your first time."

Arthur swallowed. "Is it that obvious?"

"You have to want to do this."

"You have to want me to."

They locked eyes, Arthur's with a touch of endearing entreaty.

"God, yes, I want you to," Joseph growled.

Arthur grasped Joseph's hips and slid his tongue down the underside of his shaft, then back again to tease the head with wet swirls and pulsing squeezes. The man was a fast learner. Joseph groaned his approval.

Little by little, Arthur drew Joseph's cock into his mouth, each advance wetter and warmer and tighter than the last until his lips encircled the root. Arthur swallowed. Joseph sighed at the exquisite flutter of his friend's throat.

"Breathe," he murmured. "You have to breathe." He raked his fingers through Arthur's hair, tenderly, encouragingly.

Arthur retreated then proceeded once again, languidly, too slowly. Joseph pumped his hips provokingly, wanting, needing to go faster.

"All right." Arthur's words reverberated with a chuckle.

He gripped Joseph's butt, steadying his hips. Arthur sucked determinedly, moving along the length of the shaft with the fullness of his tongue, squeezing with his lips, nipping with his teeth, keeping with the rhythm of Joseph's lust. The painful pinch of fingernails in the straining muscles of his buttocks heightened the pleasure of Arthur's mouth, now picking up speed in tempo to Joseph's muttered oaths.

Theirs was a beautiful cadence. Joseph closed his eyes, letting the sensual act lift him to a higher plane of ecstasy. Desire pumped through his limbs, taut and trembling, struggling between suspension and release. Energy coiled at his groin, tightening his balls heavy with need.

He clinched Arthur's head in his hands, bucked against his mouth, spewing his seed. Unable to pull back, Arthur sucked and swallowed, his hands falling to his sides in submission.

Joseph's heart thundered as he relaxed his hold.

Arthur sat back on his heels, gasping for breath. "I need some water."

He laughed and helped him up. "That was rather brave."

Arthur stumbled over to the basin. "I don't know about that. Interesting perhaps." He drank deeply from the porcelain pitcher. "I still prefer women, you know."

Joseph chortled as he shucked his clothing. "As do I. Especially your sister," he reminded, raising a brow.

"Shit. Look—about Sophia," Arthur said, unbuttoning his trousers. "I have a plan. We'll talk about it in the morning." He pulled off his shirt and climbed into bed, smoothing the sheet beside him. "Lock the door. The maid will know to not bother us."

Joseph had to admit it was a very restful slumber.

* * * * *

For Sophia to be invited to Arthur's for a private luncheon was a bit out of the ordinary. But this was the first time in years Arthur had been without female companionship, so perhaps such invitations were a new ordinary. Sophia hoped at least. She liked spending time with her big brother.

Sending a private carriage to pick her up and drive her to the front door was a gallant gesture too. He hadn't said anything about it being a formal affair but Sophia had dressed in a brand new frock of pale emerald with pink lace edging the neckline and frothing at the ends of the short, puffy sleeves. She wore the pearl choker Arthur and Henny had given her for her eighteenth birthday, hoping it would be a happy reminder of pleasant memories for him as it was for her.

The footman held her hand gently as he helped her step out of the carriage and did not let go until she was in the foyer with the front door closed behind them.

Arthur was concerned for her safety. Before *the incident* she would have been annoyed. Now the attention made her feel protected.

He dashed out of the library to greet her, kissing her on both cheeks.

"Sophie, I'm so glad you're here." He clasped her hand and led her to the dining room. "You are looking well."

"Thank you. I am recovered. And you?"

He was glowing with excitement about something. He must have received good news about his business.

"I'm as well as a man can be, considering…" He pulled out a chair for her next to the head of the table.

"Yes, of course."

She settled herself while he took the head seat. Just the two of them as intimate friends was quite nice.

Luncheon was excellent.

"Henny arranged for Mrs. Babcock to study under a chef from Provence. Now when she's not cooking, she's tending her newly planted Provencal-style garden in the back. Or pining for the chef."

Sophia giggled.

"How is your first Season? Have you met anyone interesting?"

"I've met the queen." She couldn't contain her smile.

Arthur laughed. "But, of course. Is she a good dancer?"

She swatted him playfully.

His eyes twinkled at her. "Who else? What about all the balls you've been attending? Geoff says he's seen you once or twice."

"Geoffrey's quite popular, you know." He had been spending time with Flora Sheffleigh, which meant his flirtation with Sophia was over. "We barely have time for a 'how do you do' these days, which is too bad since he's far more interesting than all the others I have to dance with."

"Anyone I might know?"

"Well there's been Rupert Prescott, the heir to a viscount. The Marquess of Aldersley who's widowed with a son. And the Earl of Croxley."

"They're all a bit old for you, don't you think?"

"They're younger than the Duke of Royston."

"Ah. Yes. Prescott's brother is one of my investors." He grinned at her. "But he's already married."

"Probably any one of your investors is far more interesting than the men Mama makes me dance with. They don't really *do* anything."

"What about Joseph? He's been spending more time with Geoff since…well, since I've been dull. Do you ever see him at these events?"

Sophia turned her attention to the perfectly seasoned potato salad, hoping Arthur did not see her blush. "I never see Joseph anymore."

"That's too bad. You get on quite well."

She smiled. "He did send me a book the other day."

"That was thoughtful. What book?"

Joseph had sent her an extraordinarily naughty novel involving schoolgirls, which Arthur would not, could not ever know about. "It was a lovely little book with Classical designs. Vitruvius, I believe." Joseph had wrapped that one along with the other so she would not have to lie about the contents of her package.

Arthur chewed his lamb thoughtfully. "Joseph has a lot of books sent here from Jacobs in Lincolnshire."

"Oh." She forked too much of the potatoes in her mouth.

"Sophie, to be honest, I invited you here today for a reason. I have a proposition."

Sophia blinked. "A proposition?"

"I want you to be my hostess when I hold events here. You know, dinners and such." He put down his knife and fork. "Now that Henny's gone I need a woman in the house, to balance out the guest list when I hold parties. Otherwise there's always one extra forlorn bachelor."

She patted his hand.

"I've asked Mother and Father and they have agreed to allow it, despite your age and position."

"I suppose it is rather irregular."

"Rather. Mother was mostly worried about your absence at important events—"

Sophia snorted.

"No matter how boring, dear sister, you are expected to be present at certain affairs to keep up appearances. Do you want to think it over? There's no hurry. I really haven't done any entertaining since...well, since."

He looked so much like a forlorn bachelor at that moment. And giving parties did sound fun. "Yes, Arthur. I think I'll enjoy it."

"Oh good. And you'll meet so many more people—men—to extend your circle of potential suitors. To show off your abilities as a hostess."

"I need to learn how to be a hostess first."

"Mother will teach you and I can show you what Henny used to do."

"Thank you, Arthur." She was encouraged to know he had so much faith in her.

He pushed his chair back. "Now let's repair to the drawing room so I can teach you how to drink brandy and smoke cigars."

Sophia stared in astonishment. "You can't be serious."

"Sort of," he said, pulling out her chair as she rose. "I've been known to throw some wild parties."

She giggled as he regaled her with tales of bachelorhood on their way to the drawing room. She took her place on the couch in the central conversation area and arranged her skirts around her. Arthur placed a tray with a crystal decanter and two snifters on the table before her. "This, dear sister, is brandy. You should never drink too much of it."

"Oh my. Tell me what happened."

"I think you best not, my lord."

Sophia turned to the familiar voice. "Joseph."

He beamed and went to her, taking her hands in his. "My lady."

Her heart pounded with joy, rushing heat to her cheeks. "It's wonderful to see you."

"It's been a long time." His gaze was intense. "Did you get my book?"

A tingle teased between her legs. "I did." She bit her lip. "It's lovely."

Arthur offered him a glass of brandy. "Glad you could join us, Joseph. I've just been telling Sophie about my idea to have her be my hostess this Season."

Joseph relinquished her hands. "Ah, yes. An excellent idea."

She liked that they talked about her when she wasn't around.

Arthur handed her a brandy. "Have you ever tasted it?"

She glanced at Joseph. "Once."

Arthur held up his glass. "To my hostess."

"Slowly," Joseph cautioned.

She sipped the liquor, feeling it burn on her tongue before it hit the back of her throat to burn there. "Is it supposed to taste good?"

Arthur laughed. "You'll get used to it." He took an easy chair opposite. "Sophie, I've also asked Mother and Father if I could set you up with a room here."

"A room?"

"A bedroom." Arthur crossed then uncrossed his legs. "For those days when we host a dinner at night and a breakfast the next morning."

She had never heard of such a thing. "Does that happen often?"

He rubbed the back of his neck. "I don't know really." He glanced at Joseph, who regarded him curiously. "Perhaps more often than is fashionable."

Maybe it was an American fashion. "All right," Sophia conceded. "I suppose if I plan ahead, I can pack a gown—"

"Damn it." Arthur stood and walked to the window then back again. "I'm obviously not being plain enough." He glanced between her and Joseph. "I want you two to continue your affair and I'm providing you a place in which to do it."

"What?" Joseph said sharply.

Panic coursed through her veins. "Our affair?" She dared not look at Joseph.

Arthur knelt down next to her. "Sophie, I've known about you since after your attack. The connection was apparent from the way you depended on Joseph—"

Sophia turned away, tears smarting in her eyes.

"Henny knew too. I guess she found you one day. That's what she told me before she…" He gently cupped her chin and turned her to face him. "I've lost the love of my life. I have nothing but memories. The love of your life is here." He glanced up at an utterly dumbfounded Joseph. "You two should be together." He stood and walked to the fireplace, hanging his head against his arm on the mantel. "Mother and Father still consider Royston as a possibility for you. I do not. I cannot. You will not marry that man." He glanced between her and Joseph. "I want to make it so Royston no longer wants you."

"No longer wants me?"

"Arthur," Joseph growled.

Arthur turned to him abruptly. "You don't want her to end up with Royston either."

"I don't want your house to be a brothel."

"It's not a damn brothel," Arthur bellowed.

"O.K. A place of assignation, then," Joseph snarled back.

"It already was with me and Henny—"

"What you are suggesting is far more clandestine and improper."

Arthur held his ground, red-faced, eyes narrowed. "Do I need to remind you of your promise that you would do anything to protect her?"

Joseph threw his head back and grumbled an oath to the ceiling.

"Will you two gentlemen please explain what you are arguing about?"

Joseph drew in a deep breath. "Your brother is offering a subterfuge and a location for you and me to continue doing what we had been doing in the studio at Harwell Hall." He eyed Arthur intently. "Except he would like it to go much further."

Sophia's breath hitched. "Further?" she asked Arthur.

Arthur speared his fingers through his hair. "Royston prefers virgins and if you are not one, he might reconsider his suit."

"Oh."

Joseph met her eyes and blushed.

"Oh." Realization made her blush as well.

"Sophie," Arthur said gently, "if you could marry anyone in the world right now, who would it be?"

She flicked her eyes at Joseph. "Anyone?"

"Anyone."

She couldn't possibly answer that out loud. Joseph flashed the most devastatingly sympathetic smile in her direction.

Arthur smirked. "I think I have my answer."

"Good God," Joseph muttered with exasperation.

"And you would ask her if you could," Arthur said to him.

"Arthur, I'm not allowed to marry just anyone," she reminded quietly.

"No. I know." He slowly paced before her. "But what if you had to get married?"

"Had to?"

He knelt before her, taking her hands in his. "Sophie, Henny was pregnant when she fell down the stairs. She lost the child. Our child. And…" He swallowed hard. "She didn't fall down the stairs. She was pushed."

She gasped. "Pushed?"

"By Royston."

Sophia clamped her hands over her mouth to stifle a cry. Joseph sat at her side and wrapped a warm arm around her shoulders.

"Sophie, what Royston tried to do to you was his way of ensuring you would not belong to any other man. To put it very indelicately, he was trying to *claim* you." Arthur resumed his pacing. "I will not have you marry that man. I know you do not want to marry him and I suggest we—you, me and Joseph—do everything we can to make sure the marriage does not happen. One way is to have you be *claimed* by the man you love—"

"Arthur," Joseph warned.

"Which means you and Joseph being intimate in a way that only a husband and wife should be intimate." Arthur studied them both. "Which means not concerning yourselves with the consequences."

Sophia threw Arthur a questioning look.

But he did not answer her. "I'm going to my study to work on correspondence. I'll leave you two alone to discuss this. I'll return in… I'll return." He left, closing the door behind him.

"The consequences?"

Joseph let his annoyance subside at Sophia's plaintive query. He squeezed her shoulder. It felt so good to have her in his arms again.

"He wants us to make love until you are with child."

The shock on her face was endearing.

He drew a finger along her jaw to outline her gaping mouth. "And yes, I do agree that such a request is highly irregular. Especially from one's brother."

He dipped his head, touching his lips to hers, the intensity of the sensation enlivening every inch of his flesh. She clasped her hands around his neck and opened to him, letting him explore her as he used to far too long ago. He took his time, renewing their intimacy, and she followed him every step of the way.

He could kiss her like that forever. "And?"

"And what?" she asked breathlessly.

"Could you kiss me every day for the rest of your life?"

She flushed as tears formed in the corners of her eyes. "Yes, I could. I know I could. But Joseph," she said, wiping her eyes, "I am not at liberty to marry whomever I want. Even if I am with child, Mama and Papa could still say no."

"Who on earth would they expect you to marry but the father of your child?"

Her tears flowed unrelentingly. He fumbled in his pocket for his handkerchief.

"They could send me away," she said, pressing the handkerchief to her nose. "I've heard of servants who became with child and have to leave the estate. I've never seen them again. I have no idea where they go."

They probably went home to their families but such a thought was no consolation. He took her hand. "We could run away as soon as you think you might be pregnant."

"And go where?"

Good question. Perhaps Arthur had thought some of this through. "We could go to America."

A flash of terror clouded her face.

"No. Sorry. You don't want that. I have to stay in England for a while anyway, until Arthur and I sort out all this railway business."

"Darling, don't be offended." She grabbed his arm and searched his eyes, a corner of her lips curling upward. "I've just never considered going to America. Everything about this is new to me."

"Yeah." He smiled. "To me too. We'd have to be married. Or travel with Arthur, I suppose."

She crinkled her forehead in thought. "I've only heard about this in gossip but I think girls my age can get married in Scotland."

"Scotland?"

"Henny mentioned it, after Arthur had returned from setting up a house there."

Ah. The Lamberton property.

"It's quite scandalous, you know. Only girls who *have* to get married do that sort of thing."

Joseph chuckled. "I think that's the idea."

"Oh." She blushed again. It was damn bewitching.

"But," he sighed, "you do bring up a point I think Arthur didn't consider. Not only would it be scandalous for you, it would be quite scandalous for the company. If I got a woman of my own class with child, most would turn a blind eye. But to be seen as having seduced the innocent daughter of a marquess, during her first Season… I don't think our investors would have confidence in my reputation after such a revelation."

"But maybe they wouldn't have to know."

"How do you mean?"

"Well, Mama and Papa would not want the papers to get a hold of such a story. Even if they knew, they wouldn't want anyone else to know. I think it could be kept a family secret."

"Then all of a sudden, nine months later you and I are married and have a child?"

She shrugged. "We'll be in America. How will they know?"

He chuckled and pulled her close. "Look, the other morning Arthur said he had a plan to bring you on as a hostess in place of Henny. He knows I have strong feelings for you so he asked if such an arrangement would be O.K. with me. That's all he said, I swear. I had no idea he was up to some crazy shenanigan."

"'Shenanigan'?" She fluttered her eyelashes at him in puzzlement, a look that swelled his heart. And his cock.

"Intrigue, plot. Whatever the hell it was he was thinking." He threaded his fingers through hers. "Darling, we don't have to do anything right now. I mean, I do have half a mind to carry you upstairs to my bedroom and have my way with you—"

"Apparently with Arthur's blessing."

A nerve-racking thought. "Yes." He chuckled. "But we do need to plan this out some more." He brought her hand up to his lips. "And most importantly it should be the right moment for you."

She gave him that look again, the look of innocent curiosity tinged with a burgeoning sensuality she probably did not quite understand. The look that always did him in. He pulled her into his arms and kissed her, laying her down against the arm of the sofa, helping her shift her body underneath his. He lengthened himself on top of her, skimming his hand over the swell of her breast, teasing her nipple through the silk of her bodice with his thumb. She moaned his name then pressed her lips to his.

She was his, he was hers, and they were in this together. He deepened their kiss and ground his hips against hers, mimicking the act that would seal their union.

And he didn't give a damn if Arthur walked in and found them.

CHAPTER SIXTEEN

"Oh, Sophie, you look beautiful." Mama gushed as Sophia spun around in her bedroom, showing off her new ball gown.

"Do I?" Sophia brushed down the lace collar draping across her bosom. She had tons of new dresses to wear since the incident with the Duke of Royston. She had lost a treasured dress that night but the new pale-blue silk brocade with lacy trim was swiftly becoming her favorite.

"Perhaps tonight you will meet your husband." Mama pressed a hand to her mouth, her eyes reddening.

"Mama, don't cry. You should be happy for me."

"I am. But I'm losing my only daughter. Oh, Sophie." She shook with sobs.

Sophia hugged her closely, tears forming in her eyes. Arthur's plan was going to rip their family apart.

"Let's get ready to go, Mama. Papa hates it when we keep him waiting."

Lord and Lady Hawkhurst's annual ball was well attended, perhaps too much so. The ballroom was a complete crush, as was the refreshment room, although dozens more guests could have been received if the women's skirts hadn't been so voluminous. Dancing was a chore at times but Sophia's dance card was full of fabulous partners. Unusually so. As if all the men who excelled in the waltz had decided to attend that very night.

The event was truly the height of the Season.

As she whirled a polka-mazurka in the arms of the Earl of Bedingham she spied Geoffrey dancing with Flora Sheffleigh. She couldn't help but smile for him. He looked happy.

A wave of melancholy crashed over her. Was she really going to leave everything she knew and loved behind for an unknown life? She had been excited at first but now, seeing familiar faces, seeing Mama cry made Sophia a bit queasy.

Lord Bedingham relinquished her to Mama at the end of the dance.

"Oh, Sophie, you look unwell." Mama took out her fan. "Perhaps some air?"

"Thank you, Mama—"

"Perhaps a refreshment?"

The familiar and most unwelcome voice sent a stabbing chill up her spine.

"Your Grace," Mama said with a curtsy.

"Lady Richmond, Lady Sophia." Royston bowed too extravagantly.

"Yes, Sophia, a refreshment with the duke is a fine idea."

She could not believe Mama had just said what she had said. "I think I'll remain where I am, Mama." Sophia tried to keep her cool. She whipped out her fan, waving it most obnoxiously. "My next partner will expect to find me in the ballroom." She smiled when she spied him. The Earl of Croxley was handsome and a wonderful dancer although he was a bit old for her and already smitten with Lady Skeyton. But dancing with him would get her away from her tormentor.

Lord Croxley approached and gave his greetings all around.

She held out her hand. "My lord," she said with a curtsy and an alluring smile.

"Our galop, Lady Sophia." He offered his arm.

"Lord Croxley," began Royston in an overly deliberate manner, "did I not see you in the garden with Lady Skeyton just an hour ago?"

"Your Grace?" The earl stiffened.

"Ah yes, it was you. I recall the color of your waistcoat. Your jacket was off, hanging on a tree branch. Of course the lady's face was obscured by your muscular torso but she sounded as if she was enjoying herself."

Lord Croxley flushed crimson.

"Oh dear." Mama's hand flew to her mouth.

The earl kept his head. "You were a long way off the walking path to have seen such a scene, Your Grace. One wonders what you yourself were doing there."

"Taking the air, my lord."

"Oh, Sophia," Mama said urgently. "I think you ought sit this one out."

"But, Mama—"

"Listen to your mother, my dear Sophia," the duke said too familiarly.

Lord Croxley bowed. "It looks as if I should take my leave, Lady Sophia." He walked away, his head held high.

"Now how about that refreshment, my dear?" Royston stuck out a bent arm.

"Oh yes, Sophie. After that shocking incident," Mama said, fanning herself vigorously, "you'll need a cooling drink."

Sophia wanted to throw her fan at something. Anything. "Please excuse me, Your Grace, Mama. I think I will repair to the ladies' retiring room, if you don't mind."

"Not at all, my lady. I will be waiting right here for your return." Royston leered. "Don't be too long."

She had to get out of there. But how? She had arrived with Mama and Papa. Maybe Papa could call for the carriage. She'd send it right back.

Her frantic thoughts clouded her vision and she almost crashed into a very tall man.

"Lady Sophia, you look as if you're running from something."

Geoffrey. Her savior. "Geoffrey," she said, taking his arm despite him not offering it, "could you do me the biggest favor in the world?"

"Sophie," he said quietly, "what's wrong?"

"I have to leave. I have to get out of here. Please can you take me in your carriage?"

"Yes. For you I'd do just about anything." He led her quickly to the coat room. "Home?"

She did not want to go there. "No." She needed to be with someone who would listen to her. "Can you take me to Arthur's? Do you know if he's at home?" She hadn't thought it through, she just hoped.

"I saw him at the club this afternoon, so he's possibly having an evening in."

If Arthur wasn't home, then Joseph might be. "Yes. Please. Could you take me to Arthur's?"

Geoffrey knew something was terribly wrong with Sophia. Once inside his brougham she drew the shades and slunk back against the squabs, yet, despite her efforts, hid behind her hood and fan until they were well on their way. Only when they were far beyond the Hawkhursts' did she fold the fan, revealing her twisted, trembling face. She said nothing as Geoffrey put his arm around her and pulled her against him. Her perfume drove him mad but it was clearly not the time to pursue a dalliance.

Arthur's house was dark and Wittering took forever to answer the door. Sophia tugged her hood over her face and stayed close to Geoffrey. In the foyer, with the door closed behind them, she looked around then drew back her hood.

Arthur trudged down the stairs, still sleep-addled, but perked up the instant he saw them.

"Wittering, go wake up Mr. Phillips, please," he said as he reached the bottom riser.

"Yes, my lord."

Sophia ran to him. "Arthur, I had nowhere else to go." Her eyes were studded with tears.

"Geoff." Arthur raised a brow in query.

"Arthur," he responded with a shrug.

"The library might still be warm."

Arthur wrapped his arm around Sophia and steered her through the door. Geoffrey tried to get her to sit but she declined, preferring to wring her hands and pace while Arthur stirred up the dying embers.

The door opened. Sophia stood stock still for only a second before she ran into the arms of a stunned and sleepy Joseph, kissing him full on the mouth. He kissed her back, initial surprise swiftly melting into surrender, his practiced hands skimming her curves.

Geoffrey stared, bereft of breath, as if he had been kicked in the gut. Finally he snorted an exhale. "I should have known something was up," he said, folding himself into an easy chair, attempting a smile.

"Geoffrey, no," Sophia gasped. "It's not what you think."

He chuckled, crossing one leg over the other. "It looks a great deal like what I'm thinking." He sobered. "However, you were running away from something, Sophie. I think I deserve an explanation."

"Please forgive me," she said softly. "I had to leave as soon as I could."

Arthur turned to her. "What happened?"

"Royston. Mama tried to foist me off onto Royston."

"What?" Arthur gaped.

"Shit," Joseph muttered.

"Will someone please let me know what is going on?" Geoffrey inquired politely.

Arthur flashed a glance first at Joseph then at Sophia. They nodded.

"My parents have a notion to marry Sophie off to the Duke of Royston, as you know."

"I do and I still cannot believe I've been bested by such as he."

Sophia smiled. "You'll always be the better man, Geoffrey."

"You also know Sophie's never been interested and I wasn't altogether pleased but I suppose we were both ready to accept our parents' wishes. Until a month ago."

Interesting news. "Oh?"

Arthur looked at his sister. "May I?"

She nodded.

He let out a juddering breath. "Sophia was beaten and almost raped by Royston at the Wrexham ball."

"Good God." Geoffrey made a move to get up but she indicated he should stay put. "Sophie, I had no idea."

"Joseph came to my rescue. And Arthur. Mama and Papa made sure everything was kept a secret so no one would know."

Geoffrey was incredulous. "And they still expect you to marry the man?"

"It's frustrating and strange really," agreed Arthur. "But they are equivocating on the matter so it's not a done deal. Still they have not shut him out. But that's not all. Royston was instrumental in Henny's death."

"What? Henny?" The story grew more fantastical by the moment.

"He accosted her, she tried to fend him off and in the tussle she fell down the stairs."

Geoffrey trawled his fingers through his hair. "Jesus. Does the marquess know this?"

"No. He would just say it is her word against Royston's and the fact of the matter is she's dead. But we have already reported the rape of a servant and have since been informed of another incident." Arthur swallowed hard. "The attack on Sophie should have been enough to change the marquess' mind. It wasn't. But it was enough to change *my* mind." He sucked in a shuddering breath. "And Henny's revelation that Royston insulted her when she was just a child simply reinforced my decision. Now I know I will do anything to stop the marriage of my sister to that man. Anything."

Sophia stared at him blankly. "He hurt Henny when she was young?"

"His abuse was the real reason she refused to marry him. Luckily she had a supportive father."

Knowing Arthur, there was more. "So what is the 'anything' you are willing to do, Arthur?"

"Ah, this is the awkward part," muttered Joseph.

Geoffrey turned to him. "How so?"

"Well you see," Arthur started, "it turns out Sophie's had a case on Joseph here and the feeling is mutual—"

"I gathered that." Geoffrey shook his head, ever the fool.

"Yes, well," Arthur stammered. "You see, Royston has a particular letch, divulged to me by Henny—" He stopped, stared blankly at Geoffrey, flushing crimson. "For virgins."

Geoffrey could almost feel what was coming. "And?"

Sophia's voice surprised him. "Arthur and Joseph thought that if I were not a virgin, the duke would no longer want me."

Arthur smiled weakly at his sister. "And the best way to announce a woman is no longer a virgin is for her to be…well…with child."

"Jesus," Geoffrey hissed. Unbelievable. Joseph was quite possibly the luckiest man alive. For a second the fantasy of them sharing her bedeviled him.

Arthur's voice snapped him back to reality. "We hope that would force our parents to reconsider their ill-advised choice of husband."

"And that they would let me marry the father of my child."

They were all mad. But a villain's evil would render one so. Geoffrey stood and sauntered to the hearth. "Phillips, how old are you?"

"Twenty-one."

"If what you want, what you wish is to get Sophia with child, then do that. However, as you are twenty-one, there are easier ways to avoid parental consent laws."

"Such as?" asked Arthur.

"The banns. More than likely the Richmonds will choose to ignore such a public declaration so as to avoid any attention."

"I hadn't thought of that," admitted Arthur. "But Royston being in the same parish allows him to object. We can't chance that."

True. "All right. I suppose you could go overseas to America, although I don't know what the marriage laws are over there," he said thoughtfully. "And you," he turned to Joseph, "might be accused of seduction. Unless Arthur accompanied you." He stared into the glowing embers. "You could spend the requisite twenty-one days in Scotland." He chuckled darkly. "It might appear suspicious if Sophia were with you but I'm not sure how you would get her with child otherwise."

Arthur chewed distractedly on a finger. "Looks as if we need to think this through a bit." The worry lines on his face deepened.

Geoffrey approached Sophia and took her hands. "Sophie, we've been friends for a long time. I'm happy for you and Joseph. Believe me, I am." He only partially lied. "If there is anything I can do for you, please let me know."

He lifted her hand to his lips and pressed a lingering kiss to her palm. She blushed.

"I'll return to the Hawkhursts' and look for Lady Richmond. I'll let her know I brought you here and that you are safe."

He nodded Joseph's way. The American looked dumbstruck.

Sophia threw her arms around his neck and kissed his cheek. "Thank you, Geoffrey. For everything." She kissed him again, this time on the lips.

Christ. She shouldn't arouse him so. He gently urged her away from him.

"Sophie," Arthur interjected, "I'll also send a message around to Mother and Father letting them know you were not feeling well and you came to me."

"Thank you, Arthur."

Arthur offered a sympathetic smile and grabbed Geoffrey's arm. "Shall I see you out?"

"Thank you, my lord."

Geoffrey glanced behind as he left the library. Sophia was back in Joseph's arms, looking quite comfortable.

He really had to stop thinking about the three of them together.

CHAPTER SEVENTEEN

Joseph pulled Sophia more closely to him. He had been dreaming of her before Wittering had awoken him, a very lascivious dream, which he lamented having to give up as he put on his trousers and dressing robe. But once he saw her in the library, feminine and emotional, he had no regrets.

"You look beautiful tonight, Sophie." He drew his fingers across the bare skin of her shoulders and back. "I should come to these events just to see you in your finery."

She snuggled into his chest. "You mean to see me with such low-cut necklines."

He grinned and kissed her hair. "That is definitely one of the attractions, yes. And probably the only one since I would not be allowed to dance with you."

She looked up at him. "We can have a dance now."

"Here? In the library? And me in my robe."

"Would it shock you to know I once danced with a half-dressed man in a billiard room?"

He held his arms in a waltz stance and she followed suit. He whirled her about as much as the furniture and her full skirt would allow. The first time they had done such a thing she had been abashed, uncomfortable in the arms of a man she found desirable. Now her face glowed with delight and anticipation.

"I fear I've done this all wrong, my lady," he said. "I believe the flattery comes after we walk into the dark recesses of the garden and not before we dance."

"Oh, but Mr. Phillips, you may flatter me whenever you wish."

"May I kiss you whenever I wish as well?"

She licked her lips. "Yes."

He bent over as he continued the dance, touching his lips to hers, her soft moan inciting him to deepen their union, the taste of her tongue riling his senses, inflaming his body as it had been during his dream.

"I wish to seduce you, Lady Sophia," he murmured, still moving her in the dance. "Will you allow such an outrage?"

Her eyes widened. "Yes, Mr. Phillips. But not here in the library."

"Then let us take our walk upstairs."

He held out his arm and she took it excitedly.

But the closer they got to the door the more his gut twisted, and when they were safely inside his bedroom, the door shut and locked, his heart thudded wildly.

Damn.

How many times had he done this before? But he fumbled as he unfastened her dress, faltered as he unhooked her corset, wavered as he untied her petticoats, trembled as he pulled off her stockings.

He had bedded a dozen women a hundred times but this time it was different. This time it was Sophie. She was the love of his life.

"Have you ever been with a virgin?"

Could she tell? How could she possibly? Of course she could. They had been intimate before and he had not then acted like a callow schoolboy.

"Yes, but I was one myself so I hardly knew what I was doing or what to expect." He took off his robe. "I fear I did not give her the most enjoyable of experiences. It was over too quickly."

What had changed? Nothing and yet everything. They were still in love but what was to happen would irrevocably affect their future. Their mutual future.

Once they made love it would be tantamount to marriage. The stakes had never been so high.

And he had never wanted to win so desperately in his life.

She led him to the bed and under the covers, allowed him to enfold her in his arms, let him kiss her, let him touch her anywhere, everywhere. She directed him to suck first one nipple then the other, urged him to stroke her clitoris to excitement, encouraged him to open her thighs and nestle his body between them.

She looked intensely into his eyes as he positioned himself and nodded her assent.

He entered her slowly. Her rapturous sigh swelled his heart to bursting. He tempered his movements, relishing the throbbing wetness as he pushed in, the warm tightness as he pulled out.

Her breathing quickened to a frenzied pace. She cried out as she clenched his cock, the force of it almost his undoing. She searched his eyes, intently, questioningly.

"Your crisis, love." He kissed her cheeks, her lips.

"More," she said, breathless. "I want more."

He increased his tempo, building steadily.

"More."

Her desires were one with her body's reactions, grasping, flexing, wanting, needing. She came again, her orgiastic cry goading him to join her, the force of her body almost compelling him.

But he wanted more too.

He forged ahead, giving her what she demanded, hugging her to him as he drove into her faster and deeper. Her eyes shut, her mouth slackened, lost in the bliss before climax. He pounded harder, urging her to the point of ecstasy, her cries matching the beat of his thrusts until she bucked up, gripping him with the strength of surrender.

He slammed inside her one last time, emptying himself, jerking with release, his emission making them one.

"You're mine, Sophie. No one can take you from me."

"Joseph, my Joseph," she heaved in relief.

He collapsed on top of her, still needing their bodies to remain as one. Their limbs tangled, their hearts pounded, their breaths found a mutual rhythm.

"I love you."

It did not matter who said it first.

The light poured on Sophia's face at an unexpected angle. Had she turned completely head over heels in her bed?

She opened her eyes and memories of the night before deluged her. She turned over to see Joseph, his face soft from deep slumber, the covers tossed off his magnificent upper torso, and all she could think was how wonderful he was, how beautiful their love-making had been.

And how much she had to pee.

She could make a dash for the water closet wearing Joseph's robe. But maybe there was a chamber pot under the bed…

She climbed out of bed as gently and noiselessly as possible, really only succeeding in getting as far as removing the covers from her legs when Joseph stirred. She froze. What on earth did one do in such a situation?

The mattress bounced and creaked as he got up. He fumbled around on the floor then walked around until he was in full view of her tenaciously half-closed eye, positioning the chamber pot he had hauled out from under the bed.

And then he grabbed his cock and pissed. Right in front of her. His stream was urgent and strong. He emitted a satisfied groan as he gave his cock a shake. And then he looked at her.

By that time Sophia's eyes were wide open.

He closed the lid to the commode and sauntered over to the bed. "Your turn, my lady."

She stared at him, horrified.

He grabbed hold of her arm and wrenched her from the bed. She couldn't struggle. If she had, she would have passed water all over the carpet.

He dragged her to the commode and lifted the lid. The stench of fresh urine increased her urge.

She absolutely couldn't. Not in front of him.

"Oh yes you can," he grinned.

"Joseph!"

"If we are to share the rest of our lives together, we have to perform the most intimate of acts in front of each other. Should I remind you I was, but a few hours ago, inside your person?"

He was right. Well, right enough at that moment. They could discuss it at length another time.

"Squat, my lady."

She gave in and squatted, the mere act of doing so loosening her resolve and her bladder. And when she was finished he handed her a sheet of curl paper. Her cheeks burned at the far greater intimacy of wiping.

She stood, utterly mortified, wanting to simply get dressed and go find some breakfast. But she had no other clothes than her ball gown.

"You are absolutely charming in your modesty, my lady," he said closing the lid and moving the box very carefully back under the bed.

He pulled her to him, sliding his hands tenderly along the contours of her back. His skin was still heated from their warm bed and penetrated her now-chilled flesh. She pressed her palms against his chest. His heart beat a steady, seductive rhythm.

"You should know we do not have indoor plumbing at my parents' house in New York." His eyes twinkled teasingly.

"I'll have to do something about that, won't I? Once you bring home the sister of the Earl of Petersham as your wife your parents will have to expect changes. I will not raise my children in colonial filth and squalor."

"Children? How many?"

Two—a boy and a girl—would be nice. But she wasn't going to tell him that just yet. She tapped his chest with her index finger. "Ten."

His brow crinkled. "Ten?" His eyes narrowed and a grin spread across his lips. "Well then, we had better get started, hadn't we?"

She squealed as he picked her up and threw her on the bed. The mattress sagged with his weight as he climbed on top of her. He hovered, his knees on either side of her hips, his hands above her shoulders.

"I take it you enjoyed yourself enough last night to want ten children."

"I was hoping it would get better every time we tried."

He laughed and slumped alongside her. "You little minx." He swirled spirals around her breasts, around her belly, tickling her with arousal. She rocked her hips encouragingly, hoping he would continue his path just a bit farther.

Instead he laid his hand on her belly, his warmth spreading over her, penetrating her, mingling with the delicious tingling between her legs. "Sophie, love, was I too rough with you last night? Are you sore?"

Her heart swelled at his concern. "I suppose a little. Mostly my thighs. I'm unused to such a position."

He chuckled. His hand proceeded to the spot where she had hoped he would go. He drew a finger through the cleft between her legs.

"You're wet," he murmured. "Deliciously wet."

She licked her lips as he stroked her pleasure spot, squirming with each caress, melting into the bed with each release. His gaze skated along her body then back up to meet hers. His eyes were black with desire.

"I want to touch you," she said.

"Please," he growled with a smile.

She encircled his cock with one hand and pumped slowly. The other rested on his strong upper arm, feeling the glorious muscle twitch as his fingers tantalized her below.

"You use this arm to pleasure yourself, don't you?"

"I do."

"One day I want to watch you."

He grinned. "O.K."

"But right now I want you to fuck me."

Instantly he was on top of her, stretched out between her legs, his prick in position. But he did not seek her assent this time. Instead he plowed ahead without warning. He slammed into her, jostling her. She wrapped her legs around him to steady herself, to ride with him, to experience a new pleasure, a pleasure of crude, vigorous physicality. His grunts and ragged breaths filled her ears, inciting her to cry out with abandon. Inside her, he grazed an untouched spot, deeply embedded, eliciting a luscious sensation, a new way to climb to the top of sensuality. She tilted her hips, needing him deeper, needing him to push her over the edge. He complied, wrapping one arm around her to hold her tightly against him, securing her as he drove inside her relentlessly.

She swooned, delirious with pleasure, riding waves of euphoria, gasping at the crest—

She screamed in climax. His mouth descended on hers, silencing her, drawing her ecstasy into his body. He slammed inside her one last time, growled his satisfaction into her mouth and jerked his pleasure deep inside her.

He rolled off, panting. "Oh, God, Sophie." He stared at the ceiling stunned.

"Was it good?" she asked teasingly.

"Christ, it was good." He drew in a long breath and sat up. "I'm famished. Let's get some breakfast."

"Oh." *Clothes.* "I suppose I could wear my underthings and borrow your dressing robe."

He chuckled. "I think that might be a bit too risqué for your brother."

She gasped. Arthur! Oh, goodness. Had he heard her scream?

"Look, to save you any mortification," Joseph said as he pulled on his trousers and braces, "I'll get a tray. I'll send a carriage around to get Anna. Any dress in particular you wish to wear today?"

"I have a nice new rose day dress."

"Good, that will match the flush on your cheeks." He lifted her chin and gave her a peck on the lips. "You can use the pot in private while I'm gone."

The door to the breakfast room opened and Arthur put down his morning paper. He wasn't sure whom to expect but was glad to see Joseph…alone.

He watched intently as Joseph went to the buffet and poured a cup of coffee, added milk, took a sip then proceeded to fill two plates with enough food to feed an army.

The silence was deafening. He couldn't stand it.

"And?" Arthur inquired pointedly.

Joseph looked up from the chafing dish of eggs. "Did I deflower your sister? Yes. But I find it a bit sordid to have to tell her brother."

Arthur chuckled. "How is she?"

"Probably asleep."

"Shouldn't you be there for her when she wakes up?"

"I already was the first time, about an hour ago."

"Oh."

Joseph pulled out a chair and sat next to him. He let out a sigh then placed a hand on Arthur's shoulder. "Look, Arthur, the deed is done. We have to go through with the plan. Unless you can find a more suitable man who would not care about your sister's virtue."

"Joseph," he said quietly, "I cannot think of a more suitable man than you. Sophie is in love with you. Besides, I think my parents aren't really looking beyond Royston. If the deed is done, then we will proceed as planned."

"Which is what exactly?"

"Making sure the two of you have plenty of opportunities."

"To get Sophie with child." Joseph sipped his coffee sullenly.

"What's wrong?"

"It's really a rather miserable way to begin a life together. Dishonesty, secretiveness, immorality."

"Think of it as trying to run away from a villain and doing anything you possibly can to escape."

"I suppose." He finished his coffee but remained sitting. "You know there's one thing you never considered in all of this."

Oh? "What's that?"

"Us."

"Us?"

"You, Arthur, and me, Joseph."

"You mean the business."

"No." Joseph met his eyes.

Arthur held his gaze, heat rising in his cheeks. "Of course, it's impossible now," he whispered.

"Do you regret it?"

A flush of panic prickled his neck. "Do you?"

Joseph gave his hand a squeeze. "I don't regret anything we've done, Arthur. But I am sorry we probably won't do anything like it again."

Sorrow carved a hollowness in his heart. "My sister's a lucky girl."

"She is." Joseph patted him on the back. "Because she has the best damn brother any girl could hope for." He stood. "Look, can you send a message to Sophie's maid Anna? Have her come with Sophie's new rose day dress and whatever toilet articles she needs for her hair and such. I'd do it but the missive should really come from the earl himself and not his American houseguest." He angled over. "You know, to deflect suspicions."

"Yes, right away." Arthur pushed back his chair. Their deception had begun. He just hoped to God it would work.

CHAPTER EIGHTEEN

London, 17 August 1860

Sophia held her breath and the lace edging of her corset while Anna tried to fasten the front. Finally the harried maid took a step back, her hands on her hips.

"I can't do it, my lady. You'll just have to wear the blue brocade again tomorrow night. I think that one is cut a bit fuller."

"O.K.—I mean, all right. Thank you, Anna." Sophia took off the corset and handed it to her. "Can you loosen it a little?"

"Yes, my lady." Anna eyed her queerly. "What are you going to tell Lady Richmond?" she asked as she tugged at the laces.

She desperately wanted to tell Mama the truth. "That I've developed a fondness for sweets, and if anyone asks, the brocade is my favorite dress. It's the final ball of the Season. I think I should be allowed to wear my favorite dress, don't you agree?"

Anna lowered her head to conceal her smile. "Yes, my lady."

Sophia sighed. July had proved to be the longest month of the summer and August was hinting it too would be interminable. Peers and politicians clung to London and environs as Parliament plodded on, which meant Papa, the consummate political peer, stayed in town. Arthur did as well, as most of his business associates were hangers-on to the political sphere.

The Season hadn't been as fun as she had hoped. She keenly felt Henny's absence especially as, one by one, the girls she had debuted with became engaged. Royston still dogged her at every turn and for that reason she relished her time playing hostess to Arthur. Even entertaining investors' wives was far more tolerable than anything to do with Royston.

She sometimes saw Geoffrey at balls and teas but mostly saw him at Arthur's dinners. He often inquired after Anna on those nights, wondering if she had something to keep her preoccupied as if waiting for Sophie at Arthur's house was somehow different than waiting any other place. Anna had her own room on the top floor and always had a book to read or mending to finish. Sophia reassured Geoffrey that her maid was indeed just fine.

And then there was Joseph.

She loathed having to play a part during dinner and in the drawing room when all she wanted to do was link her arm in his and lean her head against his shoulder as if they were an old married couple. Sophia knew she blushed around him. Of course he was exotic and charming and most of the women blushed in his presence but her reasons were much more deeply felt.

And then the guests would leave, although sometimes Geoffrey would linger to distract Arthur, and Sophia had to play another part. It would be unseemly to simply exit the drawing room with Joseph, even though all knew they would be spending the night in each other's arms. So she would leave first and go to her room where Anna would undress her. Not long after that Joseph would rap lightly on her bedroom door, Anna slinking past them as they embraced.

Every moment she spent with him alone was exquisite. Pleasantries and conversation were left for when they were in company. Their time alone was purely for carnal pleasures. He worshiped her body with his, each time taking her to heights she thought she had already climbed, showing her the different ways a woman and man may make love, how one position flowed into the next. She could straddle his hips and ride his cock, lifting and settling rhythmically, "as a man rides a horse". Then that position could be reversed—rather awkwardly the first time—allowing Joseph to "admire the charms" of her backside. And when he could take her slow slides up and down his cock no more, he maneuvered himself to kneeling, holding her steady, never breaking contact, then slammed into her from behind as she arched over the mattress on all fours.

And that was just one night. The next morning they explored yet more variety of love-making.

But Sophia spending too many nights at Arthur's house made her brother nervous. People might talk, he worried. He made sure Geoffrey was in attendance at every dinner he held.

"It makes it seem more official, Sophie," he had explained. "The three of us partners."

Yet her presence at breakfast, giggling as she and Joseph flashed knowing glances at each other, proved a source of consternation to her brother. He suggested Joseph go away for a spell.

"I'll visit my house in Lamberton," Joseph offered. "I've heard Scotland's lovely this time of year."

All agreed. Joseph would leave for a fortnight and to dispel any lingering rumors of impropriety involving the American, Arthur would continue to have dinners late into the night with Sophia as hostess staying over until morning.

The night before he left Joseph gave her one more lesson. They lay in her bed, skin still flushed from love-making, fingers tangling, breathing each other in.

"Of all the books I've given you," he murmured against her, "which is your favorite?"

Sophia propped herself up on an elbow. "Ooh, *The Lustful Turk.*"

Joseph's brow crinkled with his wide grin. "The one with the sultan and the English girl?"

"It's exotic. I like exotic." She drew a finger down his chest, tracing the shadowed curves of his muscles. "Like you. You're exotic.

If it were *The Lustful American*, I think I would enjoy the story even more."

He chuckled. "Well you can make that one up."

Her eyes widened. "You mean write my own naughty story?"

He threaded his fingers through her hair, arranging it to spill over her shoulder and curl onto his chest. "You don't need to write it down—you can simply speak it to your lover, guiding him through the fantasy."

"Hmm." She lay back on the pillows and stared at the ceiling thoughtfully. "You're an American privateer and you've just captured my ship." She bit her lip, a little abashed at her thoughts. "I'm an English lady. I was held captive by your freedom fighters during your war for independence and they've just set me free."

"Only to fall into my lustful clutches."

"Yes."

"Will you be easy to conquer?" He nuzzled into her neck, the tip of his nose tickling along her pulse. "Surely the patriots had their way with you and have made you wanton." His featherlight touch from her belly to breast prickled her flesh and the deep tones of his voice reverberated within, encouraging her toward a new sensuality.

"No. The rebels knew I was worth more if I remained a virgin. My husband, a colonel with the British army, died before we could consummate our marriage."

Joseph lengthened himself on top of her, pushing her knees apart. "A virgin?" He quirked a brow. "Your innocent treasures are worth more to my cock than to my purse." He pushed his erection between her thighs.

She spread her legs wider, already wet.

"Do you deceive me, my lady? A daughter of the aristocracy does not so easily open herself to criminal scum such as myself."

How wicked. She pushed against his chest. "Blackguard. I will not let you have your way with me." She clapped her thighs shut in vain, her words at odds with her grin.

He handily resisted her struggles, his legs far too strong, his desire far too eager. Yet she could be wily when she wanted.

A swift graze of her nails across the sensitive skin of his hips incited a jerk and a yelp and provided an instance for her to roll out from under him. She stumbled off the mattress, the glee of victory welling within. Yet he regained his senses quickly, lunging for her, wrapping his brawny arms around her waist, tossing her onto the mattress amidst her untempered squeals, this time on her stomach. He stretched out on top of her, his bulk weighing heavy, trapping her, his cock prodding between her legs.

"You cannot possibly mean to escape this ship, my lady. I suggest you give in—"

"Unhand me, you brute." She wriggled under him futilely, laughter melting her muscles of their resolve.

He pressed forward, the head of his cock finding its target. "And now I have my triumph." He plunged in, full force.

She sighed, vanquished, relishing her ravishment. The fantasy had heightened her senses and engorged his cock to iron-hard. She came quickly, easily subdued. He thrust fiercely, rutting as a pirate denied lewd pleasure far too long. He emptied himself inside her with a growl then collapsed at her side with a laugh.

She wrinkled her nose at him. "No fair. You'll always win these games."

He pulled her into his embrace. "Not all games involve strength, my love. I'm sure your womanly wiles can come up with some way to manipulate my senses."

"Hmm." She'd have to give that some thought. She'd have all the time in the world while he was gone. "I'll miss you."

He caressed her arm. "Sophie, while I'm gone, if you need release you should touch yourself. Don't think you can only do that in my presence."

She flushed at the notion of solo pleasure. "I can imagine you're with me. Having your colonial ways with me."

"Oh, please do." He laughed. He pursed his lips in a sober line. "And darling, if you have to, seek solace from Geoffrey."

Guilt spiked through her. "Geoffrey? How do you mean?"

He traced a finger along her jawline. "I mean in his arms, what you used to do." His finger trailed over her lower lip. "Kissing him."

"Joseph—"

"Shh, shh." He pressed his finger against her mouth. "You're a passionate woman, Sophie, and I fear I have riled those passions even further. Too far." He brushed his lips against hers. "I want you to do whatever it is you need to do to satisfy your lascivious appetite."

Returning to Geoffrey's arms seemed a preposterous notion when she had fantasy and her now-skilled hand. But after a week without Joseph and inflamed by his love letters sent wrapped up in business missives to Arthur, Sophia understood what he had meant.

Geoffrey was astonished when she first took his hand after Arthur had carelessly left them alone in the library one night. She quickly convinced him.

"Only kissing," she assured.

But it was kissing as they had never done before, he crushing her as she lay on the couch, his hips rolling between her splayed legs, his lips daring to tease a nipple, spiking arousal to her sex. Their embraces left him glazed-eyed and wobbly, stumbling out to his carriage as she fled to her bedroom, dismissing Anna quickly so she could finish by her own hand.

And when Joseph returned a little over a week later, Sophia told him everything she had done with Geoffrey despite his grins and chuckled protests stating he didn't need to hear about any of it.

But there was one secret she guarded closely. She wanted to be absolutely certain before she revealed it.

Anna knew. Anna had to know. She had said nothing when Sophia missed her courses, calmly watched Sophia vomit in the morning, took the initiative to loosen the lacings of her corsets. But then one day she blurted how she was sure the bath water was far too hot for the baby and perhaps her lady should wait a moment for it to cool. Sophia had cried, letting loose a flood of emotions she had kept bottled up for weeks.

Anna had promised she would say nothing until Sophia said she was at liberty to do so. And Sophia was about to release Anna from her silence.

She sighed at the pile of clothes on her bed. "Well, which of my day dresses will fit?"

"The brown plaid I think. The pattern will distract from your enhanced bosom."

Sophia laughed. Anna was the best lady's maid a woman could have.

And thirty minutes later the best lady's maid had worked wonders to her undergarments and her accouterments to make sure no one knew she was pregnant. It was probably the last time they would be able to manage such a deception. And the last time they would have to.

Sophia had sent Arthur a message, asking to see him about his entertaining plans for the autumn and requesting his business partner, Mr. Phillips, be present. Of course both would know she had other matters to discuss. But one could not be too careful.

"Sophia, darling sister." Arthur kissed her cheeks.

He led her upstairs to the morning room where Joseph waited by the hearth. He took her hands in greeting. Tea was promptly brought.

"To what do we owe the honor of your presence?" Arthur poured out three cups.

She sat demurely at his side and waited until he had put the teapot down.

"Arthur," she said in almost a whisper. "I'm pregnant."

Arthur's jaw dropped as he held the milk jug aloft. Joseph rushed to her side, kneeling before her.

"What do we do now?" she asked.

"First," Arthur stammered, "are you sure?"

"Of course I'm sure."

"How do you know?" he insisted.

She looked at both men. "You really want me to tell you?"

Joseph took her hand. "I think I have a fair idea, but yes. We'll need to call in a doctor so you'll have to tell him your symptoms as well. We'll need proof for anyone who doubts or challenges."

Sophia sighed. "I haven't had my courses for at least two months, I'm terribly fat, I'm nauseated in the morning and when I'm not nauseated I'm famished. I've been eating more than usual."

Joseph grinned and brushed a finger across her cheek. "You're not fat, darling."

Arthur grabbed pen and paper at his writing desk. "I've had Geoff inquire about a discreet doctor. I'll send him a note to fetch the man as soon as possible."

The doctor came that very afternoon.

Dr. Waddington was a middle-aged, garrulous chap who treated her like a granddaughter and spoke mostly to Arthur, who played the role of the terribly scandalized yet concerned brother. The doctor was indeed discreet, asking no questions about who the father might be, only gathering information about her symptoms, taking notes with the occasional hum and nod. She had to disrobe to her chemise and stockings, although was afforded a screen behind which to do so and a dressing gown to cover the sheer underclothing. He first placed his hands on her stomach, applying pressure here and there, then inserted a thick finger all the way inside her, poking and prodding. Next he inserted an instrument he called "a sort of stethoscope, my dear," to listen where his finger had just been.

And when Dr. Waddington decided he had made a thorough examination he had a private talk with Arthur. Soon after, he left.

Joseph stayed away during the doctor's visit and didn't return for a few hours. Sophia waited with Arthur in the library, wanting to be there when he got back.

"So?" Joseph asked, practically bursting through the library door.

"It's official. I am with child, Mr. Phillips."

He pulled her up and out of her chair and swung her about amidst her giggles and Arthur's protests.

"And we want her to stay with child, my good man. Put her down."

Joseph nuzzled her neck, humming his happiness.

"When do we tell Mama and Papa?" she asked over Joseph's distractions.

Arthur paced before the hearth. "When the time is right."

"Well, dear brother, it better be soon. I won't be able to hide my condition very much longer."

"Sophie, the last ball of the Season is tomorrow night. Countess Authorpe's. Can you get through that?" Arthur's brow furrowed.

"Yes. I do expect both of you to be there to support me."

"Of course." He grinned and came to her, extricating her from Joseph's arms to embrace her. "Oh, Sophie, I'm going to be an uncle."

Sophia pulled back to wipe the tear that trailed down Arthur's cheek. "You'll be the *best* uncle."

"I'll tell Mother and Father next week." He sniffled. "Let's get through Saturday night as if nothing has changed first."

Sophia hugged him with a melancholy sigh. Everything had changed.

CHAPTER NINETEEN

Arthur waited until Tuesday, or rather his parents invited him to luncheon on Tuesday, and he decided that would be the best time as any to deliver the news.

"Arthur." Mother greeted him in the foyer. "So glad you could join us. We have an exciting announcement."

Arthur pecked her cheeks. "An announcement, Mother?" Surely not as exciting as his.

She wrapped her arm around his. "Come into the morning room, dear."

As they entered Father remained standing at the window, staring out, his countenance slack.

"Harold."

He turned to greet them. "Arthur, son, good to see you."

"Likewise, Father." Arthur sat on one end of the couch opposite Mother.

Father paced before the fireplace. "Son, how has Sophia been handling your affairs this Season, hmm? She's been a good hostess, no?"

"Absolutely. The very best."

"Good, good. Parliament has been dragging on a bit late this year, otherwise we'd be home. We intend to leave as soon as it closes. Do you think you'll be needing Sophia much after August?"

"If you mean you wish her to return home to Lincolnshire, Father, by all means. I can handle my affairs here in London myself."

Father cleared his throat. "Yes, we will want her to return to Harwell Hall—"

Mother let out a clipped squeal then promptly covered her mouth with her hands.

"We'll be holding a ball in her honor in September."

Arthur did not like where this was going. "Oh?"

"Just tell him, Harold." Mother was far too excited.

"Yes, Matilda. Arthur, we will be announcing your sister's engagement at our annual hunting ball."

A chill ripped through him. "Engagement? To whom?"

"The Duke of Royston, my dear," Mother answered cheerfully. "Who else?"

Shit. Now appeared to be the right time for his announcement. "No. Sophia cannot marry the duke."

"Why ever not, dear?" Mother queried.

"Son, I know you've had some personal antagonism with Royston in the past but you must put that behind you. He is to be your brother-in-law."

"No, Father, it is not my antagonism that leads me to object." It most certainly was. "But rather some news I've just learned."

Mother paled. "News? What news?"

He better just come out with it. "Sophia is with child."

Mother yelped.

"*What did you just say?*"

"Sophia is with child, Father."

"Good Christ above," he bellowed, throwing his hands in the air. "This," he stabbed a finger in Arthur's direction, "this is what happens when I let an innocent girl be watched by her licentious brother. You could barely keep your hands off Henrietta."

"Harold—"

Father stretched out a silencing hand in Mother's direction. "And who, pray tell, is the rogue who got Sophia this way? Don't tell me it's that Peel fellow."

Arthur drew in a fortifying breath. His parents would prefer it to be Geoffrey once they heard the truth. "Joseph Phillips."

Mother gasped.

"The *American*?"

"Yes, the American. My business partner. They are very much in love and wish to be married."

"I cannot allow that, Arthur."

There was a knock on the door.

"Yes?" Father called out, not taking his eyes off Arthur.

"My lord, His Grace is here for luncheon."

"Send him in."

Arthur felt the blood drain from his face.

Royston looked chipper but scowled when he saw the dour expressions. "I fear I have just interrupted a family discussion."

"Oh but, Your Grace," said Mother, getting up to greet him, "you are to be part of our family."

"Yes, Your Grace, you will be welcomed into this family," affirmed Father.

"Thank you." Royston bowed then caught Arthur's eye at a most inopportune time. "Ah, I see not all members of the family are as welcoming as you."

"Your Grace," began Father, "Arthur has just delivered the most shocking news. Sophia is *enceinte*, done in by the American chap."

Royston's eyes narrowed accusingly at Arthur. "She's been spending quite a bit of time at your house, has she not? Did you not see fit to safeguard her from such abuse?"

Arthur controlled his rage. "Joseph Phillips is not the man from whom she needs safeguarding. In fact it was he who saved her from your continued cruelty." Arthur turned to Mother. "You will recall,

Mother, how Sophia was covered in bruises after spending time with the duke?"

She swallowed a sob.

"Arthur, it was all a misunderstanding," said Father. "His Grace has assured us he had not meant to harm her." He turned to the duke. "Given the circumstances, how do you wish to proceed? We can hasten the marriage so she will not show as much during the ceremony. Or we can delay the event until next spring."

Royston sat next to Mother, who cried silently.

"There are ways of getting rid of the child," he said casually as he fished through his pockets for his handkerchief.

"Such as pushing a woman down the stairs?" Arthur said through his teeth.

"Arthur," Mother scolded. She took the handkerchief from Royston with a brief smile.

His parents had no idea who the villain was in Henny's death. There was no use in telling them. Royston would simply deny that as well.

Royston made no overt reaction. "That is a method, yes. A little barbaric. I want Sophia to survive the ordeal. I was thinking about a surgical procedure."

"I don't follow, Your Grace," said Father stupidly.

"The child can be removed from her body via an abortion."

"Why, that's murder," yelped Mother.

"It's not murder when the child is redundant."

"What?" cried Arthur. "Need I remind you, Your Grace, you are talking to my mother about her grandchild?"

"I will not raise the bastard child of a colonial miscreant as my heir. The child needs to be eliminated."

"Gentlemen, let's discuss this civilly," Father said feebly.

"I cannot discuss the murder of my sister's child civilly, Father. It is too upsetting. I give my regrets to your staff for luncheon. I simply cannot stay and talk to a man who takes the life of a child so cavalierly."

Royston cleared his throat. "Where is Lady Sophia anyway? I wish to give my fiancée a congratulatory kiss."

Arthur cringed inside. "She's with my cook discussing a dinner I'm having tomorrow night." She really wasn't. She was with Anna at the seamstress' getting some dresses altered but he was not going to tell anyone that. He knew where the seamstress' was—his mother most likely did as well. He was not going to have Royston send a man around to fetch her and do God knows what with her.

"Ah well, when you see her give her my deepest regards." What would have been simply sweet coming from any other man sounded filthy and lewd from Royston's mouth.

Arthur left, a prayer of thanks running through his head that he chose to travel to his parents' by coach and not brougham—the latter would have been far too small for three…four really with Sophia's condition. He snorted, astounded. *Redundant*. Royston had actually used the word "redundant". He sickened at the thought.

He made sure his carriage went in the expected direction of his house, only turning for the seamstress' after ensuring he was completely out of sight. As he pulled up to the shop one word echoed in his head.

Lamberton.

S ophia loved how the seamstress Mrs. Haigh thought to simply add a frill or two to her dresses as she let them out. No use in having a whole new wardrobe. Joseph would praise her for economizing.

"And I think the green velvet would look lovely with the plaid for autumn," Sophia said cheerfully.

"And send the bill to me."

She turned at the sound of her brother's voice, her face stretching into a big smile at the sight of him. "Arthur. What a lovely surprise."

He kissed her cheek. "I need you to come home with me at once," he whispered in her ear.

She tried not to look worried. "Is the order complete, Mrs. Haigh?"

"Yes, my lady," the seamstress replied.

"And please do charge it to my brother." Sophia wrote quickly on a scrap of paper. "Here is the address. Anna," she called out to her maid, "we must leave."

Arthur took her arm as they exited. "How did you get here?"

"We took a cab."

"Good. We'll take my coach."

He was sullen on the drive to his house, barely saying a word. "Not until we are home and Joseph is present. If he's at my club, I'll send a note to have him join us."

But Joseph hadn't left for the club.

Arthur shuffled them all into the library, even Anna, requesting everyone take a seat.

He sat then stood then sat again, his elbows on his knees. He drew in a long breath. "Sophie, you are to be engaged to the Duke of Royston. The announcement will be made at the annual Richmond hunting ball. I tried to stop them but all I managed to do was let them know of your condition. Mother and Father and Royston all know you are pregnant with Joseph's child." He looked her in the eye. "Royston wants you to have an abortion."

Sophia wavered, suddenly lightheaded. Joseph held her steady with an arm around her shoulder.

"No," she managed.

"This is outrageous," said Joseph.

"It is indeed." Arthur stood and paced before the hearth. "The two of you must get married as soon as possible." He stopped, his hands on his head, and stared at each one of them, his gaze landing on Anna. "That's it!" He pointed to the startled maid. "Anna, have Wittering send a note to Geoffrey Peel to pack a bag for a short trip and get here as fast as he can in his brougham. No questions asked. And then come back here. I'll need you."

"Yes, my lord." Anna curtsied and left.

Joseph watched Arthur intently as he paced determinedly before them. "What do you have in mind?"

"Lamberton. The two of you are going to Lamberton."

"Oh," Sophia gasped. The room started spinning. Everything was happening so quickly.

Arthur turned to Joseph. "You've spent at least twenty-one days there, haven't you?"

"I'm not sure."

"But enough time for people to know who you are? Briggs and Mrs. Reed could attest to your presence."

"O.K. I see where you're going with this." Joseph patted her shoulder. "Sweetheart, it will be a long journey. Can you manage?"

Sophia placed her hand on her belly and stared blankly at the carpet. "Yes."

Arthur's pacing turned into wandering. "I doubt Royston will put forth any legal argument," he muttered.

"Is the plan for Geoffrey to join us?" Joseph asked.

Arthur stopped at the window. "Yes. He's the subterfuge. I'm fairly certain Royston has a man watching my house. You're leaving for Scotland as soon as possible. But not in my carriage."

"In Peel's," said Joseph.

"Yes."

Anna entered after a gentle warning knock. "Mr. Peel has been notified, my lord."

"Ah, Anna. Have a seat." Arthur indicated a comfortable chair the maid would never have sat in for all her days.

She sat and looked up at him with soulful eyes.

"Anna, I need you to pack two bags. One for your lady and one for yourself. Pack for a trip for a few days."

"My lord? Where are we to go?"

"You will be accompanying Lady Sophia to Scotland to get married."

Anna turned a bright smile to her. "Oh, my lady."

"But you," Arthur continued, "are going to ride to the railway station with Geoffrey Peel in my coach, which carries the Harwell crest. You need to be on your guard. You will be dressed as Lady Sophia, masquerading as her."

"Their journey should be slightly altered," Joseph offered.

"Yes," agreed Arthur. "You two will leave first in Geoff's brougham. Geoff and Anna will leave in mine perhaps a quarter of an hour later." Arthur studied the two women pensively. "You'll have to switch gowns."

"We don't know when or where Royston will strike," Joseph said.

"No, but most likely in London. You should depart from different stations." Arthur went to his map cabinet and pulled out a handful of *Bradshaw's*, passing one of the timetables to Joseph. "Thanks to the chaos that is the British railway system we should be able to find two distinct routes."

Joseph leafed through the pages, turned the book sideways, tucked in a finger to hold his place then thumbed back to the beginning. "Geoffrey and Anna should take the more obvious route." He checked a few pages. "The Great Northern from Kings Cross to…" More pages. "York."

"Yes, I see," said Arthur, flipping through his own schedule. "Then transfer to the North Eastern all the way to Berwick." He looked at Anna. "You can hire a coach at Berwick. Lamberton's not far from there."

"Yes, my lord."

Joseph's face crinkled as he muttered over his *Bradshaw's*. "Now our journey will be a bit more indirect. We'll pick up the London & North Western at Euston Square."

"The North Eastern controls the northern lines."

"Yeah," he said not looking up. "So we'll go through Birmingham and Crewe up to Leeds then catch the North Eastern there, following the same route as Geoffrey and Anna." He flashed a hopeful smile at Sophia. "I think this might work." He turned to Anna. "You two will probably arrive at Lamberton before us. Arthur can send a message to Briggs to expect you."

Arthur grinned. "Helps to know the railways when planning an escape, doesn't it?"

Sophia stared at the floor. Anything, she'd do anything to save her child.

＊ ＊ ＊ ＊ ＊

Geoffrey could not believe his luck. He and Anna alone in a coach? Then together on a first-class railway carriage? To Scotland of all places. Perhaps they could take a day to wander and get lost, deliciously lost, only each other and a stocked picnic basket. Or perhaps a fishing pole. He would impress her with his ability to fend and care for her in the countryside—

The *swoosh* of her tugging at her taffeta skirts distracted him back to the reality of her sitting across from him in the carriage.

"Miss Colney, are you comfortable?"

She smiled sweetly. "Thank you, Mr. Peel. I am but I'm still getting used to such finery."

"Today's fashions are rather extreme, are they not?"

She flushed briefly, possibly at the reference to what was under her skirt. "Yes. In this one regard I am glad to be a servant. Our clothes and underpinnings are a bit more practical."

"You look beautiful."

Her eyes widened in surprise.

Heat prickled his skin. *Christ.* Had he just said that out loud?

She looked away, not out the window as the shades were drawn, just *away*. She sucked in her lips, chewing on the bottom one for a bit, then looked down at her hands.

Surely he should say something.

Anything.

Now was as good a time as any.

He got up and moved to her side to her utter astonishment—or was it horror? Boldly he took her hand, which trembled inside her glove. He understood. His palms were sweating inside his gloves.

"Miss Colney—Anna, please, you've touched my heart. My thoughts are filled with images of you—"

She pulled her hand away. "Mr. Peel, you mustn't."

"'Geoffrey'…it's 'Geoffrey'. And what mustn't I do? Declare my desire for you?"

She gasped.

"Tell you I find you the most enthralling woman alive?"

She clenched her hands together and looked away again.

"That your honest beauty enchants me?"

"Please, Mr. Peel, you must stop." Her meek voice trembled.

She glanced at him and in that brief moment he saw she was crying.

"Darling, Anna."

He found his handkerchief and held it out for her. She took it tentatively.

Geoffrey sat back against the squabs. "I apologize. I meant no offense."

"I am flattered, Mr. Peel, believe me. And I know you are a man of honor and integrity, otherwise the earl would not trust you with his interests. But the difference in our stations may have incited you to passions that should not be expressed. I beg you not to pursue the matter."

"The difference in our stations? Miss Colney, you must believe me when I say—" He stopped. The heat rose in his face again, this time from mortification. "My God, you must think me vile. I would never, *have* never tried to seduce a servant."

She turned her head away. "I don't think you vile, sir," she said in a hushed tone.

"I'm not sure I ever thought you a servant." He crossed his arms. "It's just these circumstances that have inspired me. We've never been alone for very long. I...well, I've wanted to say things to you." He best just say it. "I mean to court you, Miss Colney."

"Court me?" She twisted in his direction, her face pale with shock.

The carriage lurched, thrusting them both forward. Instinctively Geoffrey held his arm out to prevent her from falling onto the floor. Her bosom crushed against his elbow. His body immediately and inexorably responded.

When the carriage stopped she righted herself, abashed and flushed. "I've never been courted before."

"Never?"

"Perhaps a childhood infatuation paid me mind. But nothing since."

His heart picked up its pace. "Would you like to be courted now?"

"Mr. Peel—"

"If position in society were not an issue?"

"But it is."

He drew in a breath. "Miss Colney, my father may hold a title but it does not come with much wealth or property. While he is alive I remain a commoner. I have to earn my living and will continue to do so once I inherit the viscountcy. With the Richmonds you lived in much grander circumstances than I ever did. We may have been born to different stations but now we find ourselves in the same situation with an uncertain future. So, Miss Colney, I ask with all the fervor a man of my station can muster, may I hold your hand?"

She smiled a gentle smile. "Yes, Geoffrey, that would be lovely."

His heart thrummed joyously as she tugged off her right glove one finger at a time then lay her bare hand on the seat between them. The pounding of his heart grew to a crescendo as he took off his left glove and placed his hand over hers, grasping her delicate fingers. She was soft and warm. He breathed a sigh of relief.

The driver rapped lightly on the roof.

Geoffrey opened the hatch. "Yes?"

"It's the duke, sir," the coachman hissed quietly. "It's why we're stopped."

"Thank you." Geoffrey shut the trap. "It's Royston," he muttered.

"Oh God." All color drained from her face. "I don't want to see him."

"Neither do I."

Voices—Royston's and perhaps that of a man of his—filtered into the carriage from outside.

"Don't tell me what I can do, boy!" Royston was just on the other side of the carriage door.

Anna pressed herself against the pillowed leather of the carriage seat, screwing her eyes shut, gripping Geoffrey's hand for dear life.

At that moment he knew something had happened between her and the duke. Something terrible. And he was going to do every damn thing in his power to protect her now.

The door opened with a violent urgency. Royston shoved his head inside and glanced around.

"What the devil is going on here?" he bellowed.

Geoffrey tried to steady his fraying nerves. "Your Grace?"

"You know damn well what I mean, Peel. Where the bloody hell is Sophia?"

"I really don't know, Your Grace."

Royston eyed Anna. "Where is your mistress?"

Geoffrey squeezed her hand in support.

"Damn strumpet! Where is she?"

Anna paled to ashen. "I—I do not know, Your Grace," she answered quietly.

Royston slammed his fist on the outer wall of the carriage. "Be assured that no matter what you are up to I will find her. I will find her and her indigent colonial lover and I will have him tried for seduction and breach of contract."

"But there was never an official engagement," Geoffrey blurted.

"You think you are so damn clever," Royston grunted. He gave Anna the once-over, his lips twisted in a lascivious grin. "You'll find her an easy lay, Peel. Doesn't put up much of a struggle." He shoved the carriage door shut with a crash.

Anna quivered, her breaths puffing rapidly.

"Darling?" Geoffrey wrapped his arm around her shoulders and drew her to him.

She tried to pull away then relented as she began to cry, her body shaking convulsively.

He gently urged her head to his shoulder. She slumped against him, nuzzling his chest, sobbing, her arms wrapping around his waist.

Sophia and Joseph were miles away, probably a safe distance with a good enough lead to get them to Scotland unhindered. And Royston would leave him and Anna alone from now on. Well...sort of.

Clearly whatever evil the duke had wrought would continue to dog his victims.

Geoffrey knocked on the roof, indicating they should resume their journey.

The driver poked his face through the hatch. "Where to, Mr. Peel? Kings Cross? Or back to Lord Petersham's?"

Anna needed a respite. They would go to Scotland. Do their duty as witnesses then spend time along the coast. She would be safe and far away.

"Kings Cross."

Geoffrey caressed Anna's back, looking forward to sharing a private car with her, even if he merely held her in silence.

Her arms around him, nestled in the crook of his shoulder, his hand stroking her back, Anna let the heat of Geoffrey's body imbue hers with an emotion she hadn't felt for several months.

Safe. Geoffrey Peel was safe.

Relief flooded over her and with it fresh tears. His hand at her back stilled, pressing into her, steadying her as she shook with sobs.

"Geoffrey," she began hoarsely, "what he said about me, I'm sorry you had to hear it. I understand if it changes your feelings toward me."

He drew her to him a little more, a sign he wasn't letting her go. "Tell me what happened, Anna." A squeeze. "If you can."

She sucked in a breath, the emotion of the memory catching in her throat. "I had chaperoned Lady Sophia on an outing with the duke. He was not pleased. He tried to get my lady alone and he almost succeeded but she fell or was pushed, I don't really know. I came to her aid. She told me later he tried to kiss her and she did not want to be kissed by him. Then that night…" Her voice wavered. She inhaled, detecting a comforting hint of pipe tobacco from Geoffrey's fine wool jacket. "That night he abused me. I did not struggle. He threatened violence if I did."

His chest rose and fell evenly, steadily, a momentary shudder betraying the emotion he tried to calm within. "If I ever see him again—" He exhaled and gave her another squeeze, crushing the brim of her bonnet into her face.

She giggled.

"Anna, darling," he said, lifting her chin to tug at her hat strings, "let us not talk of this now."

She let him take off her bonnet although she had to help. And when the hat was off and their remaining gloves removed he rested into the corner of the carriage bench and eased her back against him.

"Tell me a little about yourself." His deep voice rumbled in his chest under her cheek.

"My father was a vicar. He held the living at the Brampton estate." She glanced up at him. "I'm sure you know the place. It's not far from Harwell Hall. I was raised simply although educated far above my station. My parents thought I should be a governess but I was recommended to the Richmonds as a lady's maid. I've been with Lady Sophia for almost five years."

He nuzzled her with his nose, his breath hot on the crown of her head. "I suppose I was at university with Arthur when you first arrived."

"Yes, I do believe Lord Petersham was at Cambridge at the time."

He brushed his lips across her hair then kissed her lightly, the intimacy bathing her with a joyous warmth.

"Geoffrey…" She paused briefly to breathe courage. "You should know I am not a maid."

He tightened his hold. "Good God," he hissed. "Royston?"

She chilled at the thought. "No. No. A boy at Brampton. I won't divulge his name. As I said, it was a mere infatuation." She looked up at him. "I thought you should know."

He smiled. "And, Anna, you should know I am not without experience myself."

"Well, there is all that kissing with Lady Sophia."

He laughed with heartfelt amusement, dispelling the lingering disquietude. "There hasn't been much kissing with Lady Sophia since the arrival of Joseph. But there was one night… It was…" He chuckled. "Well I'm sure she was thinking of him." He lifted a brow. "I was very definitely thinking of you."

"I should like it if you would think of me in that way."

"May I do more than just imagine?" His lips parted in anticipation.

She cupped his cheek. "Yes, Geoffrey. Please."

He kissed her gently, tentatively until the flame of desire could be contained no longer. His hand steadied her head as he plunged in, his tongue seeking hers in the depths of her mouth, growling his satisfaction as she opened for him, taking full advantage of what she offered.

It had been too long, much too long, the last time with him when he thought her Sophia. Before that with Jonny Brampton. But the naive yearnings of two sixteen-year-olds were meager compared to the fervor of maturity loosed from societal dictates of self-denial. And passion shared with a longed-for lover was far more exciting than a surprise kiss in the dark.

He pulled back, pecking a trail along her tear-stained face to her neck, the raw masculinity of his rough cheek spiking lust to coil in her core.

"You're wearing her perfume."

She smiled broadly. Of course he would notice. "My lady thought it a nice touch while we were changing gowns. I'm not sure I've ever worn perfume."

"It suits you." He nibbled her neck. "But perhaps we can find something unique so I won't be reminded of her when I make love to you."

The lust unwound, spreading deliciously between her thighs, the sensual freedom heightened by his palm covering her breast. She wanted nothing more than to bare herself to him, to have him inside her, to share the joy for which woman and man were purposely created.

But she wanted so much more than that with him.

"Darling," she began. "Geoffrey—"

"Yes, my love?" he asked, lazily drawing his tongue across the seam of her lips.

"I think the courtship has gone as far as it ought for the moment."

He froze then sat back into the padded leather. "Of course," he murmured, his eyes wide in surprise or mortification. He was simply precious with his tousled hair and disheveled collar.

"Don't give me that look," she scolded softly. "What I mean to say is that I like kissing you but we are to do nothing further until you have properly courted me."

He grunted a chortle. "I suppose I was a bit too vigorous in pressing my suit just now."

"As was I." She smiled. "But, darling, there is risk in pursuing such a liaison. I need the assurance that your parents will accept such a relationship."

"Yours as well, I suppose."

"I hardly think a vicar and his wife will refuse the offer of a viscount's heir." She smoothed his hair back into place. "Your business associates as well. Lord Petersham. I'm sure Mr. Phillips and Lady Sophia won't find it shocking."

"No." He chuckled. "Sophia will be miffed you did not confide in her."

"A lady's maid does no such thing with her mistress."

He took her hand between his. "Just think of the fun you could have had switching places."

"Oh, you are wicked." She leaned forward, placing her palm on his leg above the knee, the heat emanating from his crotch sparking arousal within. That he wanted her as much as she wanted him was exhilarating, liberating. But she would not give in.

She eased her hand closer to his hip, the tips of her fingers curling around the flesh of his inner thigh. He drew in a sharp breath, his brow crinkling in hopeful expectation.

"If you feel the need to appease your urges, I will allow you to take a lover," she said quietly. "I won't be so cruel as to deny you your pleasures while we wait for approbation from your family and colleagues."

He swallowed and glanced at her hand. "I doubt I will need a paramour when you will occupy my dreams every night."

She smiled and melted into him, closing her eyes as he wrapped his arms around her, the sway of the carriage an accomplice to their forbidden affair.

CHAPTER TWENTY

When their hired dogcart pulled into the drive before the cottage at Lamberton Sophia breathed a sigh of relief. Amazingly Arthur's plan had worked. She and Joseph had arrived in Scotland without ever having seen Royston.

Which possibly meant that Anna and Geoffrey had encountered him. She shuddered and prayed he would not persist in his pursuit. Joseph put Mr. Briggs on night watch just in case.

They spent their first night alone, Joseph coaxing her into his arms, out of her clothes, to open for him. Afterward he held her, murmuring reassurances that all would be O.K. Had she really just left behind everything she knew and loved? No, not really. She loved Joseph and Arthur and Geoffrey. Anna even. But she also loved long strolls across the lawns at Harwell Hall, birds and clouds floating above, the crisp, spring air reddening her cheeks. There would be no more springs in the countryside. By next spring she would have a newborn and would be living in America.

Geoffrey and Anna didn't show up for a whole day and too late for the parson, which was just as well. Joseph was certain he was a few days shy of the requisite twenty-one and he was adamant there should be no irregularities.

Anna looked a proper lady in Sophia's clothes and acted as one as she kissed Sophia's cheeks in greeting and relief. They had been delayed twice by the duke, once in London then in Peterborough when they saw him at the station. Anna had suggested they stay in Peterborough a day, which they did. Royston was probably heading for Harwell Hall but they didn't want another encounter on the railway.

Despite their misadventure with the duke, the pair was in good spirits. Geoffrey's eyes twinkled whenever he looked in Anna's direction as he gave his account of their journey. She glowed and beamed in Geoffrey's presence, blushing when he said she should simply sit down and let Mrs. Reed serve the tea. Anna was very pretty when she smiled. It was the first time Sophia had seen Anna truly smile.

"Will the two of you be visiting the parson, as well?" Sophia needled.

Anna gasped and paled while Geoffrey looked down at his teacup. Joseph let out a guffaw.

"I promised Miss Colney a proper wedding," Geoffrey said, meeting Anna's gaze. "But only after a proper courtship."

Sophia clapped her hands to her face. "Oh, Anna. Is this true?"

"Yes, my lady."

She stood and pulled Anna from her chair and into a hug. "I am so happy for you." She kissed her cheeks. "For the both of you," she said to Geoffrey.

"We don't mean to take away from your happiness, my lady."

"You aren't. And you must call me Sophia." She turned to Joseph. "Or after tomorrow, Mrs. Phillips."

"I dare say, Sophie, you will be Lady Sophia Phillips," said Geoffrey.

"We'll see how Papa and Mama react first."

That night Joseph was seized by a sudden sense of chivalry, deciding that he and Sophia should not sleep together until after they were man and wife although it was possibly merely a ruse so he and

Geoffrey could stay up half the night drinking brandy and exchanging lurid stories of bachelorhood.

She and Anna did not get much sleep either, Sophia from nerves, Anna from giving in to Sophia's prodding about Geoffrey while they lay in bed in the dark. Anna also confided the account of her rape by Royston, leaving Sophia sullen and guilty.

"I should have done more to protect you," she said, staring at the night-blackened ceiling.

"How could you when you were his victim as well?" Anna exclaimed. "It's no one's fault but his, my la—Sophia. We'll not talk about it any longer." She turned onto her side, tucking her hands under her head. "Geoffrey's a good kisser, isn't he?"

Sophia laughed. They giggled into the night until sleep overtook them.

When Sophia awoke, the sadness for her past had lifted. Her future lay with Joseph and she was eager for their new beginning.

The marriage took place at the Lamberton tollhouse near the border with England where clandestine and irregular marriages had traditionally taken place before the law was changed to not encourage elopement to Scotland. The parson, Dr. Ardwell, a jovial fellow as tall as Geoffrey and as brawny as Joseph, boomed an exuberant welcome to the foursome, putting everyone immediately at ease. Sophia expected to have butterflies in her stomach on her wedding day. Instead her heart threatened to burst from an excess of joy, lifting her as if she were walking on air, her feet barely touching the wooden floor in the little stone building, her head in a fog, barely hearing Joseph and Dr. Ardwell discussing fees and paperwork. She didn't remember saying "I do" but was certain she did, for suddenly there she was signing the registry.

And when she looked up Anna was blushing crimson as Geoffrey whispered something in her ear, his lips twisted in a sly smile he once reserved for Sophia, a smile now suffused with a difference, with contentment and satisfaction.

Dr. Ardwell's assistant shooed them away as the next couple approached. In lieu of a wedding breakfast, Geoffrey suggested they drink a toast in a nearby pub. On the way, Joseph sent a quick note to Arthur.

After they celebrated their wedded bliss and the health of their child, Joseph returned to business.

"We'll travel to London together as quickly as possible. Arthur will want to see the marriage certificate."

"We can leave today," suggested Geoffrey.

"But what about a honeymoon for Mr. and Mrs. Phillips?" Anna pouted.

How sweet for Anna to look out for her, but they did not have the time.

Joseph caught her eye. "I think we already did what we were supposed to do on our honeymoon." He winked. "I promise we'll go somewhere, do something special."

Sophia did not doubt that. They would go to America at least. The thought made her a little uneasy but if she were with Joseph, she knew she would be, as he would say, O.K.

Arthur studied the paintings of his ancestors outside the door to Father's study. He remembered his grandfather and the oil portrait captured beautifully the glint of mischievousness in his eyes above the stern line of his mouth. Grandpapa got that same expression when Arthur did something wrong—well, something Father thought was wrong at least. Grandpapa had been far more forgiving of Arthur's boyhood foibles. He wondered if the old man would forgive the adult as well. Arthur was prepared to do something very bad indeed.

He had made an appointment with Father and had insisted Mother be in attendance to discuss an urgent family matter. He shook his head. Grandpapa had always been ready to listen. No appointment needed. Arthur missed him terribly.

All sentiment dissolved the moment Billings opened the door and invited him in. The oppressive atmosphere of the study came not just from the dark wood paneling but from the foul mood of his parents, Father in a position of power behind his desk, Mother primly poised on a stuffed visitors' chair. They gave no greeting, no offer to sit.

"Royston tells us Sophia ran away," Father growled. "Where did she go?"

Arthur stood before the desk, his hands folded behind him as if an admonished schoolboy. "Scotland."

"Oh, my word," Mother whimpered, raising her hands to heaven.

Father's eyes bored into him. *"She did what?"*

"You heard me, Father. Sophia went to Scotland with Joseph Phillips with the intention of getting married."

"I will have her brought back at once. Billings!" He stood, both hands gripping the bureau's thick mahogany edge. "She's not spending three weeks with that man."

Billings entered promptly. "Sir?"

"She doesn't have to," Arthur drawled. "I sold the Lamberton property to Joseph months ago. It's listed on our contract as his residence and usual place of business. He's already spent three weeks there, and," he had to contain a surge of victorious glee, "I've just received word they were successful in their endeavor."

"That's a lie. I'll challenge it in court." Father dismissed the secretary with a backhanded wave.

"Harold, please. Think of the scandal," Mother said quietly.

"I will have the blackguard arrested for seduction."

"And have it spread all over the newspapers?" Arthur stated coolly.

"Oh, Harold," Mother squawked. "We cannot have Sophie dragged through the mud."

Father narrowed his eyes. "Did you allow this to happen?"

"Yes, Father, I was instrumental in saving my sister from harm's way."

"You are no son of mine—"

"Harold!" Mother's screech pierced the air. She stood and approached the desk, leaning toward Father. "You are not to say that ever again."

Arthur chilled at the scene. He had never seen his parents engaged in a clash of wills. Father turned beet-red under Mother's steely stare then flicked his gaze to Arthur.

"This is outrageous." He slammed his fist on his desk.

Both Mother and the inkwell jumped.

"More outrageous than marrying your daughter to a true blackguard? An absolute brute? More outrageous than aborting your own grandchild?"

Father turned his back to him to glower out the window.

"All Royston has ever done is tell you lies, Father. I do not understand why you continue to listen to him. He beat and almost raped Sophie. If it hadn't been for Joseph, she would have been defiled by that man. Now Sophie carries the child of the man she loves, the man she wanted to marry, the man she did marry. The man with whom she will raise your grandchild. Your first grandchild. Quite possibly your only grandchild."

Mother gasped. "Arthur? Whatever do you mean?"

"I mean, Mother, that you had your chance with Henny. Henny was pregnant when Royston threw her down the stairs—"

"What?" Her jaw dropped as her hand flew to cover her mouth.

"That's right. He was responsible not only for her death but for the death of our child. She had to suffer with the knowledge of a miscarriage then suffer with the knowledge she might not ever carry another child." He drew in a breath to steady himself. "I will not produce an heir for a title whose current holder has faith in the most barbaric of men."

"Arthur…" Father growled, turning to face him.

"Does the idea vex you, Father?" he snapped. "I am well aware that I am the last of the Harwell line, the final male heir to the Marquessate of Richmond. I wonder if Sophie has a son, where he will fit into the lineage? And then if I refuse to have a son? What then?"

"I will petition for a special remainder." But the words of defiance were tinged with a touch of fear.

"In favor of whom? Some unknown fourth cousin by marriage? The marquessate as you know it will die."

His father glared at him. "You wouldn't dare."

"If allying with men of Royston's ilk is what the peerage is all about, I want no part of it."

"It's not what you think."

Arthur angled over the massive desk separating father and son. "Then tell me what it is I should think, Father."

The marquess turned a horrific shade of crimson and looked away.

"I do not know what sort of hold Royston has over you," Arthur bit acerbically, "what sort of blackmail he demands or spell he has you under, because that is all it can be. He is a most reprehensible beast, completely ill-suited for your sweet, innocent daughter. I cannot believe you continue to believe in the charade that is their engagement."

Mother sobbed quietly into her handkerchief.

"Because of him I no longer have the woman I love and we will never share the joy of children. I will not allow you to destroy Sophie's one chance at happiness. When they return to London I will shield her and protect her as I should have done for Henny. When you give up this damn pretense I will let you see your daughter and grandchild."

Arthur turned on his heel and left.

CHAPTER TWENTY-ONE

Sophia was exhausted from the journey and from the baby but giddiness burbled through her as the cab from Kings Cross headed toward Arthur's house. When the foursome arrived her brother was glum and dull. But she wasn't going to let him spoil her good news.

"I'm married, Arthur. Can you believe it?" She threw her arms around his neck and let him kiss her cheeks.

His grin was tempered with fatigue. "I'm so very happy for you, Sophie." He turned his smile to Joseph as he took her arm. "For the both of you. And I'm just glad it is you who is my brother-in-law."

Sophia squeezed his arm. "We'll not speak of anything but my future happiness, Arthur."

"Of course. Let's to the drawing room for a little celebration."

Like the best brother in the world that he was, Arthur had champagne and a small fruit cake ready to fete the wedding. The mood in the room was of weary victory, except Geoffrey was overly attentive to a blushing Anna.

"I've a small dinner prepared," Arthur announced. "I'm sure you are all famished from your trip." He turned to Anna. "You are welcome to join us, Miss Colney. I fear you are embroiled in our plot now."

Anna curtsied. "Thank you, my lord."

Arthur twisted his lips and sighed. "Let's not use such formalities in private. Please just call me Arthur."

Anna blushed again with a smile.

Dinner was simple. The three men discussed business and Anna occasionally flashed Sophia questioning looks. Sophia explained what she could but was quite distracted by just watching Joseph engaged in conversation with Arthur and Geoffrey. He had an intensity of conviction and a camaraderie with the other two men that was quite appealing, quite…arousing.

She picked at her peas. Food cravings had become routine in the last few weeks but she hadn't expected to crave Joseph—her *husband*—and his virile charms. Her hunger for him was increased by the fact they hadn't had a proper wedding night. And she couldn't stop thinking about what they might do on that special night.

Heat rushed to her cheeks. She flicked her gaze around the table to see if anyone could tell she was at that very moment, at the dinner table, having very naughty thoughts. But the men were guffawing over something and Anna was clearly enjoying wearing a low-cut gown and eating at an elegant table rather than in the servants' hall.

After dinner they all repaired to the library, the men forgoing cigars but not Arthur's port as he kept the finer liquor near his books. They drank another toast to Sophia and Joseph, then Arthur invited everyone to take a seat.

"Sophie, not to put a cloud over your happy day but I do need to mention a few things. Mother and Father are not happy. However, I don't think they will threaten a legal suit against Joseph—"

"Why would they do such a thing?" Sophia was horrified.

"For seduction," Geoffrey said softly.

"But he didn't…I mean, I did too—"

"It's a legal term, Sophie," Geoffrey explained. "You are not an adult in the eyes of the law. Until a young woman not in her majority is married her father retains all legal rights over her person. The marquess could sue Joseph, essentially, for loss of his property."

"Repugnant," muttered Joseph.

"Yes, but he won't," said Arthur. "The scandal would be horrendous. Libelous attacks on the honor of fifteen generations of Richmonds would be utterly shameful to him." Arthur sipped his port thoughtfully. "You'll live here with me—and Joseph—for the duration of your confinement. You too, Anna," he said to her.

Sophia stared at him in disbelief. She was never going home again.

"I've sent for the rest of Anna's personal property. Unfortunately for you, Sophie, everything you have is essentially owned by Father. I don't want to upset him further."

"Everything? My new gowns?"

"We'll have a modiste visit whenever you wish."

"May I write to Mama?" She longed for her advice. It simply hadn't sunk in that mother and daughter would not share in the joy of a grandchild.

"Yes of course," he said curtly.

The sullen silence was broken by the rustle of Anna's silk skirts as she got up from the sofa.

"I think I'll retire now, if I may."

"Yes, Anna," said Arthur. "Thank you."

Anna glanced at Geoffrey, who got up immediately and walked out with her.

Arthur sat next to Sophia and took her hand. "We've put ourselves in a terrible mess but it's a damn sight better than you being married to Royston." He gave a little squeeze. "I'm just happy you're safe and with me."

"Oh, Arthur." Sophia flung her arms around his neck, tears stinging her eyes.

He patted her back. "We'll get through this together."

"Thank you."

"I'm going to bed. This is your house now, Sophie. You do as you like."

He kissed her forehead then left her and Joseph alone.

* * * * *

Joseph drew Sophia against him on the couch. "We haven't had a proper wedding night you know," he murmured.

"I know." She snuggled more deeply.

"I think we should do something special."

She looked up, coyly biting her lip. "Oh? Like what we used to do?"

What he had in mind they had never done before. "Something like it."

The coyness faded as a wicked gleam flashed in the green of her eyes.

The door opened. Sophia pulled away, her abandon replaced by decorum.

Geoffrey walked in with a heavy sigh, catching sight of them on the couch. "Sorry. I suppose Arthur's gone upstairs."

"Come sit." Joseph tapped the space between him and Sophia.

"I'm not disturbing you?"

"No. Tell me about Anna."

Geoffrey slumped on the couch. "She's frightened. Nervous perhaps is a better word. She knows no other life." He cast a smile at Sophia. "She's absolutely loyal to you, Sophie."

"But what about you and her?" Joseph asked.

"Ah. There is the class difference." Geoffrey blew out a breath. "She admires the two of you but feels there's too much risk to our business if I also upset the social order. It's one thing for an upstart American to aspire to the ranks of privilege, quite another for a proper English servant to attempt such a move. Servants who marry up are presumed to be parvenus or fallen women. Or both."

Joseph wrinkled his brow. "Upstart?"

Geoffrey casually crossed his long legs, his mouth twitching to a half-smile. "I think she used the word 'democratic'. She's quite astute."

Joseph chuckled.

"Which means I remain a celibate man until she's settled in her heart and mind about us. Otherwise it's just another scion of the aristocracy abusing his misconstrued rights." He leaned his head back against the sofa and stared up at the ceiling. "She even suggested I take a lover. Or a mistress."

"How scandalous." Sophia laughed.

"And why don't you?" asked Joseph.

"A mistress is far too expensive and a lover, well, the last time I had a lover she broke my heart."

"Oh, Geoffrey." Sophia placed a hand on his shoulder.

He linked his fingers through hers. "Don't worry, it's well past." He sighed. "Last Season. Celia Perkins, already widowed at the ripe old age of twenty-nine. She ran off with an Austrian graf twenty years her senior. I supposed she likes that sort of thing."

Sophia tugged at his fingers, her expression softened with concern. "What about Flora Sheffleigh?"

"Ah, Flora. Pretty little thing, isn't she?" He winked at her. "She's already secretly married and I've been her subterfuge. Wealthy Jewish chap. Made his fortune in textiles. The plan is to run off to Paris."

"There is one woman you wouldn't mind taking to your bed," said Joseph, eying their continued intimacy.

"Oh, bollocks, don't—"

Sophia's eyes widened. "Who?"

"And now she is married, her innocence is no longer an impediment."

"Phillips," Geoffrey groaned. "That was told to you in drunken confidence."

Joseph laughed. Indeed it was, the night before his wedding.

"Oh, Geoffrey, how shocking. Do tell."

He narrowed his eyes at Joseph. "Perhaps I should let her husband do the honors."

It took a second for Sophia to catch on. "What?" She tried to release her hold but Geoffrey did not let go.

"It's no secret, darling," he said, stroking her palm. "I've wanted you for a long time. I almost had you too. There was that one night when Joseph was up at Lamberton and you and I..." He hummed a moan. "Right here on this very couch." He let go of her to smooth the velvet upholstery.

Sophia blushed a most exquisite shade of rose. "Joseph said I should…with you."

"Sometimes I regret my honorable streak."

"And," Joseph said, arching an eyebrow, "whom did you think of later that night?"

The rosy blush crimsoned. "You, love, I thought of you."

Geoffrey sighed. "Once again I've been bested."

"I thought of you too," she blurted.

Sophia's hand flew to her mouth as the two men chortled.

"At once, darling?" Joseph tormented. "Or one at a time?"

The blush paled to ivory, her gaping mouth slackened then pinched shut. "More like a melding of the two of you, sometimes you, sometimes Geoffrey." She narrowed her eyes at him. "Sometimes I didn't know who it was pleasuring me."

Her words shot straight to his cock. *Damn, she's good.* Joseph grinned.

Geoffrey rubbed her thigh. "Thank you for including me in your fantasy, Sophie. I haven't shared a woman since Cambridge."

Which was the very memory that had sparked their drunken conversation a few nights ago. Frustration in the wake of Anna's continence had Geoffrey reminiscing about his caterwauling with Arthur during their university days.

"I don't think you ever kissed the bride for luck, Peel."

Geoffrey cast him a dubious look. "Is that an American custom?"

"Among some of the Scandinavian settlers of New York, yes."

"Ah," he said with a smirk.

Geoffrey stood and gazed down at Sophia, a yearning hunger in his eyes, and pulled her to him. Sophia's slight jerk of reluctance and sidelong glance at Joseph were enlivening, acknowledgment of his precedence. But Geoffrey's commanding strength quickly eased her into submission until she relaxed in his arms, arching into his palm at her back, pressing into his hips as his other hand cupped her butt and urged her forward. She gripped his collar, holding herself steady, staring up at him. He bent over and kissed her mouth, her neck, dipping to her décolletage. She closed her eyes and exhaled a soft moan. Her cunt would be dripping wet, ready for her seducer's cock.

Joseph was rock hard. Another man was ravishing his wife and it was arousing as hell.

He slid behind her, wrapping his hands around her waist. Geoffrey took the cue, relinquishing his control slightly to allow Joseph's incursion, following his lead as Joseph crushed her skirts with his thrusting crotch.

Shit. He was harder than he had ever been in his life. "Let's continue this upstairs."

One moment Sophia was kissing Geoffrey, his lusty growl reverberating all the way to the desire pooling between her legs, when the heat of her husband's body permeated her, his respiration, heavy with arousal, filled her ears, his lips, hot and demanding, assaulted her neck. Then before she knew what was happening they were in Joseph's bedroom, the three of them. Four hands undressed her with care and determination as excited, erratic breaths joined in synchronized rhythms.

As she stood before him nude and willing, Geoffrey stared reverently, murmuring oaths in praise of her body, touching gingerly, as if not quite certain she was flesh. Joseph had abandoned her to Geoffrey's lascivious need, undressing slowly on the slipper chair in the corner, watching the scene before him with as much lust in his eyes as if he were a participant, his gaze raking over not just her but Geoffrey. Tall and thin, he appeared lanky when dressed, his clothes hiding muscles honed by his active sporting life, his endowments sized to match his height.

Geoffrey lifted her into his arms and carried her to the bed, laying her down gently, climbing next to her and extending himself alongside. He kissed her languidly while his hand weighed a breast, then gazed intently as his finger drew spirals around the areola, exciting her nipple.

"Magnificent."

She smiled. "You're rather wonderful yourself."

He sighed. "This is simply beyond fantasy." He bent over her and took the hardened peak into his mouth, swirling his tongue, sucking eagerly. He turned his attention to the other breast, his hand sliding over her belly to dally in the thatch of hair at the apex of her thighs. She closed her eyes to luxuriate in the heat of his mouth, the tickle of his questing finger.

He returned to the other breast. Then there were two mouths.

Sophia's eyes flew open. Two mouths, two tongues, two pairs of lips, each sucking a yearning nipple, throaty growls of satisfaction intensifying the pleasure with vibrations. She closed her eyes again as shivers of pleasure rippled through her, coiling at her clit. A hand reached to stroke between her legs, skillfully taking her to the precipice of climax, holding her steady in agonizing ecstasy, and then freeing her to burst in glorious, wanton release.

She cried out, bucking up. She opened her eyes to see Geoffrey licking his fingers.

Geoffrey. He had brought her to orgasm. He had just encountered her body and was already master of it.

He moved over her, separating her legs with his knees, positioning his prick at her entrance, slipping it through her slickness, moaning his eagerness. He glanced up at Joseph, who sat at the head of the bed, propped up by pillows, gripping his rampant cock. He nodded his assent.

And then Geoffrey pushed inside her.

"Oh, God," he gasped, repeating the oath as he thrust in and pulled out, groaning breathlessly when she clenched and released to his rhythm. "It's been too long," he murmured. "Darling Sophie, you feel so good, so very, very good."

Sophia cupped his face with her hands and kissed his lips tenderly, encouragingly, working her hips below. She was the master now.

Geoffrey increased his rhythm, his eyes boring into her, glazing over, beginning the slide into joyous oblivion.

Joseph sidled up and reached his hand between Sophia's legs. He grabbed Geoffrey's cock when he pulled out.

Geoffrey yelped.

"Switch," Joseph commanded. "You on bottom."

Geoffrey eyed Joseph for a moment before smiling. "Yes." He rolled onto his back, pulling Sophia on top to straddle him. She wriggled until his prick nestled in the slick folds of her sex.

Joseph retrieved something from his nightstand. "Lift up, Sophie."

She positioned herself on her hands and knees. From behind, Joseph massaged her clit, expertly taking her to the point of luscious delirium before sliding through her slit to draw the sticky wetness to the crinkled hole of her arse.

Oh, God, yes.

She poked her butt out in invitation. One finger breached the tightness then another, moving in and out gently, slowly. He stopped for a moment only to return to his ministrations with a cool, creamy substance.

"Cold cream," he murmured. "Better than butter."

Excitement shot through her.

"Remember to relax, love." Joseph's gentle words were laden with arousal. His prick nudged her behind.

He pushed in, tenderly but resolutely, the pain exquisite. Sophia gasped, tried to relax. Geoffrey touched her cheek, comforting her, an expression of wonder on his face. She held his gaze as Joseph continued to work his way inside, teasing her clit with his fingers.

Geoffrey gaped. "Christ, I could spend just watching you."

A sharp pinch sent her lurching forward with a clipped cry. Now fully embedded inside her, Joseph held his position as she relaxed around him. A moment later he commenced a slow, sensual rhythm.

"Geoffrey," he said, "it's your turn."

Geoffrey grinned and grabbed his cock. "Sophie, lower yourself onto me."

"But Joseph is still inside me."

"That's the point," he chuckled.

Unbelievable. Joseph stilled as Sophia spread her legs to let Geoffrey guide himself. He pushed in with a groan, his hands gripping her waist, holding her steady.

"My God, it's so tight," he breathed.

Her head spun at the double invasion, every nerve sparked, setting off a riot of sensation—pleasure, pain, hunger, satisfaction. Her breath staggered, her heart raced as she was swept into a whirlwind of orgiastic delight. She grabbed Geoffrey's hands at her waist and wailed in ecstasy.

Geoffrey beamed at her, wide-eyed.

Joseph resumed his movements, spurring Geoffrey to begin.

Incredibly the men moved inside her at once, inciting a new wave of sensuality to rise within, goaded by Joseph's attention to her clit and nipples. She pulsated around Geoffrey's every stroke, her breaths puffed with the exertions of all three.

Beneath her Geoffrey lolled on the pillow, his gaze dreamy, his hands pawing frantically at whatever part of her he could reach. Behind her Joseph moved steadily, determinedly, his ragged exhales filling her ears, his hands forgetting her as he raced to his own culmination.

Geoffrey emitted a low, guttural grunt. "Oh, God—I can't—"

He bucked up, piercing her to the core, emptying himself with a loud, unwavering growl. He crashed down onto the mattress, trying to catch his breath, still embedded inside her.

Joseph drove into Sophia with more determination, lost in his own need. Geoffrey watched, his expression one of utter fascination, then held her gaze, stroking her clit resolutely, willing her to the brink. Still hard, he thrust deeper. She clenched around him forcefully, slumping forward, her body powerless to the onslaught of lust controlling her, taking her once again on a journey to sensual oblivion, racing to the end with Joseph.

But she needed something to take her over the edge.

She pleaded to Geoffrey with her eyes.

He reached for a nipple, twisting it cruelly, sending a shock wave of delicious pain to meld with the pleasure below. She came with a howl, every muscle straining in orgasm, compelling Joseph to join her.

She collapsed on top of Geoffrey, breathless.

Joseph chuckled with relief. "That was magnificent." He pulled free and drew her to lie alongside him. "Perhaps a somewhat unique wedding night, my wife," he murmured, kissing her cheek.

Geoffrey laughed. "Wonderfully unexpected and thoroughly enjoyable." He kissed Sophia on the other cheek.

She lay between the two men, sated and amazed, marveling at a husband who would permit such a pleasure for his wife.

Already everything about their marriage was unique.

CHAPTER TWENTY-TWO

The drawing room at Arthur's house droned with the grumbles and growls of more than twenty men. Wittering scurried about, making sure each had what he required—tea, coffee, something stronger—repeatedly explaining that the windows were closed on the August afternoon to maintain absolute privacy. Joseph slumped in the corner near the door, acutely aware not one man would meet his gaze and trying like hell to maintain his composure.

Repercussions from his marriage to Sophia did not take long but were of an entirely unexpected nature. He was adamant Sophia's reputation not be besmirched. "I'll take the blame," he had told Arthur and Geoffrey.

"We're in this together, Joseph," Arthur reminded him. "Each and every one of us."

"I'm surprised it took all of three days before Thuxton sent a note requesting clarification on the matter," Geoffrey said. "But what Royston lacks in funds he makes up for in societal connections."

Arthur had insisted they immediately call a meeting of current investors and invite important parties of interest. They needed to ascertain what had been said about whom and lay any and all rumors to rest.

With a chime of his silver spoon against his porcelain teacup, Arthur called the room to order. "Gentlemen, gentlemen." He waved his hands to suggest they take their seats. "Now it has come to my attention that there have been rumors of impropriety surrounding Harwell and Company, involving our engineer, Mr. Phillips, and my sister."

"Impropriety, Petersham? Well that's putting it mildly." The Earl of Thuxton remained standing, his normally casual air replaced by a rectitude at odds with his personal notoriety. But vast sums of money were at stake.

"How's that, my lord?" Arthur asked.

"I dare say abduction and violence on the lady's person can hardly be called 'impropriety'."

Joseph met Arthur's gaze with a raised brow. The gossip was worse than they had imagined.

"Can you elaborate on these rumors of abduction and violence, my lord?"

Somehow Arthur was able to maintain his calm. Joseph just wanted to lash out at every damn one of them.

"Does that man have to be present, Petersham?"

Thuxton nodded in Joseph's direction. The icy stares of a dozen men sent a chill up Joseph's spine.

"Since Mr. Phillips is the one accused of such crimes I think it best he hear the accusations directly, my lord." A faint tremor had invaded Arthur's reserve.

"Very well." Thuxton returned his attention to Arthur. "It is said he carried off the Lady Sophia and had his way with her."

The oppressive silence that followed was only slightly marred by Leonard Prescott's cough. "As a fallen woman she was forced to marry him," he said.

"Rumor has it she is expecting his child," added Harland Moseby.

"And from whom did you hear this, gentlemen?" Arthur had regained his cool.

"The Duke of Royston," said Thuxton. "He claims he heard it from Lady Richmond."

The silence became an eerie buzzing in Joseph's ears.

"Royston said you and Mr. Phillips have been at odds since the death of Lady Henrietta," Thuxton continued. "That the rape of Lady Sophia was the only way a fellow of low birth knew how to gain leverage in such a situation."

The buzzing swelled to a roar, drowning out the murmurs and exclamations of incredulity whirring around him.

Geoffrey clamored for quiet in the room. "Gentlemen, please. We asked you all here so we could clear up these preposterous rumors."

"Preposterous, Peel? The Lady Sophia has been missing from her home for weeks."

Geoffrey raked his fingers through his hair. "Days, my lord. She's been in hiding for several days."

Thuxton's brow furrowed. "Hiding? Whatever do you mean?"

Geoffrey straightened. "Her parents have expressed a wish for Lady Sophia to marry the Duke of Royston."

"And what, pray tell, Peel, is the matter with that?"

"Everything is the matter with that, Lord Thuxton," Arthur said. He faced the room. "Unfortunately, gentlemen, the rumors of rape pertain to Royston himself, not to Mr. Phillips."

Thuxton blanched. "You had better be able to defend such a serious accusation, Petersham."

Arthur inhaled deeply, releasing the breath slowly. "We have evidence the duke brutally raped two servants."

"Rape?" Thuxton narrowed his eyes. "Are you sure such allegations were not spawned from the consciences of girls desperate to repair stained reputations?"

Arthur's fingers flexed, the sign he was girding his emotions. He wouldn't be able to answer without impolitic bitterness.

"The girls in question, Lord Thuxton, were beaten in the course of the crime," Geoffrey said.

"Yet they allowed it to happen. That implies consent."

Geoffrey's lips thinned. "I will not argue the particulars of a legal anachronism, Lord Thuxton. But that is not the worst of the duke's offenses. He attacked the unmarried daughter of a peer earlier this Season. Her injuries took two weeks to heal."

Silence once again weighed heavily in the room.

"Was this witnessed?" Thuxton asked, greatly subdued.

"Yes," Geoffrey answered, holding the earl's gaze.

Thuxton stared back. "The girl's father has every right to press charges."

"The girl's father does not want the scandal," Geoffrey said pointedly. "You yourselves see how Royston can turn a situation around to his favor, regardless of the truth."

Thuxton colored. "I want to see Lady Sophia. I want to question her myself." He turned to Arthur. "Do you know where your sister is, Petersham?"

"Yes, my lord, I do. She is here."

Joseph started but Arthur flashed an admonishing glare. "Wittering, please call down Lady Sophia."

"Yes, sir."

Geoffrey sidled up to Joseph as a murmur spread like a wave across the room.

"Thuxton is a longtime friend of the family's. He's known Sophie since she was a child. He'll be gentle."

"They're putting her on trial, Geoff. I don't like it. She's not the villain in this affair."

"I don't like it either," Geoffrey grumbled. "I'm thinking as quickly as I can."

The room fell silent as Sophia entered, wearing an austere, pale-mauve dress, the two-tiered skirt cleverly adding volume to hide any signs of pregnancy, the exquisitely tailored silk with lace and fringe declaring the lady had suffered no change in circumstance and still held her position as a daughter of the ton. Arthur took her hand and led her across the carpet, the susurration of her skirts punctuated by murmured greetings to the men she passed. He offered a chair vacated by a stunned viscount, then took his place at her side. Anna had accompanied her mistress, remaining near the door, averting her eyes from Geoffrey's furtive attentions.

The consummate young lady of society, Sophia sat with a dignified air. She scanned the faces of the occupants of the room, nodding as she caught a familiar eye, her face registering no emotion.

Until she saw him.

Their eyes met and not for the life of him could Joseph control the grin that spread across his face or the flush that crept up the back of his neck. The color rose in her cheeks, plumped from her own smile, her lips twisting in a vain effort to maintain her earlier solemnity. Finally she allowed herself the freedom to express her joy then quickly looked down at her hands.

Thuxton approached. "Lady Sophia, you are looking well."

"Thank you, my lord."

"In fact I might say you look almost glowing."

"You are kind to say such a thing, Lord Thuxton."

The earl cleared his throat. "You see, we had heard rumors that you had been abducted—"

She gaped. Her hand flew to her mouth.

"And abused by a certain man who is known to you—"

"Oh, God, no." Sophia grabbed Arthur's arm.

Joseph's heart clenched. Geoffrey placed a warning hand on his shoulder.

"The consequences of which threaten Harwell and Company. We need to know the truth, Lady Sophia."

The poise broke and tears streamed down Sophia's face. Arthur knelt at her side and offered his handkerchief.

"Arthur, do I have to?" she asked quietly.

"Yes, my lady," answered Thuxton.

The cad.

She sucked in a sob. "It was at the Wrexham ball—"

Shit. Alarm spiked Joseph's gut, panic prickled every pore. They hadn't meant *that*. Arthur should have told her. She should never have to relive that night.

Geoffrey grabbed his arm. Joseph slumped against the wall. He had been ready to go to her aid.

Thuxton gawked. "At the Wrexhams'? Why, that was months ago."

"I didn't want to go with him but he forced me." She looked at Arthur. "Please don't make me say it."

Her entreaty broke the stunned silence of the drawing room. Joseph closed his eyes at the desperation in her voice. There was no way to regroup. She would have to move forward with the story she was about to tell.

"No, no, sweet. They just want to know who." Arthur's voice shook. "There have been rumors about who attacked you."

"Someone other than the duke?"

Gasps and murmurs filled the room.

"Which duke, Lady Sophia?" Thuxton asked gently.

"The Duke of Royston, my lord," she quavered.

The murmurs grew louder.

Thuxton colored. "That is not the name we have heard, my lady."

Sophia looked at Arthur with a crinkled brow. "I don't understand."

Thuxton placed his hand on her shoulder. "We heard that another man attacked you, my lady. Not the duke. I see we have been misled." He paced before her, staring at the carpet, then stopped. "Tell me, my lady, what is your relationship with Joseph Phillips?"

She glanced at Arthur, who nodded.

"I am his wife, my lord."

Sharp exclamations punctuated the growing babble.

"And when did this occur?"

"Last week, my lord."

"Was this of your own choosing?"

She tilted her head and bit her lower lip. "Are you asking if I had my father's permission?"

"Ah, no. I am asking if you were coerced in any way."

"Well yes, in a way—"

Shit. Joseph held his breath.

"Because despite the duke's insult my parents insisted on our marriage. Such a fate was abhorrent to me. I would have preferred a longer courtship with Jo—Mr. Phillips and a grand wedding but time was of the essence."

She looked his way, hope in her eyes. He exhaled.

Prescott coughed again. "It's obvious, Thuxton, there is a great affection between the two."

"The rumors appear to be just that, rumors," added Moseby.

Thuxton sighed and shook his head. "It appears we owe you an apology, Mr. Phillips," he said.

Everyone present turned to Joseph.

"Say something, damn it," Geoffrey muttered under his breath.

Joseph straightened, steadying himself against the anger and frustration boiling within. "It is unfortunate that Lady Sophia had to be subjected to such interrogation." All eyes were on him as he traversed the length of the room toward her. "It is equally unfortunate that our business associates did not trust my actions and instead relied on the slander of a known adversary." He took her hand in his and kissed it, raising the color in her cheeks once again. Still holding her hand, he turned to face the room. "I understand, gentlemen, in your eyes I am not only a foreigner but of low birth. It must be shocking that Lady Sophia has chosen thusly. How can I earn your trust?"

Thuxton approached. Sophia gripped more tightly.

The earl bowed. "I humbly offer my congratulations, Mr. and Mrs. Phillips."

The room erupted in cheers and applause. Joseph glanced sidelong at a relieved Arthur then toward the door at Geoffrey.

But Geoffrey's face was twisted in worry as he watched a flustered Anna scurry from the room.

Anna could watch the heart-wrenching romance no longer. She'd quietly opened the drawing room door and had left as quickly as she could, hoping Geoffrey wouldn't notice.

Once in the hall she closed her eyes and drew in a breath. If only it were as simple as Mr. Phillips made it seem.

She rucked up her skirts and scurried up the cramped staircase to the servants' floor, taking the steps two by two, slowing as she reached the fourth-floor landing.

"It's a damn good thing my legs are longer than yours. I don't think I would have caught up with you otherwise."

She turned around at his voice. Geoffrey stood on the landing below, looking up at her with a smile and a crinkled brow, the door ajar behind him. She had hoped he wouldn't think to take the servants' stairs.

"It's not going to work," she said.

"What isn't?"

"Us."

"Us? And why is that?"

"He's exotic, foreign. A man. It's acceptable. I'm a servant in their own country. If I were exotic, they would accept me."

Geoffrey drew his hands over his face. "Anna, darling, they were concerned about his integrity. Not his social standing."

"And if the duke spreads rumors about me?"

He stared at her. "He wouldn't dare."

"Whom would they believe?"

He drew a breath through his teeth. "Darling, can we talk about this somewhere else?"

She motioned for him to join her then led him down the hall to her room. When they stepped inside, she measured his reaction to the modest space.

"What a cozy abode," he said, taking it in with a gentle smile.

"Yes, the governess' quarters. Right next to the nursery. That's mine, too. I read by the fire in there." It *was* cozy. She turned the lock and leaned against the door with an exhale of satisfaction.

The bed loomed large against the wall, seemingly occupying most of the room. She indicated a chair by the fireplace and he sat, staring at his feet as he stretched out his legs along the floor. She paced the rag rug by the hearth, trying hard not to look at the bed.

"Darling," he began, "Joseph will be staying in London for Sophia's sake. Arthur doesn't want her to travel. Wants her under his care." He looked at her. "They need someone to go to New York to set up the American segment of the business. We discussed the matter and the task falls to me."

The air was sucked out of her lungs, dizzying her. "When?"

"End of September."

"So soon?"

"I need to be settled before winter."

"Yes, I understand."

"Anna," he said quietly, staring at his shoes, "I won't take a lover in New York."

She hardly knew what he meant. "Oh?"

"No. I intend for my wife to be at my side."

The dizziness spun into a dream. She stood still, trying to feel her feet on the floor.

He rose and went to her, taking both her hands in his. "As Sophie said, I would have preferred a longer courtship but time is of the essence."

America. "Scotland was the farthest I've ever been from home."

"It will just be until Joseph is able to leave here, after the baby is born. Maybe until next spring or early summer. I'm to negotiate the legal aspects of setting up a company in America, find a house for the Phillipses, that sort of thing."

"You won't remain there then."

"No." His gaze was intense. "Unless you feel otherwise. You'll be Mrs. Peel. No one will know you were a servant." He placed his hands on her shoulders. "He can't touch you overseas. Royston has neither the funds nor the social connections to do any damage in America."

Safe. With Geoffrey she was safe. She squeezed her eyes shut to dam the tears but they spilled through her lashes.

"Darling."

His arms went about her, hugging her closely, the steady, strong rhythm of his heart filling her ear.

She looped her hands around his neck, drawing him down to her, kissing him, he kissing her back tentatively, her whimper releasing his passions, his mouth and tongue distracting her as he tugged at the buttons of her dress. She started on his waistcoat, his shirt, the waistband of his trousers—

"No. Not yet."

He led her to the chair before the hearth. "Sit," he said. He removed his jacket and knelt before her.

He bunched up her skirts over her knees then took her right foot in his hand. He untied and loosened the lacing of her short boot and eased it off, then repeated the action with the other shoe. He cupped one unshod foot in a palm and drew his other hand up her calf, over her knee, his light caress thrilling, shooting shivers up her spine. He untied her garter, slowly stripped off her stocking, stroking gently along the way.

Anna flinched. "It tickles," she giggled.

He smiled and proceeded to undress her other leg. He urged her thighs open, grabbed underneath and drew her to him. She slumped in the chair, pushing down her skirts for a view of him. He licked his lips as he untied the string of her drawers to loosen the garment and slip it off.

And then he pressed his mouth to her sex.

Anna yelped in surprise then gasped at the new sensation. His tongue slid through her nether lips as it had with her mouth, opening her to his invasion. She bucked up, grabbing the arms of the chair for purchase, but he held her steady, his hands cupping her butt, tilting her to him. He sucked on her clit, swirling his tongue over the nub until her gasp became moans, became cries, her head lolling, her mind spinning, reaching the familiar peak in a new and glorious fashion.

"Geoffrey!"

He hummed his pleasure against her sensitive flesh. He once again drew his tongue through her, delving into her quim, pressing into her more fully to mimic a lover's thrusts.

She had never wanted a man so much.

"Geoffrey, please. Please," she moaned, hoping he understood, hoping he felt the same.

He chuckled, the reverberations resounding in her core. He sat back on his heels, his mouth wet and smiling. She could do nothing but stare in incredulity, panting from the sensual exertions.

He held out his hand and she took it. He easily lifted her from the chair then proceeded to unbutton, untie and unhook her garments. She watched, fascinated.

"I've never been undressed before."

"There appear to be many firsts this afternoon."

She stood before him naked, unashamed as the expression on his face was one of awe and admiration not unbridled lust. Her offer to help him undress was met with a polite rebuff, proving he was not a man who relied on his valet to do menial tasks. He could take care of himself and he was asking to take care of her.

The last article of clothing dropped to the floor revealing the nude man, a fine figure displaying an athleticism belied by his profession. Muscled shoulders curved to thick arms, a sculpted chest, tapering to his slim waist and hips. The fine brown hair of his chest narrowed its path down his abdomen, curling densely at his groin, his desire apparent from his prick erect with anticipation.

She caught his twinkling eyes observing her observing him.

"You have to want this, Anna."

"Oh, Geoffrey." She flung herself into his arms. "I want this, believe me I want this."

He grasped her hand and led her to the bed, under the covers taking his place alongside. He stroked gently, exploring, his fingers delving intimately. He moved on top, spread her legs with his thighs, slid his cock in the folds of her wetness. She swallowed hard.

He pushed inside, his face twisting in wonderment and joy. "Anna, my Anna."

He thrust in and pulled out, bending over to kiss her neck, she unsure where to touch, as she wanted to touch him everywhere. The hair of his legs brushed the tender flesh of her inner thighs. She opened for him, wrapped her legs around his hips, the feel of skin against skin mesmerizing in its sensuality.

His hair fell over his forehead and a wicked glint shone in his eye.

"Darling, I fear you have me undone."

He was at his crisis, the moment two would become one.

"Spend inside me."

He held her gaze as he pounded toward his culmination then lifted his face to heaven, his eyes screwed shut in ecstasy, and let out a growl. The heat of his seed sparked her climax. She clenched around him and he juddered inside her once more.

He held himself aloft for only a moment before he relaxed on top of her. She clung to him, tears of joy and relief streaming down the sides of her face.

He rolled to her side, nuzzled against her neck. "Does this mean we are engaged, Miss Colney?"

She laughed. "I believe so, Mr. Peel."

Sophia had spent the last half hour exchanging mumbled pleasantries with mortified business associates of *Harwell & Co.*, maintaining her composure, smiling and laughing at poor attempts at levity. Now an annoying stiffness twinged all the way from her low back to a point between her eyes.

At least she had garnered a few more promises of financing from amongst those who had previously only expressed keen interest in the business. Apparently insulting the daughter of a marquess was enough to rile them to economic action.

Joseph remained standing behind her throughout, his hand on her shoulder while she sat as if she was the queen presiding over a presentation at court. Now the men had left and Joseph knelt at her side.

"How do you feel, love?"

"Tired." She sighed. She wanted to stretch out and take a nap.

He rubbed her hands between his. "You did well, Sophie. Too well. See, they had thought I was the one who had abducted and abused you. They just needed to hear it wasn't me. But now they know the true depths of the villainy of Royston."

Tears spiked in her eyes. "You mean I said the wrong thing?"

"No, darling, you said the right thing. I admire your courage to do so. It was very, very brave." He kissed her palm.

"Now that the others have left, gentlemen, I have a proposition."

Lord Thuxton's voice boomed in the quiet drawing room, the only other sounds coming from Wittering and a maid gathering teacups and plates. The earl glanced around.

"Where's Peel? He needs to be here."

"He's—" Joseph started. He thinned his lips. "Wittering, please tell Mr. Peel to join us when you see him."

"Very good, Mr. Phillips." The butler exited, ushering the maid out.

"Where's Geoffrey?" Sophia whispered.

Anna, Joseph mouthed.

Sophia stifled a grin.

"What's this about, Thuxton?" Arthur was wary.

"Let's repair to this cozy corner, Petersham, shall we?" Thuxton indicated a corner by the window where a day bed was set near a couple of overstuffed chairs. "Mrs. Phillips." He held out his hand and helped her up.

The earl led Sophia to the day bed. "We're practically family," he said. "Why don't you put your feet up?" His eyes flashed with a knowing twinkle. "How far along, Sophie?" he asked gently.

She flushed. "Around two months, my lord." She stretched out, grateful for the opportunity for familiarity.

"Ah, well, it's none of my business, really, but I suspected. I offer my heartfelt congratulations." He nodded to Joseph. "To you both."

"Thank you." Joseph moved a chair alongside her and sat.

The door flew open and Geoffrey came in, flushed and slightly disheveled. "They've all gone?"

"Mr. Peel, please join us."

Geoffrey sauntered over and took a seat next to Arthur, glancing at him with raised brows. Arthur shrugged.

Lord Thuxton cleared his throat. "Gentlemen, and Sophia," he nodded to her, "I've had my suspicions about Royston for quite some time. Rumors of abused servants and shop girls abound. But the peerage has its privileges, both legal and psychological, making it difficult to defeat a duke." He looked at her, sadness in his eyes. "I've known you since you were a child, Sophie. I can't let this outrage go unpunished." He glanced at the others. "I have a plan to destroy Royston. It's rather unconscionable really." He met her gaze. "He's your villain, Sophie, what say you?"

"Not just me, my lord. He's been a villain to each one of us."

Arthur stood and walked to the window. Geoffrey shifted in his chair.

"All right then." Lord Thuxton thinned his lips. "We have few options to pursue. Even if Royston were not a duke, an attempt to convict him of rape would be a harrowing experience for his victims. As a duke, he would be tried in the House of Lords and the peers would most likely find in his favor."

"There's only ever been one trial for rape in Lords," grumbled Geoffrey, "and that was over two hundred years ago."

Sophia hesitated a moment. "What about murder?"

"Murder?" Lord Thuxton raised his brows. "Is there evidence?"

Sophia tugged at her skirts and glanced at Arthur.

"No," Arthur said with annoyance.

Lord Thuxton shook his head. "And we must be careful of what we say in public so as to avoid any criminal charges of slander."

"*Scandalum magnatum*?" Geoffrey snorted. "That law is obsolete."

"Trust me—Royston knows more about his rights as a peer than most lawyers. If an ancient law is still valid, he will seek to be shielded by it." Lord Thuxton paced pensively. "As I said, we have few recourses to defeat Royston. Two will be most effective." He glanced around at his audience. "Ostracism and financial ruin."

Arthur narrowed his eyes. "Get him expelled from the Merchants and Industry Club?"

Lord Thuxton smiled. "A task which will be fairly easy as he hasn't paid his dues in years, as I understand. The other is a bit more complicated." He drew in a deep breath. "I have a friend from university days. Viscount Oakham. He's a cheat and a scoundrel. When one is twenty those characteristics attract. When one is nearing fifty and has developed scruples, such antics are considered disgraceful. Until one realizes how useful they can be."

Lord Thuxton gripped the back of a chair and leaned in. "I won't invest in anything he does despite his reputation for garnering vast sums with his successes. What most don't know is that the sum of his gains equals the sum of his losses, rendering one, at best, right where one was to begin with. Some, however, end up deeply in debt. He seems to thrive on such destruction."

"And you still call him 'friend'?" Arthur asked in astonishment.

"I do." He chuckled. "We have a past. Don't worry—he has no hold over me. Some friendships are simply based on longevity. You'll see." He winked. "If anything, Oakham is beholden to me. He follows my advice to his great advantage and has become a very wealthy man. He'll help us."

"What do you have in mind?" asked Geoffrey.

"Oakham owns a railway in the States." He turned to Joseph. "In your state of Ohio, the Ohio Short Line. He needed a canal for a right-of-way so he formed another company, the Cleveland Canal Company, and purchased a canal under this name. He's owner of record for the canal but the railway is untraceable to him."

"Is that illegal?" Sophia asked.

"No," Geoffrey answered. "We'll be doing something similar. It just depends on what one's goals are with such an arrangement."

"Precisely," said Lord Thuxton. "Oakham needs financing to fill in the canal and build his railway. Cleveland Canal was operating at a loss when he purchased it. So it would seem he would simply bankrupt the canal company and use financing via his rail company for his construction. However, he had a better idea.

"East of his canal, the Erie Canal is still viable, still profitable. He wanted Cleveland Canal to appear profitable as well. So Ohio Short Line secretly loaned Cleveland Canal vast sums of money. He's been showing these accounts to potential investors with stories about the success of the Erie Canal, along with false drawings of plans to extend the Cleveland Canal. The fools are falling for it."

"Royston?" Arthur asked.

"Not yet. But that's the plan."

"So how does this hurt the duke?" Sophia was keeping up but just barely.

"Eventually Oakham's railway will call in the loans from Oakham's canal. Some of the money will have already been spent so they won't have the money to cover the payment. Cleveland Canal will be bankrupted and its assets forfeited to Ohio Short Line."

"And as owner of the railway Oakham walks away with the money provided by the canal investors." Geoffrey seemed impressed.

Joseph snorted. "Anyone who knows anything about transportation in the States will see right through this. The canals are slowly dying. No one is extending them."

"Yes, of course," Lord Thuxton agreed. "The savvy investor will simply walk away. The novice investor only knows America as the land of unending wealth."

"Royston may be stupid but he's no novice," said Arthur.

"He's easily swayed, Petersham." Lord Thuxton paced slowly. "Royston has two weaknesses—he's mired in the past to such an extent he despises modernity, and he actively invests contrary to whatever I do. If I get word out that I won't invest in Cleveland Canal, Royston will, once approached by Oakham. Plus the investment is attractive in that it involves a relic of history."

It seemed like quite a bit of effort for little gain. "So he loses money, my lord," Sophia said. "How does this destroy the duke?"

Lord Thuxton smiled weakly. "Royston is obsessed with money. To not have any is a weakness, perhaps even a threat to his manhood. Oakham will require an overwhelming contribution when he spouts his seductive promise of riches." He sighed. "It is no match for what he has done to you, Mrs. Phillips. But it's the best I can do."

"I suspect he's blackmailing my father," Arthur said. "If he is, he'll still acquire an income from that."

"Blackmail?" Lord Thuxton exclaimed. "What's his game? He's already tried to ruin Sophie with slander."

"To be honest I don't know."

"Papa is constantly loaning him carriages and such," Sophia added.

"Ah…" Lord Thuxton steepled his hands under his chin. "I'll have a talk with Richmond. If there is blackmail involved, we'll work something out where he ostensibly invests in the canal to reduce his payments. If it is misplaced generosity, I'll give him a piece of my mind."

Joseph took her hand. "If Sophia allows the deceit, I'm all for it. I don't want any of it traced back to us, though."

"It won't be. I'll make sure of it." The earl turned to her. "What say you, Mrs. Phillips?"

Was it really the best that could be done? Ruining his pride in exchange for his assault on her, on Anna, on countless others, the murder of Henny?

She sighed. "Yes, Lord Thuxton. Please do your worst."

Sophia offered apologies as she took her leave while Lord Thuxton stayed to chat with the men. Once in her room she rang for Anna then stretched out on her bed in relief.

Anna entered directly.

Sophia patted the mattress at her side. "Geoffrey is a lucky man."

Anna blushed crimson as her hand flew to her mouth. "Everyone knows, don't they?" She sat on the bed. "Oh, I am mortified."

Sophia grinned. "No. Only Joseph noticed his absence. But that's not why I called for you." She slowly drew in a breath. "Anna, do you know the Duke of Royston's valet?"

Anna paled. "Jasper? Not very well. Just from working below stairs at Harwell Hall."

"From your brief association could you ascertain his estimation of the duke?"

Anna shook her head with a heavy sigh. "Poor Jasper has a sturdy streak of tolerance. He seemed to abhor the duke. All the servants did."

"How difficult would it be for you to get something to Jasper? An object that might implicate the duke in a crime he claims never happened? Of course you should not put yourself in any danger."

Anna lifted a brow as if comprehending. "I can manage such a task, my lady."

Sophia smiled. "Good. First I'll tell you my plan, then you can tell me all about Geoffrey."

CHAPTER TWENTY-THREE

Arthur crumpled the invitation to a private interview with his father. Not a message scratched in Father's own hand, no, but a formal request written by Billings addressed to "Lord Petersham" no less. He threw the missive in the library fire. They would never truly be father and son if this was any indication of Father's familial affections.

He should have walked but he took his brougham instead. The drive was not nearly long enough to cool his indignation. He arrived still seething. Billings, the ever-stalwart secretary, ignored his curt tone and thinned lips as he led him into the somber study.

"How can I be of service, my lord marquess?" Arthur said snidely.

"Don't start, Arthur. I've got Royston watching me. I had to use my general correspondence as a safeguard."

"Oh? Have you changed your mind?"

"Not about Sophie, no. I still think what she did was…" He threw his hands in the air. "Ill-advised."

Arthur kept his mouth shut. If they were ever to reconcile, it would be best to listen.

"He's got me. He's blackmailing me down to the very farthing." He slumped into a visitor's chair. "I'm ruined."

Arthur took the chair opposite. "If it's money you wanted to talk about, I can certainly help."

Father offered a weak smile. "I've heard your scheme is moving ahead. Not one of your investors defected due to the scandal."

"I tell you this in the strictest confidence, Father. We explained the situation truthfully and no one backed out. We're not profitable just yet but if you need money—"

"No. Royston is calculating enough to not bleed me dry. More than likely I will have to keep paying for his lavish lifestyle until the end of my days."

The irony was not lost on Arthur. "And had you married Sophie to that man she would have had to endure your burden until the end of hers."

"She's young. She would have outlived him."

Arthur stood and paced the carpet. "Henny did not."

Dubiousness glazed his father's eyes then melted into realization. "He would not have destroyed that which was truly his. That's why he stopped at mere rumor where it concerned you."

"'Stopped at mere rumor'? He could have ruined me."

"But he did not. He knows you're clever and diplomatic enough to extricate yourself from a difficult situation. He is potently aware that I raised you properly no matter what your circumstances of birth."

Arthur rounded on him. "My what?" And then Father's words from the week before sank in. *You are no son of mine.* "What the hell is this about, Father?"

"Matilda."

"Mother?"

"And Royston."

Mother and Royston? Arthur's gut churned. "What about them?" he asked icily.

"Royston claims you are his son. Your mother, of course, denies it."

Arthur staggered backward, falling against the desk. "No. God, no."

"And there, I've said it." Realization dissolved into tears.

Arthur had never seen Father—his father, he was absolutely certain—cry.

"Yes," Father croaked. "I've been a fool. I was fond of your mother at the time, she was—and is—a fine companion. I was never 'in love' with her, as you children today feel is so important for a marriage. Such sentiment was not important for us. The partnership was primary. So when she developed a fascination with Royston— who was not a duke at the time, mind you, only the heir—I let her. That is the unspoken rule when one marries for duty. I didn't know him at the time—I didn't know his tastes, his predilections. I also did not know my own wife's predilections." He drew in a shuddering breath. "I've since adopted those tastes to keep her from straying again."

"Father, you don't need to tell me such things."

"Yes I do," he bellowed, the deep lines of his forehead twisted. "The affair was about twenty-five years ago."

Arthur stared at him incredulously.

"Yes, your mother and I did have relations at the time. We were both young and it is natural for young people to be intimate. But we had been married for a little over a year and had not had a full life in the bedroom. Matilda met Royston—Giles, as she called him then—at a party. He was an older man, in her eyes a sophisticated man, a handsome stranger who was paying her mind and she fell head over heels for him. After that our own intimacy grew as he was riling up her passions as I had never done. She was insatiable."

Arthur really did not want to hear *that* about his own mother.

"And then she became with child. Royston realized she was no longer his plaything. She was fully my responsibility. So he left. When you were born I could barely look at you." His father met his eyes. "I can barely stand your presence now."

Arthur stood frozen. No wonder the man before him had never been a good father. "I am not his son," he spat. "I am not Royston's son. Can't you see that?" They needed a mirror.

The entryway, where women checked their bonnets.

He grabbed Father's arm, hauling him out of his chair, out of the study, past a stunned Billings and frightened servants to the entryway, stopping before the enormous mirror that hung above the hall table. He wrapped his arm around Father's shoulder and drew his face alongside. Father averted his eyes.

"Look at me. At us."

Father reluctantly stared at their reflection.

"I am your son, Arthur Harwell, the one who is your heir, who will one day be what you are now, the Marquess of Richmond, who, until that time, is graced by courtesy with your title Earl of Petersham. Can you not see this?"

Father stared at Arthur's brown hair then his own faded with gray. He studied their eyes, both rounded pairs set with greenish brown irises, Arthur's perhaps a bit more green like Mother's, separated by the same broad bridge. His gaze trailed down his nose, the twin of Arthur's except with a tiny quirk of the tip to one side then arrived at the mouth, a wide slash with neither upper nor lower lip too generous. Father's complexion was uneven, his skin sagged with lines of age and worry, his lashes still damp from tears.

"Tell me you see a likeness, Father."

"Arthur, please—"

"And if you do not believe this reflection, you may gaze upon the faces of our illustrious ancestors. I'm certain you will see my own image painted there."

Father pulled away. "But why do you insult our family, first with Sophia and that man and now with threats to end the title? My son would have respect for his heritage."

"You have never treated me as your son, Father."

The marquess stared at him through narrowed eyes. "No. I will admit I did not." The lines on his face softened as he sighed.

"You don't need to suffer his blackmail anymore. Tell him you have realized I am your son and he holds no sway over you."

"He would still spread rumors to cast doubt."

"We would both deny them."

"Ah, but then he would expose Matilda."

"He would expose that the Marchioness of Richmond had an affair when she was a young girl of twenty?"

Father held his gaze. "He would expose that the Marchioness of Richmond enjoys being tied up, whipped, and fucked in the arse."

"Good God." Arthur's head spun.

"Whatever you do, don't tell Sophia."

Arthur shook his head in grim astonishment. "No. Of course I won't." He grabbed his hat from the hall stand. "Let me at least invest something for you."

"No. I won't be part of that. He'll know and raise his fee for continued silence."

"All right," Arthur conceded. Of course Father could not prevent him from secretly investing in the name of the Marquess of Richmond. "Sophie misses you. She misses her papa."

Father's eyes reddened, the corners pooled with tears. "I never wanted to hurt her. You must believe that. Duty compelled me, Arthur, not cruelty."

Arthur settled his hat on his head. "Know that she's happy now, Papa."

Arthur nodded his goodbye, his final image of his father sobbing into his handkerchief.

CHAPTER TWENTY-FOUR

London, 22 March 1861

Joseph checked in with the aged concierge at the Merchants and Industry Club, unable to stand still as the man dragged a frail finger slowly down the roster of expected guests.

Arthur dashed into the lobby from the main club room and grabbed his arm, shooting the concierge an apologetic grin. He led Joseph into the smoky, oak-paneled room.

"This had better be important, Arthur. My wife is about to give birth any moment now."

"I know, I know. Thuxton's asked for your presence."

"Thuxton?" Joseph arched a brow.

"Yes. Also I have great news from Geoffrey. Just follow my lead."

Business. Always business. Yet today a not-unwelcome distraction from the stress of imminent fatherhood. "O.K."

Arthur smiled and waved overtly at Thuxton, who waved back from across the room, Leonard Prescott and Harland Moseby at his side. Everyone present—well anyone not with his nose in a newspaper or snoring in a too-comfortable chair—knew the Earl of Petersham and the Earl of Thuxton were meeting and had invited the man who had scandalously married Petersham's sister.

Everyone…including the Duke of Royston.

Royston sat in a leather club chair, chewing on a cigar and loudly turning the pages of the *Cleveland Canal Company Annual Report 1859-1860*, the cover prominently displayed, each rustle of paper accented with snorts and chuckles. Otherwise the room was, as per usual, rather dull and quiet.

"Ah, Phillips." Thuxton shook his hand. "Glad you could join us. I've just heard of your great success and I wanted to congratulate you before your departure for America." He spoke in his normal conversational tone, which resounded in the hushed room.

Joseph glanced at Arthur, who offered an encouraging nod. "Thank you, my lord."

"And Lady Sophia…is she well?"

Royston stopped turning pages.

Joseph understood. "She is very well indeed. We are excitedly awaiting the birth of our child."

"Splendid," Thuxton said with far too much enthusiasm.

Several club members looked up.

"Petersham here tells me Peel has sent some good reports from New York."

Arthur grinned a genuine grin, which meant the news was truly good and not part of whatever game they were playing. "Peel says your designs are causing quite a stir. There's been some bidding for exclusive contracts. Apparently railroad magnates are impressed with the idea of artistry and elegance on a mere undercarriage."

Joseph's heart skipped a beat. "Sophie. That was Sophie's idea." He broke out in a grin bigger than Arthur's. He couldn't wait to tell her.

"The New York office of Harwell and Company is working diligently on all the contracts. Peel does mention the name of the company with the largest order." Arthur fumbled through his pockets, pulling out objects and pieces of paper, an obvious stall for dramatic effect. Finally he found Geoffrey's letter. "Ah, yes, here it is. The Ohio Short Line." The last was said with too much flair even for Arthur.

Joseph struggled to not look Royston's way.

"Ohio. That's one of your Middle Western states, is it not, Phillips?" Thuxton's voice boomed.

"Yes, my lord. Very prosperous agricultural area."

Royston stood and came toward them. Joseph's stomach churned.

"What's that you say? Ohio Short Line?" He brandished the report he had been perusing. "I'll have to have a word with them. Surely your artistic nonsense doesn't make the railway trains go any faster."

"Ah, Your Grace, so good of you to join us." Thuxton dripped charm. "I'm rather fond of Phillips' designs. Passengers will prefer to ride a railway with a touch of refinement, I'm sure."

Royston grunted.

"But if you have their ear, this Ohio Short Line will certainly listen to you. Are you a stockholder?"

"I'm a major investor in their subsidiary, the Cleveland Canal Company."

"Canals? That was a risky move."

"I rather think it was a wise one." He flipped through the pages of the report. "They increased their profits just this year."

Joseph and Arthur remained silent during the exchange. Thuxton was clearly running the show.

Thuxton placed his hand on Arthur's shoulder. "Well, Petersham, perhaps you better telegraph Peel to hold off on that Ohio Short Line order."

Arthur nodded and was about to speak when a club errand-boy called out.

"Your Grace." The boy approached and presented dispatches on a silver tray.

Royston picked up the envelope on top. "What's this?" he asked unpleasantly.

"A notice, Your Grace, that your membership dues are in arrears and credit is no longer extended."

Royston's eyes widened. He raised his hand as if to strike the boy. "You little—" He stopped abruptly.

"And, Your Grace," the boy continued with a tad less enthusiasm, "a telegram for you. From Ohio in America."

Royston took the card.

The boy hesitated. "Will you be wanting to send a reply, sir?"

"No. Go," Royston growled and turned his attention to the communique.

The boy exchanged a surreptitious glance with Thuxton before he left.

Suddenly Royston turned the darkest shade of crimson Joseph had ever seen on a man.

"Your Grace, is everything all right?" Thuxton oozed concern.

"Bloody bollocks," Royston rasped. "Bloody, bloody bollocks!" He crumpled the telegram then shoved it into his pocket. He slammed his book to the floor. "You." He turned to Joseph, their eyes meeting at the same level, and stabbed a finger at his chest. "You and your damn ideas."

Thuxton held his hand between them. "Your Grace, please. How, pray tell, has Phillips caused offense?"

Royston turned his wrath on Arthur. "Your father is ruined."

Arthur paled. "My father?"

Thuxton intervened again. "The Marquess of Richmond? What has happened, Your Grace?"

Sweat beaded on Royston's brow. "Bankrupt. Cleveland Canal is bankrupt and your father was an investor. Seems Ohio Short Line is to blame." He threw down his cigar and ground it out on top of the report. "You and your damn railroad."

"What a shame," Thuxton said coolly. "Surely there's a bit left over for club dues, no?"

Royston seized his handkerchief from his jacket pocket and whipped it up to mop his forehead, flinging an object into the air in the process. A metal object. Gold metal.

It fell to the carpet.

Silence descended as all inspected the precious item, a woman's gold necklace and locket.

Joseph stared, incredulous, horror and hatred prickling his skin.

"My God," Arthur gasped. "That's Sophie's. The one she lost the night of the Wrexham ball."

Thuxton picked up the locket. He opened the compartment with trembling fingers and studied the pictures inside. "Sophia and Lady Henrietta. So it's true." He glared at Royston. "You blackguard," he huffed. "You despicable cur. How could you?"

"Bloody scoundrel," Prescott snarled.

"Loathsome miscreant," Moseby muttered.

Royston paled. "I don't know where that came from—"

"*You fucking bastard.*" Joseph swung back and slammed his fist into Royston's nose, the crack of bone startling those seated to stand.

Royston wobbled and crumpled to the carpet, holding his face, blood streaming between his fingers. "You'll pay for that, Phillips! You'll pay!" He waved a bloodied hand in the air. "You all are witness to the assault of a peer!"

One by one, the club members filed out of the room. Thuxton turned his back to the scene, indicating with a quirk of his head those remaining do the same.

Joseph watched from the corner of his eye as two very large club guards grabbed Royston and dragged him from the room.

Thuxton draped his arms around Arthur's and Joseph's shoulders, drawing them into a huddle. "They'll throw him out the back door. For your peace of mind, gentlemen, I've posted a man to watch your house should the duke do something rash." He gave them both a quick squeeze. "Phillips, go home to your wife." He placed the necklace in Joseph's palm. "Petersham, telegraph Peel with my immeasurable thanks."

Joseph dashed out.

Sophie. He couldn't wait to see Sophie.

* * * * *

Southampton, 18 April 1861

Arthur inhaled the pungent, salty air then exhaled in satisfaction. It was a beautiful spring day. Perfect for setting sail or rather, setting off on a large steamship across the Atlantic.

He would really miss Sophia and Joseph. He would especially miss his perfect little niece, Helena.

As they packed for the journey Joseph had confided he was worried about the road ahead, that the business would fail or the business would be a ripping success and he wouldn't be able to handle all that money. Arthur had assured him Sophie would know precisely what to do with all that money. Besides, Geoffrey and Anna—Mr. and Mrs. Peel—had paved the way for them in New York. Geoffrey had set up the American subsidiary of their firm, had found a lovely brownstone in fashionable Greenwich Village a world away from the squalor of the port, had moved Joseph's parents there, and Anna was busy readying the place for the new baby. Feathering a nest came naturally to her as she was now with child. Joseph had beamed at the news. Fatherhood suited him. It would suit Geoffrey as well.

In the railway carriage to Southampton Joseph's excitement for the journey home had provoked a flirtatious giddiness on Sophia's part, prompting Arthur to take his darling Helena to the far corner of the private car while Sophia and Joseph trifled and teased. He ignored them. He wanted to spend a few moments with Helena, *his* Helena, for she was, most likely, going to be all he would ever know of children. Over the last few months he had struggled with his rash ultimatum to Father. But he would never find love as he had with Henny and without such love he could never bring children into the world.

Now before him loomed the gateway to the vast Atlantic. Waves broke against the pier as melancholia crashed over him. He had relied too much on Sophia, Joseph, and Helena for his happiness. Geoffrey and Anna would return, of course, but they would be busy with their own lives as a family. He had not seen his parents for months and was not likely to see them in the near future. He'd have to seek camaraderie in his club filled with dull men and a mistress who would want diamonds and God only knew what else to keep her legs spread and the conversation going on a regular basis.

He wasn't the only solitary figure gazing out at the sea. On the edge of the quay stood a woman, bent a little from age, dressed entirely in mourning, her black veil covering her face, obscuring her view of the port from whence her lover, a soldier heading to the Peninsular Wars, had been ripped from her life.

Arthur chuckled to himself. His despondency had made him maudlin.

The woman turned and saw him. She stilled a moment, hesitating, thinking, and then came toward him.

And when she got close enough for him to see beyond the veil he recognized his mother.

She made no bold movements, did not rush to take him into her arms. She approached calmly, an action completely at odds with the emotion twisting her face and the tears streaming down her cheeks.

"Arthur," she said, her voice a hoarse whisper. She cleared her throat.

"Mother," he greeted in return, struggling against the lump welling in his own throat. "Is Father well?"

"Ah, yes, the mourning," she chortled. "Your father is fine. I'm incognito. I just wanted to see them, even if from afar. I was worried I would be too late. I'm not too late, am I?"

"No," he said with a smile. "You're early in fact. The ship doesn't leave for a couple of hours."

"Good." She glanced side to side. "Where is Sophia?"

"Over—"

"Don't point. Don't move. I don't want to cause a scene."

"You do want to see your grandchild, Mother, don't you?"

"Yes, dear. I do. Very, very much. But I came to tell you something first. Something I have to say to you in person. No letters and no one else who could hear."

A chill of foreboding crept up his spine. "Go ahead."

"I know what Harold told you and I know what he believes about you. All these years I have been telling him who you really are and he won't believe me."

"Who am I, Mother?"

"You are your father's son. You are the son of Harold Harwell, the Marquess of Richmond."

"And how can you be sure?" Arthur suddenly thought he might not want to know.

"Because Giles never spent inside me."

"Oh, God. Don't tell me such things," Arthur groaned.

"I will tell you and you will listen because you need to be convinced as well. Giles needed the violence to maintain his, well, his potency. But he couldn't control it. I became very handy with a birch rod, almost too good really. I could make him spend while he was spread-legged and doubled over a flogging bench. That's why I always went to your father afterward. Not because I was excessively lustful but because I was unsatisfied."

Arthur's head spun with disgust and fascination. "Did you not explain this to Father?"

"I did. But Giles sustained the fiction with lies and falsehoods, taunting Harold, comparing them, which one was the better lover, which one was man enough to father a child, to father a son. In the end Harold refused to believe me. His pride was hurt and he's carried a grudge for twenty-five years."

"He's still carrying it."

"No. Something you did made him think it all over. You were brilliant to make him look at you the way you did. He'd never really looked at you before. I kept telling him you have his eyes and nose. Now he is beginning to believe it. But now it is you who's hurt his pride, standing up to his decision to marry Sophie off to that monster, forcing him to give in to Royston's blackmail, refusing to give him an heir. I hate to think of how long it will take him to come around this time."

"Yet it seems you and Royston have equal cause to blackmail. You should be at a standoff really."

"Royston is demanding money not only to keep our affair and your supposed dubious parentage secret but to not perpetuate any more rumors about Sophie and Mr. Phillips. It is a lot of money but we can certainly afford it. Your father did something clever with Lord Thuxton and that American canal investment. We lost nothing while Royston lost virtually everything. He has no desire to bankrupt his only source of income."

"Surely his stubbornness with that investment has tarnished his reputation enough. Is he really worth the bother?"

"If I took Royston down, I would take myself and our family down right with him. I refuse to do that to you and Sophie. Or to my new grandchild."

"It's a girl."

Mother swallowed hard. "A girl?"

"Helena."

"Such a pretty name. Do you think I could see her?"

"Yes of course."

Arthur offered his arm. They walked casually, Mother's step uneven, quickening and slowing in fits and starts, never taking her eyes off Sophia and Joseph sitting on a bench, fussing over Helena. Joseph grinned and held the baby in his arms while Sophia trifled with her bonnet and booties, the perfect picture of domestic bliss.

Joseph saw them approach and said something to Sophia, who looked up. Shock and love filled her face at the sight of Mother. She ran to her with open arms.

"Mama, oh Mama, I'm so happy to see you." She pulled back. "But why the mourning? What has happened?"

"All is well at home. A woman traveling alone must have a disguise, my sweet child." She looked longingly at the baby in Joseph's arms. "May I see her?"

"Yes, my lady."

Mother took Helena, cradling her, gazing down at her, tears wetting her lashes. "She's beautiful." She rocked her gently. "Helena, my Helena."

"She is, Mama, she's yours. She must be part of your life, if you will allow it."

Mother's tears fell to her veil.

"She will be well cared for in New York. Joseph is an attentive father and a wonderful husband."

Helena made a gurgling sound and reached for Mother's veil.

"Lift it, Sophia."

Sophia lifted the veil. Mother beamed at her granddaughter and kissed her pudgy cheeks.

"Mama," Sophia choked. "I'm so sorry I hurt you and Papa. I never meant to do so. I did not disobey willfully."

Sophia fumbled in her purse but Arthur was quick with a handkerchief.

"I wish there was something I could do to show you I'm still your loving daughter."

"You've done it, Sophie. You've given me Helena." Mother turned to Joseph. "Make sure she's happy. Spoil her but not too much."

Joseph's lips curved upward. "Yes, my lady."

"She's part English, Mr. Phillips. I want her to know that."

Joseph nodded. "Of course."

"Your country is in rebellion, Mr. Phillips. I expect you to take care of my Sophie and my Helena."

"My parents and the Peels assure me we will be safe, my lady."

She turned to Sophia. "You must write me. Send your letters to Arthur until your father has swallowed his pride."

"Yes, Mama."

Mother kissed Helena on the tip of her nose. "And now I must take my leave." Her soft goodbye trembled with emotion as she handed Helena back to Sophia. She squeezed Arthur's hand. "Don't mention this to your father." She turned and walked away.

Sophia hugged Helena, nuzzling her cheek to cheek. "Arthur, I've hurt her terribly."

He put his arm around her. "You'll make up for it. You already have really. She sees how happy you are." He poked Helena in the stomach and she flailed her tiny arms with a squeal. "Time heals all wounds. You'll see."

He could only hope such a sentiment was true.

* * * * *

New York City, 7 May 1861

Sophia burrowed deeper against Joseph's chest as she cradled Helena in her arms on their bed. "My Helena, my beautiful Helena, the most beautiful girl in the world," she purred, kissing her tiny forehead.

Joseph chuckled. "Every mother says that, don't they?"

She smiled. "Yes, but in my case it's true."

He leaned over and kissed Helena's chubby cheek. "Yes it is. My Helena is indeed the most beautiful baby in the world because her mother is the most beautiful woman in the world."

"Oh stop." Sophia pushed him aside. "You'll crush her."

Joseph kissed her hair. "I'd like to be crushing you," he murmured. "Perhaps give Helena a brother." He gently stroked her unbound breast through her dressing gown.

She shot him a scowl. "Darling—"

But her protest was stopped by his mouth, ravenous from inattention. His tongue plunged inside her slowly, rhythmically, tempting her. She gave in only briefly then pulled back.

"I think you should visit a courtesan," she said blithely.

He chuckled. "I can't imagine anyone sucking my prick the way you do, my sweet."

"We should not be doing this in front of the baby," she scolded, unable to stop a smile from spreading on her lips.

"She won't know."

"Joseph! Surely you're joking?"

He laughed softly. "Yes, but only partly." He touched the tip of his nose to hers. "I miss you. I miss us." He pecked her lips then settled back against the headboard, pulling her and Helena alongside. He sighed. "Sophie," he said quietly, caressing her back. "I'm scared."

"Scared?" She looked up at him. "Darling, why?"

"It's always been just me. I don't need much. I always got by. My parents counseled to never rely on anyone but myself. And yet here I am, relying on the good graces of your brother and the money of a dozen men I barely know, and I have a wife and child to protect and care for. Just over a year ago I was a rash youth with some drawings and an idea."

Sophia sighed. "And I've never known such independence as you have. So I feel a bit of the opposite. New York is simply filled with possibilities. And it's exciting to be the wife of a very important businessman."

Joseph gave her a little squeeze.

She slid her hand inside his unbuttoned shirt. "When you were young if you got sick and couldn't work, your mother took care of you, right? And your father allowed you to sit at his table, even if you couldn't pay him rent that week?"

"Of course. My parents would do what they could."

"Because that's what family does. That is what they are supposed to do anyway." Papa had yet to contact her after the birth of his only grandchild. "Arthur is your brother now and Helena is his niece. We are a family. We rely on each other."

"Yes of course, love." His voice strained with emotion.

"I'm frightened, too. Frightened Papa will never forgive me for what I've done."

"If what you say about family is true, he will come around. He'll see what you did as benefiting the Harwell name."

Tears spiked her lashes. "I hope so," she murmured.

A quiet knock on the door roused them.

"Yes?" Sophia called.

Anna poked her head inside the room. "I'm not disturbing you, am I?"

"No, no, Mrs. Peel. Come in." She loved to call Anna by her married name, especially now she was with child.

She stood before them and held out her hands. "It's time for Helena's bath, Mrs. Phillips." Anna always reciprocated the honorific.

Joseph took Helena from Sophia and deftly laid her in Anna's arms. "And then bed?"

"Yes, Mr. Phillips. I'll put her to bed." She cradled Helena as if she were her own, cooing and kissing her as she left for the bath.

Sophia smiled. Anna was going to be a wonderful mother. "I wonder if Geoffrey will be as randy as you after Anna has her baby?"

Joseph guffawed. "Oh, probably."

"We should invite him to our bed in those first few weeks," she teased.

"You forget, madam, that they will have returned to England by then," he deflected.

"That's a shame, isn't it?"

He pulled her dressing gown open to reveal a breast, cupping and weighing its new fullness. "I'm not quite ready to share you again. Perhaps when our daughter is married."

"Or you leave me alone when you go out west."

A frown pulled at the corners of his mouth. "Sophie…"

"Darling, I'm not naive. You've said you've had lovers in St. Louis, in San Francisco. I don't expect you to be a monk when we're apart."

"I can try," he said with a whimper.

She laughed. "Like you tried to stay away from me? It didn't take long for you to ravish me at Harwell Hall."

"Your eagerness was far too seductive." He bent over her and took a nipple in his mouth, twisting his tongue over the tender peak.

She melted under the wet warmth. "A man of your lustful nature needs his outlets."

"And a woman of your lascivious temperament? I expect you to do the same." He sucked harder, swirling her into a state of sultry relaxation.

"Although with the baby I'll not have the time or the inclination."

Joseph lifted his head. "Unless of course it was Geoff."

"Of course," she said with a smirk and a lift of a brow.

He thinned his lips. "And how often is it that when I make love to you, Mrs. Phillips, you're thinking about Geoffrey Peel?" His rebuke held a devious edge, a tone he used when he wanted to play.

Sophia's skin prickled in anticipation. "Does it really matter whom I fantasize about when I'm in your arms?"

"You are very impertinent, madam. Perhaps you need a lesson in obedience to your husband."

With the strength of a stevedore and the nimbleness of a dancer he scooped her up in his thick arms and turned her over his lap. The bend at her hips cupped his massive thigh, the heat of his crotch like fire beneath her breasts. Above her his breathing grew labored as he slowly lifted the hem of her dressing gown, his fingers tickling the backs of her legs.

Her quim, already moist from his earlier attention to her breast, grew heavy with lust. It had been too long since the last time. She hoped he would be harsh.

He pulled the fabric to her waist, exposing her bottom to the air. She turned her head to see his gaze fall to the sight before him. He licked his lips audibly as his palm curved over the flesh of her buttocks.

"I seem to recall we made vows to one another." His touch was featherlight.

"Yes, sir."

He lifted his hand. "Do you remember what we said?"

"No, sir."

His hand came down hard. Sophia flinched before sighing in relief, her skin tingling, wanting more.

"Let me remind you, then."

"Please, sir."

"Matrimony was ordained as a remedy against the sin of fornication."

Smack.

"A wife promises to obey her husband."

Thwack. The burn smoldered deliciously.

"To serve him."

Whack, whack. He opened her legs a little wider, peeling apart the lips of her sticky and swollen sex.

"To love and honor him."

He struck at the base of her buttocks, the blow reverberating up her flexing cunt.

"To forsake all others."

Swat. Her breasts slid over his aroused cock straining against his trousers.

"And keep thee only unto him."

Slap. The hardest yet. Her buttocks would be pink by now.

He stroked her sore flesh with a light touch, drawing circles with his fingers, trailing spirals down the backs of her leg, to the softness between her thighs.

"But I too took such vows."

He inserted a finger in her wet passage, then two, languidly pushing in and pulling out.

"To love you."

She clenched around him with a gasp, surprised at the depths of her need.

"To honor you."

He withdrew his hand and grasped her by the hips. In one movement he lifted her off and positioned himself behind her.

"To comfort you."

He smoothed his palm against her buttocks then eased her legs farther apart to briefly tease her clit.

"To forsake all others."

The bed bounced gently. She turned her head and watched as he slid off his braces and pulled off his shirt then tugged at his fly. He held her gaze as he popped the buttons one by one with deliberate slowness.

"To keep you all to myself."

His cock bobbed free of his clothes. He grabbed it and positioned himself at her entrance.

"With my body I thee worship."

He slammed inside her, the force shoving her into the mattress, each thrust more savage than the last. She dipped her back to take him deeper, his sharp exhale the proof of his approbation. He repositioned, rising above her to drive into her with rough determination, his hips slapping her tender buttocks, his stones swinging into her clit. He had never been so savage, so rough, so deep, so utterly a part of her.

He snaked his hand around to slap her clit before he pressed the tender nub with a strong finger. She came with abandon, screaming into the mattress, her cunt squeezing him until he let loose his seed. He growled his satisfaction and gripped her hips cruelly, steadying her as he jerked every drop inside.

He bent over her, panting in her ear, his heart pounding into her back. She pushed him off to lie on the mattress, her legs and butt sore from his passion.

He stretched beside her and drew her to him, encircling her in his strong arms. As she nuzzled against him, the fine hairs of his chest tickled her cheek.

"Joseph," she said, spreading her fingers on his rippled torso. "It won't be like that with the others, will it?"

"No, love, it won't." He kissed her hair. "That is what makes what we have so special. Something so much more than a momentary pleasure."

The warmth of love coiled inside her. "As long as we both shall live."

EPILOGUE

London, 10 September 1879

Sophia stared at Helena poised in the lobby of St. George's church, Anna perfecting the position of her veil, while Anna's daughters, Molly and Lilly, stood at the ready to adjust her train and hand her the bouquet. Helena really was the most beautiful girl in the world, especially on this, her wedding day. Her dress was exquisite. The bodice, silk damask of the palest rose, was flawlessly fitted to her lovely figure. Three-quarter-length bell sleeves were trimmed in a froth of ivory French lace, while the ruched ivory satin underskirt was trimmed with gold fringe, the damask train trimmed in more lace and fringe. Sophia sighed, wishing she could have worn so elegant a dress when she was married. Helena looked every bit the perfect bride.

Joseph had spared no expense for the wedding and as a wealthy industrialist he was expected to provide a lavish affair. Both he and Sophia were determined to give their daughter the spectacle they never had, a ceremony and breakfast befitting the marriage of the granddaughter of a marquess to a handsome and honorable earl.

Tears wet her lashes. Everything had turned out fine as Joseph had said it would so many years ago. Including the much-longed-for reconciliation with Mama and Papa.

Over the course of eighteen years Mama had written when she could. Papa, though, had barely said a word. They had spent time with Helena—Sophia made sure of it—and Mama always gushed about how pretty she was, how intelligent. It was painfully obvious Papa wanted to get to know Helena better but pride kept him at bay.

And then Nicholas, the Earl of St. Albans, asked for Helena's hand in marriage. The title was old, older than the Marquessate of Richmond and the new earl promised to reinvigorate his estate and duties to crown and country. Papa suddenly had a change of heart.

"Sophie?"

Sophia turned to the sound of Mama's voice behind her. The moment their eyes met Sophia's stomach knotted with the pain of regret. She held out her hands and when Mama came forward regret melted into joy.

They hugged. "I'm here to give my granddaughter a good-luck kiss. We've only just got to know her and now she's being taken away."

Sophia took her arm to stroll to Helena. "I'm sure she'll want you to visit her at St. Albans."

"Grandmama." Helena's face brightened the moment she saw her grandmother.

Mama took her hands, not daring to muss the tulle veil. "You've become such a beautiful woman. I remember the day I held you in my arms when you were just a few weeks old. You were stunning even then."

"Oh, Grandmama. You'll spoil me with such flattery."

"I'm sure the earl will spoil you every day. Your Nicholas appears to be a wonderful young man. I hope he will make you happy, dear." She held out a hand to Sophia. "Like your father made your mother happy."

"Thank you, Grandmama."

"Now, my dear, I need to have a few words with your mother. But before I do I have something for you. A present." She reached into her purse and drew out a bracelet made of two curved bands of gold, a medallion etched with leaves and flowers holding the bands together at one end. "Something new. The design matches your earrings." She slid the medallion to widen the bands then placed the bracelet on Helena's wrist and tightened it closed.

Helena studied the bracelet with a smile of admiration. "It's lovely."

Mama once again took Helena's hands. "As are you. I'll see you at the breakfast." She gave Helena's hands a squeeze.

Sophia blinked back tears. She had never had a moment like that on her own wedding day. Her heartache was short-lived when Mama grabbed her arm and motioned toward a private corner.

"Sophia," she began soberly. "My dear, I've just had word and I wanted to let you know before any of your guests brought up the horrible subject. It's finally made the morning papers so someone is bound to have read it already."

"Read what, Mama?"

Mama looked her in the eye. "Royston is dead."

Sophia gasped. She had never wanted to hear that name again. The knot in her stomach tightened.

"Rumor has it a former servant killed him. A young girl. No one is speaking up and the staff he once had is scattered to the winds. There were no signs of violence, no blood. The official report says he died in his sleep, reeking of alcohol. Trouble is, Giles was never much of a drinker." She snorted a laugh. "He came to a pathetic end, living with only a man-of-all-work and a cook, and burning furniture for fuel."

Dead. She should feel glad. She felt nothing. Absolutely nothing.

"Your father received private word as he was still paying the duke's bills. He's not been the same since. He wrote to Arthur directly to make amends. He's been talking about the wedding like a giddy boy. And we'll be having a hunting ball once again. October. I expect to see you and your husband there."

Sophia smiled. "In a month? Well then perhaps I should alert you to my news."

"Oh?" Mama's brow crinkled in concern.

"Mama, I think I'm pregnant—"

Mama clapped her hand to her mouth.

"Well I'm pretty sure of it but it is too soon for an announcement. I've not even told Joseph yet." Sophia grinned at the excitement contorting Mama's expression. "And you are not to tell anyone on Helena's special day."

"I won't, I promise I won't." Mama pursed her lips in a vain attempt to quash a smile. "Oh, my dear. After all these years. Another grandchild." Mama threw her arms around Sophia.

The joy of Mama's touch warmed her. They should have hugged long ago. A mother's love was a precious gift. But she had to let go. "Mama, the wedding is about to start, you must find your seat."

Sophia sighed. Helena's special day was becoming the happiest day of *her* life.

"Oh, Nicky, so very handsome. Now, darling, I know you don't want to hear any of this—"

Joseph paused outside the door to the vestry at the sound of Lady Foxley-Graham's voice. It was rather rude to be listening in on private counsel between intimates but something compelled him to want to hear Lavinia's advice.

Probably because there had been no such counselor on his own wedding day.

"Whenever you quarrel or if Helena does something against your wishes or when she's simply in a bad mood because women often find themselves in a funk, you must remember this day, this moment and how you feel about her."

"Vinny—" Nicholas' voice held a note of abashment.

"At those times you must take a deep breath and remember she is the love of your life. And you are hers."

"Yes, Vinny."

Joseph grinned. Poor Nicholas was probably blushing beet red. It was time to save the lad.

He entered the vestry. As he had thought, Nicholas was looking askance as Lavinia brushed off imaginary specks from his jacket, his face a little flushed.

"It's all true, son," he said, winking at Lavinia.

"Mr. Phillips." Nicholas nodded.

Joseph smiled. Nicholas, the Earl of St. Albans, looked everything like a groom ought. Sleek, pressed trousers and jacket of fine black wool, a waistcoat of the same damask worn by Helena, white cravat with a subtle stripe. Until that moment Joseph hadn't realized how magnificently handsome the earl was. He was the precise man with whom he had imagined his daughter would spend her life.

While he himself was the man Sophia's father had feared.

The low tones of male conversation drifted into the room just before Bertram Atherley, the Viscount Ravensburgh—Nicholas' best man—and Arthur entered. Nicholas and the viscount hugged and exchanged a few quips as Arthur sidled up to Joseph.

"Almost time," Arthur said. "The bride—your daughter—is putting on her veil."

Lavinia started at that. "Oh. I must go to Helena. I've something for her."

As Lavinia left Arthur glared after her with a wolfish eye. "Where on earth have you been hiding *her*?"

Joseph chuckled. "She's a friend of the groom's family. Sophie knows her through her Society connections. I'll introduce you two at the wedding breakfast."

"Oh?" Arthur stared at the door.

"She's widowed and I'm certain your mother will consider her too old for you."

Arthur shot him a beleaguered look. "My mother is probably at this very moment scrutinizing every unmarried girl under twenty-five sitting in the pews." He sighed. "It's disgusting really."

Joseph laughed and offered Arthur a pat on the back. "Tell Helena I'll be but a moment."

"Congratulations, Joseph." Arthur offered a wide grin before he left.

Joseph approached Nicholas and Ravensburgh, nodding a greeting to the latter. "I must take my position in the lobby to escort your lovely bride. But I wanted to say something first." He took Nicholas' hand, wrapping both of his around it. "I don't think I could have imagined a better son-in-law."

Nicholas flushed and futilely tried to suppress a grin. "Thank you, sir." He bowed slightly. "I will take care of her, sir."

"I know," he said gently. The poor lad had already witnessed his protective wrath when he had asked for Helena's hand in marriage.

Joseph crossed the chapel along the south aisle, perusing the congregants. The cream of London Society was there, including the Marquess and Marchioness of Richmond, the Marquess of Norrington, the Earl of Petersham, the current and future Viscount Bucknall, the Viscountess Foxley-Graham. Amazingly, the Marquess of Richmond and Papa—Grandpa Phillips as Helena called him— stood in the central aisle immersed in conversation, laughing and grinning as if they were old friends. Joseph blinked back tears. He had to be strong. He had a daughter to marry into the ranks of the ton.

And when he arrived at the lobby Sophia came to him, gripping his hands in emotion.

"Oh, Joseph." Her tears were uncontrollable. And too affecting. His eyes smarted.

He drew her against him. "Shh, shh, Sophie. I know. It's been a long road. But we're here. We've arrived at the station to begin a new journey."

They were no longer alone on their path. Now they had the love and support of a vast nexus of friends and family. He was still astonished that he, a lowly port worker, mingled with marquesses and earls.

Sophia pulled back, smirking at his maudlin metaphor. "I can think of no better traveling companion for the way ahead."

He lifted her hand to his lips to kiss her wedding ring. "Neither can I."

About the Author

Regina Kammer is a librarian, an art historian, and an award-winning, international best-selling, multi-published writer of provocative historical romance and contemporary romance with a touch of history. Her short stories and novels make history sexier, whether the era is Roman, Byzantine, Viking, American Revolution, or Victorian. She's even sexed up contemporary settings, Steampunk, and Greco-Roman mythology. She has been published by Cleis Press, Go Deeper Press, Ellora's Cave, House of Erotica, Story Ink, Loose Id, The Naughty Literati, and her own imprint, Viridium Press. She began writing historical fiction with romantic elements during National Novel Writing Month 2006, switching to erotica when all her characters suddenly demanded to have sex.

Keep up with Regina

Check out her website: https://reginakammer.com/
Never miss a new release! Subscribe to *Kammerotica News*:
https://reginakammer.com/newsletter/

Historical erotic romance by Regina

Victorian

The Pleasure Device (Harwell Heirs Book 1)
Disobedience By Design (Harwell Heirs Book 2)
Where Destiny Plays (Harwell Heirs Book 3)
The Westerman Affair (Art & Discipline Book 1)
The Demonstration
The Invitation
Disputed Boundaries (Stories from the San Juan Islands)

American Revolution

The General's Wife: An American Revolutionary Tale
Winter Interlude: An American Revolutionary Novelette
On the Eighteenth of January, '78; or, A Night At Valley Forge

Ancient World

Hadrian and Sabina: A Love Story
Ancient Shorts: An Ancient World Romance Collection

Steampunk

One Cheek Or Two? (Ockham Steam-Works Laboratory Chronicles 1)
Delia's Heartthrob (Ockham Steam-Works Laboratory Chronicles 2)
Swing Follies (Ockham Steam-Works Laboratory Chronicles 3)